TELLAFROG

PART ONE

TORIN MACRATH

TORIN MACRATH

I would like to dedicate this series to all of my family and friends. Without them and all of the lessons, both good and bad, my wonder at the world would not be what it is. A very special thanks to my beautiful wife, who quite literally, took what I wrote and made it into something we could share. It was no small feat, as I had never written before and neither of us had any experience with editing, formatting, copyrights, etc. Thanks, shorty, I love you three much!

CONTENTS

PREFACE

These stories are compiled from journal notes, rec-
ollections of those involved, firsthand accounts, and
my memory, assembled to the best of my recollection over
the years. I was born in 1801, and I began writing these
in 1869. Regarding the purpose of these volumes, I began
with the series of events which led me from a rather dull,
clinical life as a field researcher into the properties of
plant, mineral, and animal life considered to be in the cat-
egories concerning magical peoples, to standing sentinel
with an eclectic alliance over the world.

I would learn in the course of this volume that my
entanglement in this sphere of adventure began when I
was only eleven. I would end up standing guard with a
few others who had fallen into involvement by chance,
watching the world over for signs of relics and those who
sought to use them for evil. Even those who sought merely
to advance science, when exposed to it, could wreak un-
intended havoc.

1

Because I was not alone, and this is purely my account of events, I will title it simply by my family name, so parallel tellings can enlighten parts I did not participate in and may differ from my account.

CHAPTER ONE

S urely I am asleep. I roll onto my left side and continue deeper into the dream. I know this memory, although it has been a while. I remember holding the rail of the ship, made of American Live Oak, worn dark and smooth over its grain and knots by years of seamen's hands. I was looking towards the East, where dark clouds churned over a rainstorm ahead, and heard small rumblings of thunder. There was a cooler breeze from the North, cool especially for late August in the North Atlantic. My father was taking me by sea for my first term at a magical school in the British Isles. We were 3 days out from Boston in 1812. It was about midday, my father, John Tellafrog, holding my shoulder.

"British Man of War 3 o'clock!" a sailor from the crow's nest yelled. We both swiveled our heads in the direction he was pointing to, then forward and to the right, and I detected something.

The captain came out of his cabin, down onto our deck, and extended his spyglass. Sailors rushed forward. They were likely hoping to outrun orders to station, and some did, gathering in their mismatched garb common with non-commissioned ranks aboard ship as far forward as they dared go.

"General Quarters, men! Be ready for command. Prepare starboard guns!" the captain bellowed, steady but in charge. I looked at my father. He, too, was calm but attentive to the British ship. Sailors ran fore and aft, up ropes to the sail and below to the gun. After that alarming command, I ceased to recall any specific details of the ship and crew. I had gone from the cusp of an adventure to cross the sea and attend a real school, to the real prospect of death. Relations in 1812 between the Americans and the British were at war footing, and at sea, any ship was subject to firing on or seizure. Despite the salty spray of the ocean crashing into the oaken hull of the ship, my mouth went dry. That I remember. It was the first time fear had an unsettling effect on me physically.

Father stated calmly, "We are aboard a commercial ship, Son, just passengers, not a concern to that naval vessel." His eyes narrowed as he spoke, but he continued watching the other ship. I could perceive that my father, a pillar of stalwart fortitude to my young mind, may have told me a fib to ease my troubled mind. I, however, knew "commercial" vessels, as he had put it, weren't actually armed, as such, so why the cry from the captain to man the guns? That may have been added by my subconscious later, as a question I might have asked but didn't.

Sometimes, dreams and actual memory merge, and we remember things the way we want, not always the way they happened. It was many years ago, after all.

4

I too looked towards the British ship ahead, only to spot puffs of white smoke around the bow, and huge splashes of water showered the ship, followed by the slower sound of the shots. Father swung his left arm off the railing and around me, hustling us towards the rear of the ship.

"Helm, hard to port! Into the storm!" the captain shouted as we passed each other near the rear. "Starboard battery, prepare to fire!" Now I was sure Dad had tried to calm my fears, but the danger was about to become real, and there was no sense in trying to avoid it. Perhaps the captain had seen their gun doors opening and being rolled out on the British ship.

The rain began spattering all around us, and then it sheathed us in a blinding downpour. Father and I reached the top of the rear of the ship, barely soon enough to grab the railing as the port turn lunged the ship hard. We could neither hear the other ship nor see its flashes now because of the rain and the thunder of the storm.

Father reached into his rucksack and pulled out his broom. I glanced around because of the rules of magic in the sight of non-magical people, but between the storm and the unfolding conflict, no one was around. He slung one strap of his rucksack over his left shoulder, grabbed me with his right hand, and instantly we shot straight up into the clouds. I held on as tightly as possible, father looking up and ahead. I looked below, where we had come from, and saw our ship faintly outlined; the British ship was closing the distance. They were no more than a half mile apart now. More flashes from their cannons. Then the American ship's right side fired.

5

The flight began to level out, so I took a look around. We were still in some rain, but surrounded, like in a courtyard, by dark, heavy clouds, lightning passing within them, the colors of which changed depending on the density of the clouds and strength of the flare. Thunder ripped around us, alternating between tremendous cracks that jolted my chest with changing air pressures and low rumbling like a boulder rolling down a hill of hard rock. We came to a halt, still, but bobbing a bit in the gusts.

I heard a sound which wasn't thunder, more like a raspy, rough wind slicing to our left. Father, hearing it, promptly turned away from it.

"What was that sound, Father?" I asked

"Rather not ...," he stopped, looked left, then above us, and was silent.

It was the unmistakable form in those grey clouds of a dragon. I had never seen one, but had the feeling it would be best had I not. Its motion suggested it was either circling us or the ships below. Neither made sense, but Father was concerned with getting the pair of us out of this situation and nothing else. So I kept my grip as tight as I could.

Father turned left and right swiftly. My small 11-year-old hands were beginning to show the limits of their strength. I winced, pinched shut my eyes, and trusted my father. When he slowed and began to hover again, I opened my eyes for a second—only a second—but I remember thinking. The dragon was right in front of us, and Father let go with his left hand and pulled his wand with one motion and cast a spell I still can't remember the name of.

An enormous cone of pure white light went forth from it, I guess, blinding the dragon who veered to our left out of the cone. No sooner had it turned, in fear, I suppose, its wing caught the front of the broom, and I fell off, ripping my small hands and crossed feet with painful force from the wet handle of the broom. The dragon dove as it went away. I could have mounted it like a horse, I thought as I fell. Silly mind of a child.

I was falling, and there was nothing I could do. All of this happened so fast, but it seemed slow in my few dreams of recollection.

I suppose that is how we absorb amazing things—every sensation, every aspect—so clearly. A blinding flash of lightning came from those rolling black clouds above and around us, striking the side of the dragon, then encasing me in its crackling blue-white energy, and then towards the sea below. I looked at my father, who was already pointing his broom straight at me, racing to try and catch me, and everything went dark. And quiet.

****

That was twenty-five years ago, and also the event that coincided with my loss of magical ability.

Screech! Screech! Came the unique sound of my owl, McCort. The light coming into my tent was quite bright, unusual, as I'm usually up quite early. Deciding to indulge that dream—or memory—had cost me perhaps half an hour. I always feel, for some reason, it is important to relive the episode when it presents itself, never sure why. Maybe it's healthy to be reminded now and again that you aren't as special as you thought you might be at one time.

7

Nevertheless, I must get up and to work, as it is. After all, it's the only way to catch the female emerald glow worms of this area, and they're quite important to why I am here. I may still find some at this hour. And, I guess McCort wants his breakfast as well.

The fire in my small stove is out. Usually it lasts all night—one of the drawbacks to not being magical anymore, I guess. Mother and Father always raised me to actively look for the good things every day, but so many things are made simpler by magic. Like not getting cold at night, or having a fire that tends itself, so you can have hot water and cook eggs when you wake up.

I sat up and went to the door flap of my tent, opening it so McCort could come inside. He glided in and sat on the perch, a letter in his beak. I took the letter and set it on my travel desk, opened the jar of night crawlers, and set it on his hook so he could have some. He will go find some field mice later I'm sure, or a nice shrew, but luckily my strange owl likes the worms I give him.

With a few sticks of firewood standing up over the left-over pieces of charcoal, then using a large splinter of rich pine in the flame of the lantern to light it, off my little fire goes. I shut the door and change into my clothes, lacing my boots tight in case I get a chance to head up the rocky face along the north side of the lake today. I still need some red-headed rockgripper feathers, and those little birds only nest here, amongst the scree along the mountain face of Lake Königssee.

After dressing and eating some breakfast, I finally turned my attention to the letter. It's from Magnus Templeton, a former teacher at my school and a family friend. He is the one who convinced the school to allow me to study there to completion, even though I had lost the ability to see, use, or create magic, spells, charms, and the like. There are very few who have lost their ability to use magic, and although I can use some magical or charmed objects and tools, they were hoping to study my case to determine if it's a reversible condition. Although we discovered the things I can do, and that my physical and sensory abilities are heightened somewhat, no recovery of the inherent magic I was born with was made.

Professor Templeton's letter was brief, merely stating that my father had sent word to him that he wasn't feeling well and asking for his advice. Templeton asked me to come to him at once. He had arranged for me to travel on Austria's first long section of railroad and both carriage and ferry ship transport back to London, with tickets paid for at each station. Hmm. Another advantage of magic—his couriers can dislocate to anywhere in an instant. I can't. Oh well, now that I'm 35 years old, I'm not only accustomed to it, I rather enjoy it. Father can't travel if he isn't well. The use of great magic, such as dislocation, requires physical cost. Besides, as warden of a territorial prison for criminal witches and wizards, if he isn't well, Mother also can't leave. Besides, maybe there isn't a thing to worry about.

I wrote a brief response to Professor Templeton, thanking him for the accommodations and asking him to please forward my concern and anticipation of returning home to my parents. His methods will result in much faster word to them than any of my means. After McCort finishes his breakfast,

I give him a good drink of water and send him off with the letter.

I begin to pack things up, and with all the sample jars, notebooks, drawing materials, and canvas bags of foliage and feathers that are valuable, I have far too much to fit into the two cases I have. I have often thought it was a fault, collecting so many discoveries. Even though upon each return to the school, the sheer number of samples and notebooks of new information is greeted with happiness. I have served in this capacity, receiving grants for my research, for several years now. There is still considerable resistance to my actually teaching, and I suppose they are right. Little interest lies in physical sciences relating to magic being taught by one who cannot perform any magic.

Walking outside, the sky is quite blue with bright sunshine, not a cloud in sight. Honestly, the stone and wood of the mountains surrounding this incredible lake are so beautiful that I can imagine myself living here one day. The meadows are full of aromas and life. The summer's warmth seems to make everything bloom brighter. Food is more delicious. And the autumn, oh goodness, is even more incredible—its colors and the wild fragrances as wind direction changes for the season, winding between the mountains. I can never have enough time spent in the mountains here.

I walk over the small rise to the west of my campsite, through the fir trees, and down to the small farm trail to look further down the valley. After a few minutes taking it all in, the carriage comes by, heading to Königssee. Seeing he has no passengers, I ask if the driver can stop, waving him down.

Obliging my request, I inquire if he can come back here to load me up and take me several miles into town.

"Yes, sir. I have one fare to take to the next village north of Königssee, and then I can come help. It should be this evening if that's alright," he said.

"Of course. One thing further. If you'll allow me to pay you now, I appear to have collected more samples than I have trunk space for. Can I give you enough money to buy two large trunks as you pass through the village and bring them with you?" I asked. This is the only carriage driver in the area who travels between these small villages and is the one who brought me here. I wanted to make sure he had the time today.

He thought for a moment, hand on chin. "Certainly, there is a shop in the other village I'm going to which has some cases that are handmade and very sturdy, for about the same cost as the ones in Königssee."

"Excellent, sir! Will five gulden be sufficient for the trunks and your help?" I asked.

"Oh, definitely, sir," again showing his honesty.

"Well, here," he said, handing him the coinage. "It's worth it if we can have me in town tonight so I can catch the train in the morning."

A wide, thankful grin spread over his face, nodding as he urged the horses off.

I finished packing and labeling the materials and took down the tent. About midday, I walked to the edge of the lake and sat on a fallen pine trunk to try to catch a perch or two for lunch. It wasn't until I had two caught and cooked that it occurred to me there may be more to my father's illness

11

than I had first thought. Why wouldn't Professor Templeton want me to head straight home instead of coming to him first? Why hadn't my mother sent anything? She would surely do so if it were warranted. She had sent me correspondence before, against Father's wishes. I'm sure I'm worrying too much, a side effect of knowing how little help I can be to good magicians.

It should be about two hours until the shade of the mountains passes over the area, so with some time to spare, I decided to walk up towards the sheer mountainside to see if I could find those rare feathers. As I cross a steep meadow I hadn't been through yet, I notice a clump of brown amongst the grasses. Picking it up, I'm quite surprised to discover it's orox dung.

A quick crack open and sniff, and YES! It is! Rarest among the dung specimens in the region are droppings from orox that have fed heavily on new-growth honeysuckle watered by snowmelt. No one knows why, but only this beast, and this diet at this elevation, yields a magical property. When a mere ounce is brewed with Tibetan tea leaves, a single cup can prolong the life of those suffering from elderly illnesses in wizardry by a whole year.

It is highly prized in southern European cities, where many retirees reside. This amount alone can finance my study for another entire season in my favorite and most beloved country to visit—Austria. Pausing, taking in the air, those crisp mountain breezes, to my special nose, also rarest of all the places I have been, I can observe the St. Bartholomew Chapel's red cap roofs atop the white walls from here. But from where I had camped, it was beyond a small wood, across another meadow, and obscured. Additionally, the green appearance of the water from ground level doesn't reveal the clarity and white rock bed below the surface. However, from this height and distance, the water in bright sunlight appears in various shades of clear blue, green, and deep green, transitioning to black with increasing depth.

I was unable to find any of the feathers I wanted, but with the orox finding, I was supremely satisfied with my expedition here. I did come across an old friend, a Ravenel's Stinkhorn. I let a little chuckle loose when I noticed it, remembering the controversy that led to my current employment. That mycological oddity has a unique shape, virtually identical to a part of a man's anatomy, with a pungent odor of raw, or sometimes, cooked meat.

Beneath the surface of the medium in which it grows is a gelatinous blob, roughly the size of a guinea hen egg, commonly called a witch's egg. While both are edible, they serve no known benefit to ordinary people. For individuals with magical abilities, especially women, it can aid in conception.

The whole atmosphere of the silly mushroom is comical—its medicinal use, phallic shape, and all. During medieval times, most clergy demanded that it be destroyed on sight, thereby significantly diminishing the supplies for magical people. One day, during a discussion on this practice in my last year of school, Professor Templeton turned to me and assigned me to develop a plan to educate ordinary people on the Ravenel's Stinkhorn and try to stop this outdated and prejudicial behavior. I did so by having a cleric who was qualified to minister to magical and non-magical people allow me to prepare them in public for consumption and shackle me

13

to a table in the town square for two days. This way, any ill effects on me were going to be for all to witness.

I was met with some spittle and ridicule, as well as harangues of mocking and shouting, by the least civilized among them. However, after the crowd sniffed the divine aroma of it sautéed in butter and realized I was wholly unchanged after the ordeal, the town was convinced, and they were left unmolested and readily available in that region.

As soon as I can, I would like to return and spend a winter here, in all its resplendent majesty, bathed in snow and glistening ice. I would very much like to spend a great deal more time around Lake Obersee, to the south and east of my current location, and on the east of Lake Königssee. I genuinely think I could spend twenty years between these two lakes and not learn all they have to offer. Even the most perceptive person, as my mother would often say, cannot recall all they've seen, but the longer they spend observing, the more they can perceive. I am drawn to mountains of stone, the woods they wear like clothing, and the alpine waters they hold in their hands. All stone and wood and natural waters call to me, but here most of all.

It was early evening when the driver returned, and his selection of trunks was perfect. He had also arranged for my room at the inn close to the Royal House, where he had noted the flag of the Counsel was up, meaning the Counsel was in residence. I suppose Harold— the driver's name, I remembered—recalled my arrival in early spring, when he collected me there as a guest of the Counsel.

As we loaded and secured the trunks and the roll of canvas tent and its poles in the trailer, I thanked him several times for all his help. And, with the discovery of the orox "gold," I gave him another full gulden and shared the last two apples I had with the horses, at which he smiled again broadly in appreciation.

I tried to absorb the last of the scenery and scents on the way into town, only a few miles, insisting on riding atop the carriage with Harold. Unfortunately, I was constantly distracted by all the things I wasn't able to accomplish on this trip, and made brief notes in my notepad with a pencil as we rode along. My nose perceived at least thirty plant species which I hadn't detected before, and at least one type of pine bark beetle I didn't recognize the sound of. By the time we crossed the first bridge and made it onto the brick and cobble roads, it had become dark. The surrounding mountains were now shrouded in a blanket of clouds. What I could see of them was bathed in deep blue, and I would have to wait until my next visit to witness them again. Little did I know it would be several years, if at all, before I could think of returning.

The village marshal was lighting the lamp posts as we entered the first row of buildings. Residents were enjoying a walk through the streets, talking and making the most of the shortening summer days before fall arrived. As we rounded the corner to the street with the inn, I thanked Harold again for all his help.

"Whoa, whoa there." Harold gently pulled the reins, and the chatter of the hooves and wheels slowed and stopped.

"With the hour as it is, I believe I will stable the horses and carriage here tonight, right down the street before the next bridge, and stay at the inn as well. Which trunk will you be needing tonight, sir?"

"Oh, only this one satchel I have with me. I will try to cross the road to visit the Imperial Counsel right after nine in the morning," I told him. "I shouldn't be there for more than an hour. Afterwards, can we go to the train station?"

"Absolutely, sir," Harold said. "I hope you rest well."

"You as well, my good sir, goodnight," I said and stepped off the carriage, tipping my hat to him before he lightly popped the reins to clatter off.

I stood stationary a moment, knowing it was going to be a while before I returned, and looked about to examine and remember as much as I could of the town—the mighty oak timber frame buildings, wattle-and-daub walls coated with whitewash lime. Bathed in waves of flickering, golden light of the street lamps, the reflections of the damp stones of the roadways and alleys, so different in appearance from the same buildings during the daytime.

Since my first visit to northern Europe as an adult, I felt a deep kinship with the land and structures, which, even now, is hard to explain. All those friends and acquaintances who have studied engineering and enjoyed the new structures of great cities confirm, in confidence, their attachment to these buildings and hamlets, some more than two thousand years old, which makes no rational sense, but is present nonetheless. The moon had not yet crested the mountains, and the stars were brilliant with the clear sky over the town, when clouds broke. The aroma of all the flowering plants and grains ready for harvest still filled the air, which is so much more pleasant than the winter-to-spring months. When everything is covered in snow, it is brilliant visually, but the air is always filled with the scent of wood and coal smoke, boiled vegetables, and various kinds of salted meats. I turned my head and shoulders a bit to look at the stark stone structure behind the high, intricate wrought iron gate of the Royal Residence in Königssee. Moving lazily atop the standard pole was indeed the flag indicating the Counsel, one of my closest friends, was in residence.

After waiting for another couple of people of high means to exit a carriage and enter the hotel across the street, I walk over and thank the doorman with a smile as I enter. The rough-hewn stone exterior, with its protruding oak beams, is very traditional, but the lavish carpets and lamp work chandeliers in the lobby highlight the exquisite, handcrafted, and upholstered furniture befitting the high status of its guests. Before I can approach the manager's desk, he, in fact, gently touches my right elbow from behind, and quietly begins to speak.

"Are you here to meet a guest, sir? Might I have your name?" obviously stating without saying, he felt I was not a usual guest, nor from a status he would expect surveying his lobby.

I turn to face him and notice that he is dressed smartly in a thick, wool jacket and pants, tailored to fit him perfectly in dark navy blue. His vest was made of blue silk with gold buttons, and the gold watch chain was predominantly displayed from the buttonhole to the watch pocket. His high-collared, stiff white shirt allowed the bright red cravat to stand out. Highly shined, well-heeled boots completed his professional appearance, and his frequently combed hair and manicured beard indicated status in any room.

"Tellafrog, sir. Raileanu Tellafrog," I said as quietly as he had spoken to me. A good manager would remember I was here not four months ago for a whole week. He should also remember I was here as a guest of the Imperial Counsel to research the nature of the area. However, I feel it is polite to allow a man who meets so many to think quietly for a moment.

"Oh, certainly! The carriage driver came and made arrangements for you earlier!" He took the bag from my hand and was now speaking in a normal volume. "Ah, there is a letter here for you as well, brought by the page of the Counsel not an hour ago."

"Yes, good sir, thank you. My work is quite important to the Counsel. Could you give me the key to the room and my bag? Within are a few things I would like to retrieve before I take it to my room, and then, sir, I must have something to eat. It has been hours since I dined, and I am quite hungry," I said, gesturing for my satchel, which he gently returned to me.

"Of course. I will find you in the restaurant and bring the room key. Please let me know if there's anything else I can do," he said, eyes looking over my shoulder to the counter where another guest was waiting.

"Thank you, please do not let me keep you," I said and headed toward the right-hand hallway, which led to the restaurant.

I found a table near the stairway from the restaurant to the upper floors. The waiter arrived, and I placed my order. Honestly, I can no longer remember what it was. Around the far corner of the bar, I spotted someone whom I had not expected. Monika. As with the first time I encountered her, almost three years ago, I forgot to continue breathing for a few moments. I was awkwardly staring, possibly like a child does watching a magician, wondering how it's feasible I am seeing what I am really seeing.

"Sir, your key... Ahem, your key, sir," the manager said, clearing his throat.

"Ah, thank you," stammered out of me, still trying to break my gaze at her. I took the key and put it in my chest pocket.

Approaching from the left was a waiter with my dinner plate and a stein of drink. I was finally able to break my gaze and try to focus on the plate of food, which was so important only five minutes before. I didn't succeed. I looked back, and she was looking at me with an adorable, slight smile. She could observe how befuddled I was, and it amused her. She had a piece of pie of some sort and a cup of tea, probably.

She waved her fork at me, stating clearly she could tell I was hungry and she was going to wait. Fine, but the food wasn't my main concern. So strange how our souls work in conjunction with this mortal body. Agreeing with myself to not waste her generosity, I begin to eat, but with a desire to finish expeditiously, the opposite of enjoying every bite as I had intended initially.

Ah, it was roast beef with potatoes. Very good order. The yeast rolls here are similar to the ones made at local bakers back home in America. With sweet cream butter, washed down with good Austrian stout, that's gemütlichkeit, for sure.

Now she laughed to herself at how I pretended to eat politely while obviously in a hurry to speak with her. I finish quickly, approach the bar to pay, and ask for an order of rolls to take with me on my trip. From here, I can see that her table is in a small corner by itself and is also not visible from any point before halfway into the room. The dining area was "L" shaped, and we had been at opposite ends. She motioned for me to come over.

As I was walking around the corner, I felt a bit unsteady for a moment and sensed a shimmer on the last step, almost as if I were walking through a completely smooth, almost invisible sheet of water. Steadying myself, it's obvious now what is going on. I hadn't remembered the small corner, nor the table she was at last time I was here. I turned around and looked at where the shimmer occurred, and sure enough, it was an illusion.

From here, I can observe the entire restaurant, but the image is wavy, and this is only noticeable from this side. Monika had allowed the illusion to weaken so that I could spot her here. Turning back, the whole pub for magical people is in plain view. Equal in size to the restaurant for non-magical people, with fifty small tables filled with magic folk, Monika was at the one closest. She must have known I was coming.

This pub was possibly 1,600 years old, and all the original building, furniture, and everything were basically timeless. The scent of the hundreds of years of beeswax on old oak is one aroma I'm glad I have stronger senses for.

Smirking at her silly trick, I walk the last few steps to her table and sit down. I am sure that anyone reading my story would like me to describe her in great detail, but I am afraid that the detail of her crafting to perfection by the very hand of God is less consequential than the soul that resides in her, and the overwhelming effect of the two on me. Her grip on the root of my heart was immediate on our first encounter, and I had no hope of escape. The details of her earthly shell are mine, and mine alone.

We first met three years ago, in the spring of 1833, at the Hapsburg Ball in Vienna, in the world of polite society. That instantaneous sharp stab on me was the same; it is every time we encounter each other. The youngest of four daughters of the Binder family, originally from Hungary, Monika's family is always distressed at her not having married again, her first husband dying of fever only three months after marriage. The income guaranteed through the marriage, however, allowed her to open several bookbinder shops throughout the Austro-Hungarian Empire, as well as one each in London and Stockholm.

She began, "Now that you have eaten your fill and fallen like a lovesick puppy through the shimmer wall, I promise to stop torturing you. It always amazes me how you look at me, oblivious that everyone around you can detect it."

I whipped my head around in an undignified manner to see who it was that noticed me staring at her like that, inciting another giggle from her. No one was looking.

"Alright, alright. I was teasing," her grin softened to a simple smile. "Are you already done with the study this year? It is a bit early, and last I heard, you had wanted to stay all winter. Trust me, when you are able to, it is incredibly inspirational."

"Yes, I had intended to. I received a letter from Professor Templeton this morning stating my father had contacted him, feeling unwell and asking for advice," I explained.

"I understand, it might explain why I am here as well," she stated, leaning back a bit in her chair, nodding. "The Imperial Counsel has retained my services to collate your findings and bind them into textbooks over the winter for my role as a guest instructor at the school in the far north of the British Isles for next term. He is quite impressed with your work and findings. It appears the peculiarity you share gives him the ability to discern the immense value in your studies that cross magical and non-magical lines. So often, if plant or animal products don't have magical value, our world completely ignores them. Several of your discoveries, in fact, have given rise to shops, particularly in Nordic villages, to benefit both through horticulture."

"Incredible. There is plenty to consider. Despite, or perhaps because of my condition, I can say with certainty that there is little that separates us, and any path forward will require us both to find solutions that benefit the whole world, not just one or the other. I am quite glad you will be compiling this work. The last editor the school used sent me more correspondence asking questions, whose answers could be found a page further in the text, than I could count." I leaned back into my chair, waving my right hand outwards, trying to restrain my frustration. "I spent more time dealing with pointless blithering two years ago than I did on new research. I know now this collection is in the best hands." Here, I retracted my arm and interlaced my fingers in my lap. "That being said, I wish I had the volume of letters from you I did from that nincompoop."

She pursed her lips and lowered her eyes. I'm sure I detected a bit of blushing. Then, with a widening smile, she said,

"I shall be writing to you as often as I can find appropriate regarding this project."

"So, no gentlemen callers? Anyone whom I should place my analytic perception against to test out for you?" Hoping both for a no, but also for someone worthy of her whom her family can agree on.

I secretly, but wholly, will find happiness in her happiness. Her family had made it quite clear I, being of no noble family, reasonable income, nor possessing any magical ability, stood no chance of courting her. Apparently, at the ball, her mother had seen the way I reacted when I first saw her. After her queries and whispers at the ball, her mother had made up her mind. I understood, for the prospects awaiting her were vast and gilded. I offered little, and any successes we would have would undoubtedly be attributed to the wealth she had access to, not my ability.

"No, I am and have been committed to the tomes and binding of new works which advance the world we all share. Not one caller sent by a friend or family can tolerate the hours I spend. Not one has intrigued me enough to stop this work, and honestly, the numbers have dwindled to none this year at all." She reclined all the way back now, sighing a few times before she continued. "I think the family has acquiesced to the state of my mind, and no doubt, word around the pool of eligible bachelors is that I am not worth their time. When I realized it was happening, I agreed to teach the visiting lecture course." She now looked at me, less emotional and more resolved. "Klement has told me this week he should have all the materials for me ready, and I suspected your humble nature would bring you here, and you wouldn't be

23

staying with the Counsel," she stated plainly, waiting to read my response.

"There is no hiding from you, Monika." Time to let her know I am okay. "You perceived every part of my soul at our first encounter, and I—after recovering from blindness—saw yours. I have and always will want you to be happy and content. I can discern no way in the structure of our orbits in this world to change them to suit my courtship. I pray that even if it were to change, you will find someone you can love, that the connection and deep friendship we have will never fail. That outcome would make me very happy."

She lightly rolled her eyes, leaned forward, and put her hands on the table's edge. "You are one melodramatic gent, you know it?" She sighed and sat back against the chair again, folding her arms. "We feel the same about each other, and the friendship I promise will remain intact." She stretched her right hand across the table, "Shake on it?"

I had never dared touch her. Not politely, not at the ball, not in civil society in any way. I had intentionally avoided it. After all, the effect of seeing her is difficult enough on me physically. Hesitating now, I looked at my hands. They were still dirty from the work of loading and packing everything, much of which included the soils in which I found each specimen. Worse still, they were quite coarse, cracked, and dry. After spending a month in South Central Afghanistan investigating the quality of their black tea leaves, I encountered a lack of humidity level like nothing I had ever experienced before. The fine dust, which masqueraded as sand, would infiltrate into the dry cracks and chew away until every wrinkle of skin bled. In the small town of Qalat, which lay in the shadow of a fort built atop a hill by Alexander the Great, the family hosting me showed me how to mix raw sugar, or jaggery, with goat butter and use it as a scrub to abrasively remove dead dry skin and moisturize my hands so they would survive until my body adjusted it's oil levels to accommodate the environment. They weren't as bad now, but I certainly wish I had some of the butter sugar scrub and had washed up before eating.

She politely waited while I inspected the sandpaper mitt, which used to be a hand, then I looked at hers, there on the table, reaching toward me. Even her hand and wrist were incredibly beautiful. I stretched out my arm, and took her hand ever so gently and only applied pressure with my thumb on the webbing of her hand, before shaking up, down, and let go.

"Deal," she smiled. She could tell the ridiculous route I had taken in my head to shake her hand. But she understood. "I will meet you tomorrow at the royal residence, perhaps. I will be with Klement's wife most of the day. I promise to write, and look forward to seeing you again soon."

She stood up and went through the shimmerwall and towards the front entrance. As I watched her leave, the manager came up and had something to say.

"Sir, the letter we received earlier from the Counsel was in fact payment for your stay, your meals, and to thank us for accommodating you on short notice. I hope you will call on me if you need anything else," the manager stood stiffly and attentively as he spoke.

"Of course, thank you very much," I assured him in my tone and words that I was not expecting anything more than any other member of his guests.

I reached into my pocket and retrieved the key. I could tell by the key's ornate nature that it wasn't the room I had stayed in before; on the non-magical side, this was a magical room. Good. The silence spells, as most spells and charms which work on physical things, still work for me. I will sleep warm, comfortable, familiar, and in deep, silent slumber.

Engraved on the turn of the key was the number "31." I crossed the room, not another soul, save the barkeep, in attendance, and up the stairs to the third floor. The first room on the left was mine. Unlocking, opening the door, and locking it again, I walked to the narrow bed in its cove along the wall and sat down. Within was also a small writing desk with a lamp, a small table with a white porcelain pitcher, a towel, and a wash basin. The window to the left was narrow, perhaps three feet tall, hinge-armed, and open. On the opposite wall was a tall, wardrobe-like cabinet with an open front, featuring an owl perch on top and three shelved sections below, each with a small pad on it. Between it and the bed cove was a low table, wider, for the working of an open trunk, no doubt. The small cast-iron stove on the wall opposite the window was ready for a fire with kindling sticks of rich pine inside, but it was not used normally this time of year. As I began to dress for bed, pulling my nightclothes from the top of the rucksack, McCort flew in the window with a letter. Likely a response from Klement. I finished changing and took the letter, exchanging it for four large nightcrawlers from the jar in my pack. I sat on the bed, now realizing how exhausting the day had been, packing everything up and simply getting this far.

The letter was from Klement, briefly stating that we indeed needed to meet first thing in the morning. There had been updated news about my father, which he had received from Professor Templeton. Interesting. I had intended only to hand over my research materials and his ring. It's strange that he would be involved with my father's news. Regardless, had it been urgent news, he would have sent for me immediately. I am, after all, only across the road from his main gate. I blew out the lamp and sat heavily on the bed. I lay back and pulled the heavy blanket and quilt over myself, exhaled, and closed my eyes.

McCort's low, rocky, gurgled cooing woke me. It was still dark, but the orange glow of the sun's imminent arrival in the East was barely noticeable out the still-open window. The number of things I needed to do today looming, I dressed rapidly, fed McCort, told him where to land at the royal residence, and headed downstairs. I found the manager and inquired what the bill was for my stay, wanting to be certain I owed nothing.

"Sir, the Imperial Counsel has insisted that from this day forth, you are to be extended every courtesy, and he will be sent the bill. It is my honor to have you at any time," he said proudly and professionally. His early consideration of my status need never be mentioned again by either of us.

I proceeded out of the front lobby, as it was closer than the magical side of the building. The sun's warm glow was settling on the morning mists and was beginning to crest the hills behind the royal residence from where I was standing.

Not a single carriage in sight, so I crossed the road and approached the main gate.

CHAPTER TWO

A mazingly, Klement Metternich, my old friend, was present, in quite a bit more casual dress than I had seen him before, speaking with the guards when he spotted me approaching.

"Ah, here is the gentleman I was speaking of! Officer of the Watch, please remember this man is a good friend of the monarchy and of me personally. Offer him any and all assistance he may ever need," the Imperial Counsel ordered them.

"Yes, sir!" They snapped heels and saluted, their palms forward at their right eyebrows.

"Welcome, Raileanu, welcome!" he said, putting his arm across my shoulders and directing me to the main entrance.

The structure was austere—beautifully crafted from large blocks of white limestone, with exposed beams and framing, and enameled black steel appointments that resembled eagles. Lantern hangers and shutters were bound with wooden planks and blackened steel bands. The six-story structure featured a large, round turret on its north corner, approximately eight stories tall. Although no longer used, the original torch cups were meticulously maintained.

The entire road path, which led around the house and intersected with the straight entrance path, was precisely fitted with light-colored slate. Round river rock was set in cement to fill the edges and any oddly shaped gaps. Two tall, slender conifers stood on either side of the doors. Polished brass ring handle adornments graced the main double door, standing twelve feet tall with a rounded top. Royal guards opened the doors for us, and we were beckoned in by butlers. As I entered alongside Klement, he removed his arm from my shoulder and went towards a third butler off to our right. He spoke low and in German to him, and with those two combined, I couldn't make out what was being said. The butler bowed silently, and all three of them walked away through one of the front rooms.

"Is everything alright, sir?" I asked.

"Yes, I instructed them to ensure we are not disturbed, and I will be unavailable until further notice. Also, I instructed one of them to retrieve your trunks and other items from the carriage driver and make sure he is paid fully for his help," he said, extending his left arm towards a door at the back of the foyer, to the left under a staircase which circled both sides of the room.

Klement unlocked the door. It led into a narrow staircase that arced similarly to the one above, but this one led down. It was wide enough for only one, and while it was clear the stair was not regularly used, the lamps in polished brass alcoves along the stairway were lit, and the way was easily seen.

The walls, stairs, and ceiling—by odor alone in this light—were in fact mahogany, masterfully carved in scenes which were obviously magical in nature. Perhaps even magically created. The arc of the steps continued into a steep spiral, with three full rotations, and opened into a large, round room made entirely of white marble with streaks of blue. Tapestries hung from bright brass rods all the way around, from the domed ceiling, likely sixteen feet above the floor, each depicting a scene of magical historical significance from central European history. The room was at least seventy-five feet in diameter. Thick rugs, lavishly embroidered, with long, furred animal skins lined the floor, all except the massive fireplace and mantle, which was thick cedar planking smoothed and oiled to a sheen. Oil fire basins hung above eight feet, suspended by well-smithed chains attached to silver arms extending about six feet from the walls, emerging from between the tapestries. Polished, concave steel shields mounted to the arms at the wall in front of the tapestries increased the light in the space.

Smooth, bright white limestone was used for the ceiling dome, making the space exceptionally well lit. There were twenty-five thick, pillow-buttoned, light brown leather chairs with armrests and high backs in a semicircle facing the fireplace. Small tables sat between each chair, again with thick, cedar slab tops, covered with knit draping. Several large, low tables sat perpendicular to the fireplace in the center.

When he realized, politely, I had finished surveying the room, Klement invited me to sit in a chair next to the hearth on the left side of the semicircle. On the table in front of me was a stack of extremely old books, with marker note pages sticking out, and a silver tray holding coffee and tea pots, along with their associated condiments. Knowing my love of Turkish coffee, Klement had prepared one in a small cup and saucer and handed it to me. Then, he sat on the edge of the table facing me and sighed.

"You know why we became friends, and why I have funded your work over the last few years. I lost most of my magical ability as a young man, at only seventeen, not a month after graduation from our wizarding school. Not many of us have lost any or all magical ability," he stated plainly and paused.

The rich foam of the coffee has such a powerful aroma, I had forgotten how much I enjoyed it, and I always use up my supplies on any trip too quickly. I waited patiently for him to begin again.

"A book exists which only a few of us use, and I—now you as well—have knowledge of. We are the only two who are not in possession of magical ability who are in this circle. Here is that book." He reached back, got the second book down in the stack, and handed it to me.

It was a large codex, black leather, quite old, with heavy, expensive paper stock. There was no writing on the cover, spine, or back. *Hmmm.* I opened the cover; there was no writing on the first few pages either. I thumbed through half the volume and found no writing. Not that curious in reality, magical chroniclers often hide their writing from the non-magical, especially important works, and are therefore invisible to people like me.

"When Professor Templeton was contacted by your father and apprised of the particulars he was experiencing in his illness, the professor contacted me. He is the one who brought me the book. Although I cannot read the texts within, like you, it is here for safekeeping. Not even my father, brother, or emperor knows of its existence." Again, he paused, and cradling his short beard in his hand, he continued. "Anytime someone encounters, or is told of events or conditions which defy current magical and ordinary scholars' knowledge, the details are inscribed here. I can write in it, and the words are instantly also inscribed in the master volume, where they are compiled in a single place. The writing in this book vanishes, and, in truth, nothing is retained in this book at all. No one can read this, nor any other version held in secure vaults worldwide. Your father's symptoms are similar to those recorded over three hundred years ago, but no cause, cure, or explanation was found at that time. Several hundred people, magical and ordinary, were claimed by it." He paused, guessing I would have questions at this point.

"My father's condition is not good, is it?" I asked.

He continued, "No. As we speak, the professor is traveling to where the master volume is located, to try and glean whatever he can to help. But no, I spoke to your mother through their portrait before you arrived. It is nightfall now, and he still has a high fever. No spell, charm, or potion available to them has shown any effect," he said calmly. "I know you were due to travel by train to its northernmost stop, then to London to speak with the professor, but he has explained the course you must take to reach your father and render whatever aid we can collect in the meantime. I know the travel required for this endeavor is painful to you, but speed is imperative. You must runeshift to London to meet

33

the professor with whatever information he has gathered and any supplies he may have. After you've regained your strength, head straight to the runestone thirty miles north of Wormwell. This is as close and as fast as we can get you home."

"Pardon, sir, but cannot a ministry warden, or American territorial ranger, immediately dislocate there to at least manage the prison, and render aid for my father?" Trying to be polite, but asking the obvious question that anyone here, along my way, or already there will also ask.

"Your father has intentionally not corresponded with you directly about any of this. He spoke with the professor to send you word, so you would come hastily, but with no alarm to anyone else. Also, on the first day, he felt ill, and he enacted the security measures in the prison; they are quite secure. The facility was already at the end of its usefulness, scheduled to move further north and west early next year, so no surprise guests are expected. The reason for these steps is directly related to the book and his ailment. If this is unknown magic, or some contagion unobserved by us, word can reach the shamans of Central Mexico, who still support Aztecan groups who gain power from death and suffering. Additionally, the medicine men of the Comanche would certainly utilize it against Texians, as both groups fear this new nation. He paused, poured himself a drink, and took a few sips of it, considering how to explain things in a helpful way.

"If we send a high-level magical inquisitor, that act alone can incite tensions. No, every possible tool will be brought to your father's aid and given to you before you leave London. I dearly wish it were possible for you to speak directly to your mother at this time. I would give anything to lend you this one weak ability I still retain. This is most urgent, and the professor and I feel you, being family—essentially ordinary in the eyes of all observers and a native born Texan—are the only one who can go immediately, with clear intent, and assuage the concerns recorded for a thousand years in this book." He let out a heavy sigh at the end and looked me level in the eye. "I honestly believe it must be you, and it must begin today."

"I understand, sir. I do not wish to linger here any longer than I must. I do wish to return your ring, which, a short time ago, was the reason I came here. Additionally, all my research is to be left in your keeping, including samples of all pertinent flora, fauna, and minerals. I did come across something of value. It is in a large glass jar amongst the trunk. Orox scat, completely suitable for an age ailment potion. If possible, can the sale of it be sent to me? I have no idea what troubles I will encounter on this trip, and I may need additional funds. If not, please deposit in the appropriate bank in London, please." I paused to give more thought to what was relevant within the time constraints now upon me.

"Definitely, my friend," he began. "I am financing this entire trip for you as the interests of us all are at stake here. I will also be employing your old acquaintance Monika Binder to collect and begin publishing your work promptly. She is already in our house, working with my wife, Laverne, to compile our family portraits and genealogy into a work using her transcription and artistry skills through magical conjuration, which will be a gift to the family this Christmas season."

"Very good, sir. Shall we have time for lunch before I must depart?"

"Yes, indeed, it is being laid on as we speak. It shouldn't be more than thirty minutes more, and it will be ready," he said, slyly smiling. "And, yes, Monika will be in attendance."

"You know our history and difficulties well, my friend. I will be grateful to see her again, if only for a polite meal with your family." That was as overtly gracious as I dared be, even to a close friend in private.

He stood up, slapping his knees, and turned around to the stack of books still on the table. He opened one, which was a book box, so it wasn't actually a book. From it, he laid several items on the small table next to me. A small coin purse made of dark leather with copper colored stitching in a diamond pattern, with copper hardware and closure, and a copper keeper chain with a clasp. Next was a finely tooled silver pocket watch, which seemed to have a keeper and chain, both made of sterling silver. The third was a small flask with the house crest from his secondary school in Austria.

Not wanting to forget, I removed the large ring I had been wearing on my left index finger, which he had lent me at the start of my work nearby. I handed it to him, thanking him for it and his consideration of our shared malady. He put it in the small pocket on his waistcoat and picked up the coin purse.

"This is something I have made, using your knowledge learned these last ten years, combining your working under-standing of how to use elemental ores, magical creatures' products, and charms or enchantments which wizardkind and we can use. None of these will be helpful or valuable were they to be found by unscrupulous persons."

He reached over and picked up a coin purse. "This coin purse is made from a ten-year-old hedgehog hide who died of natural causes and is stitched with copper-nickel wire. I have found that using copper from different orebodies, along with the charm on this, that anything placed in this purse will be sent to the exact copy, made from the same animal and orebodies of copper, and vice versa. So you can send me small items, and I you. In fact, the distance of separation has made no change in ability, as though the materials are bound at an elemental level, more so than any applied magic. This is how I will fund your trip and also keep your reserves safe while you are in the territories you are visiting. If you can send me ore from the lands of Texas, I will endeavor my silversmith to fashion a small box, and we can try it on your return."

"Second is this," he said, setting the purse back in the hollow book and picking up the watch. "It was made for me by a Swiss lady, who my wife and I were in school with. It has six functions." Clicking the clasp open, it revealed what looked like a watch with five dials, and the opposite side was a liquid-filled compass.

"This side, which looks like a compass," he began, "is in fact a compass. It will always point north. However, if you hold it open, cupped in both hands, it will point to the nearest runestone you can use for travel. Now, I know you are accustomed to runestones allowing you and me to dislocate, but without full magical powers, we are never certain to which runestone we have shifted.

"I have spoken with Professor Templeton about this for some years on and off, and he has discovered if we put a drop of blood on the specific rune on the dial which points to the one you need for your trip, it will send you to the nearest runestone which also has a drop of your blood. It will only work with you, and only for three moons' time. This is adequate, because Templeton sent me a vial of your blood from the accident when he attended your recovery when you were a boy.

"This morning I sent my younger cousin—who is young and virile—to dislocate from here to London near Professor Templeton's home, and on to the runestone due west of the old Spanish copper mine, thirty miles north of Wormwell. He has also been instructed to stay and look after your parents until you arrive.

"His name is Arterous Metternich. He is quite capable and has served as a captain in the cavalry regiment for several years here. His horsemanship and resourcefulness will be notable, I am sure." He set the compass down next to me.

"This is absolutely incredible, I am speechless. After all these years of contenting myself with ordinary travel and finding the beauties in walking holidays, horseback riding, and such, I am relieved in this dire circumstance, I can return home to my father and mother so promptly!" I stuttered in amazement. "Runeshifting is truly so hard on me. Most of the time I've tried it, I actually end up further from where I intended than if I had just walked. The considerations on my part, sir, are so generous. I am so thankful to God for knowing you and for the advancements we share and discoveries we can continue to contribute to research often ignored by current academics."

Klement continued, "The other features of this watch are as follows: The five dials, as indicated by the markings around each, are for moon phase, storm detection, magnetic inference, and a clock, of course. The fifth dial is similar to the ring I lent you. It is also the only function which requires the winding knob to work properly. It must be wound each day, and the hands will indicate how many hours and minutes it can conceal you from non-magical persons and animals. You arc not completely invisible, but an unimportant distortion—or, perhaps, mirage—in their subconscious. Anyone in sight range will not detect you, your sounds, scents, or even your shadow. However, the perception-blocking quality only lasts up to twelve hours. Its magical-mechanical properties require the internal motion of lunar stone and magma-formed quartz discs to be wound. I have used one for a year, and its function is flawless."

"Good Lord above, sir!" The gravity of the items is making something abundantly clear to me now. These are rather expensive, meticulously crafted, and rare devices made from ore, which few have even considered manufacturing. "Sir, I am beginning to understand my part is quite a bit more than helping a longtime friend return to his ill father. I promise the utmost demeanor and attention to all parts of this trip and its aims as I can gather."

"Finally," he said, closing and setting the watch into the book box and retrieving the flask, "this silver work flask has but one magical property. Based on your descriptions and my research on the Texas region of the United States, it may be your true lifesaver. It is always full of clean water. It can only hold two pints, but its sister is located in a basin which rests under the waterfalls on a ledge near Davos, Switzerland, and is fixed permanently. The ledge it rests on is three hundred feet above the valley floor below. I was exploring some nearby caves and noticed that the spot was always wet and was not visible to anyone but those standing next to it. The waterfall is fed by snowmelt runoff all year and transmits the water to the flask consistently."

"Truly, sir, no greater gift could any native-born Texan receive," I said humbly. The times even hardened woodsmen from eastern states have found themselves bushwhacked by nothing short of thirst cannot be counted. I fidgeted and shifted my weight in the chair, becoming increasingly nervous that more was happening, and I had a growing feeling that I needed to return home quickly.

"This is your gift, my friend, and the coin purse. You can now assume the tenured professor of my employ henceforth—Professor at Large of Magical & Ordinary studies. I will support you without end on a regular stipend of whatever you require, based on our years of friendship and your numerous academic contributions, which you have produced on your own. Know the balance of your book sales and valuable horticultural finds, as always, will be put on your account in London as well."

He grew a wide, open smile, and said, "You can accompany me now to lunch, specially prepared for your difficult runeshift ahead, as PROFESSOR Raileanu Tellafrog!"

"I'm sorry," I stammered. "What?"

"I have spoken with the Board of Regents of the school. Your work has been used in every associated class in the last five years. Every professor has found and included at least one element in their coursework that came from your discoveries. Some of the courses have not had new elements added in decades," he said with a wide, proud smile. "They are the ones who suggested it to the Board, who contacted me." Klement stood, looking down as he walked over to the huge fireplace with his left hand raised.

"I am sorry, there is no agreement on your teaching. Only a few suggested it, and the majority still refuse to allow it. They want you to continue your work, and the results of the last few years have convinced them of its value. I concurred with their decision only yesterday." He dropped his hand and raised his chin, placing his hands behind his back and straightening.

It is entirely likely that at this point, my mouth was agog—like an imbecile—without me realizing it. Flies could have been coming and going in and out of it, and I would not have known or cared.

Even more amazingly, it occurred to me Monika would be at the lunch, and while my shock would undoubtedly prevent me from mentioning it aloud, my friend, fifteen years my senior, my compatriot in having lost magical ability, would tell everyone. Right now, at least, the shock of my father's illness, the ability to travel as a real wizard again—sort of—the weight of the incredible gifts, and why they are to be used now, seemed a bit crowded with all this additional input. I genuinely did not know how to respond. Surely I had some- thing to say, if not offer...

41

Of course! The orange-violet striped trumpet orchids!

Klement had not been able to consistently speak directly through portraits; the regularity of his ability was not discernible, and it had troubled him for a long time. He could almost always hear the other party speaking, but he was not always able to respond.

"Sir, I do have one discovery made recently which may, in a small way, encourage you and your family. The rare orange-violet striped trumpet orchid grows near the lake on the steep edges, which are well watered, and can work much like the magical portraits for normal wizardkind. If ones from the same family rootball are raised in other areas, and kept healthy, you can speak into them, and the other orchid, say at your ancestral home estate, can repeat it for magical people to hear. You, conversely, can understand their speech from yours! I have a pair in my trunk for which I had thought of you specifically. They are labeled as such. Please allow me to give those to you, so you may hear your father and mother's voices anytime you choose." I sat right on the edge of the seat, both my hands out, feeling my gift inadequate when measured against his help for me.

"This is why, my friend, you are now a Professor! You are researching and solving issues which can benefit wizards, but especially non-magical people of wizard heritages who truly need it," he said quite seriously.

"Now, let us go upstairs, have a hearty meal, and then see you off."

"Sir, have you told Monika," I wondered, "about the new title?"

"No, honestly, I have considered it for some time, but it was only decided yesterday. Would you like to tell her, or would you like..." he started. "As Imperial Counsel, I can assign anyone I wish to such posts with the blessing of the Board of Regents."

"No, sir, please. Let me attend to my parents and return without difficulty before I inform her. I don't want either of us to concern ourselves with anything but the crucial tasks at hand."

"Very well, I understand," he acquiesced. "Let us head upstairs and enjoy our last meal together for some time." He stood and began to move towards the stairs, with me right behind him.

After coming out into the foyer, we proceeded towards the back of the house and into the large dining hall. The places were set for seven, and Monika, Mrs. Laverne Metternich, and Klement Metternich's three children were waiting for us. As always, and as the unmistakable fool for her I am, I had paused too long staring at Monika, my hint being when she smiled as she looked down and away.

The meal was brought out—venison and mushrooms, carrots, potatoes, and a side which made little sense given the rest, sauerkraut—all on the finest polished silver.

My friend spotted me looking at it confused and said, "That, my friend, is for you. I know you like it, and the chances of you having a meal included that is properly prepared where you're going is quite low." Wine was served, along with a sweet cake at the end, accompanied by a delicious, aromatic Turkish coffee.

The children asked me more than a few silly questions about America, their mother giggling lightly at most of them. Mrs. Laverne Metternich was a keenly intelligent and powerful lady in her own right. No doubt, most of my friend's successes can be attributed to her cunning and wholly charming nature. Fully trained in Austrian law, fluent in French, Italian, Flemish, and English, and precisely finished for every courtly occasion, it's true in my company—and possibly only in my company—allowed common talk and the children to be silly. She was over ten years Klement's junior, and her children were schooled with her and their mistress instructor. The travel requirements of the counselor meant they were never in one place for long. They were oldest to youngest: Stephan at fourteen, Danielle at eleven, and Daphne aged seven.

To their parents' relief, I think, none were magical. It is becoming increasingly complex to have a family in such a high station that combines the magical and the ordinary. Invariably, it leads to questions of schooling abroad or their absence. They also cannot be themselves, which causes its own problems. Had they been of the royal family, the discretion around the whereabouts of children would have been more accepted by non-magical inquisitors. Additionally, while ninety-nine percent of ordinary people are unaware of the magical population, royal families from all nations are aware and support the separation for the sake of all.

"When must you leave for America?" Monika asked.

I looked at her and it must have been obvious again I was trying to avoid looking at her and being ensnared by her beauty for all to witness.

"As soon as our meal is completed, I'm afraid." I began. "I do not wish to leave my parents alone with this illness any longer than necessary. Though leaving the company of my friends, and of course, you, is always difficult." Glancing around, it's clear it was blatantly obvious again. Danielle and Daphne snickered, so yes, it is uncontrollable for me with Monika.

As I prepared to leave, saying goodbyes to all, the Metternichs turned back into the parlor for a moment—all except her. I stood as straight and professionally as I could, hands behind my back. She looked past me, seeing that the family had rounded the corner out of sight. She reached around my side and took my hand from behind my back, holding it.

Honestly, the rush of emotion from touching her hand almost made me rethink leaving, but I must. I looked right into her eyes. Again, the description of her beauty and power over me in her soul and her form will forever be mine alone. I could tell she perceived everything about me, and none of it needed to be said by either of us. She leaned up and gave me a small kiss on the cheek, at the same time putting something in my hand.

Prying my eyes away from her, I looked at my hand. It was a small silver locket. In it was a tiny picture of her.

"I know you cannot speak through it, as magical people can, but I don't want you to forget me, for I will not notice even the sunshine until I can see you again." She said quite seriously, looking intently at me.

"I, I..." my voice breaking, mouth dry, "I will return to you as soon as I can." I took her hands in mine. "I have never been able to go a day without thinking of you, not even for a day. Thank you for this."

Klement came around the corner again and smiled, looking at his feet for a moment. I set her hands down, both of us smiling.

"Shall we set a date then?" he joked, hopefully.

"No, sir, not yet. We can save that discussion for my return."

"Indeed," Monika agreed, smiling as well.

"Well, Raileanu, we should head towards the center of town where the runestone resides. Also, if it helps, I have a few things which might be of use," Klement said.

"Goodbye, Raileanu," Monika said as she walked away, looking back at me.

"Not goodbye, only farewell for a time," I said to her. Right or not, I burned her smile at that moment into my mind. As she watched, she could see the smile in the corner of my mouth. She told me later she knew what I was doing.

"Let's go," Klement suggested.

"After you, sir," and out the front doors, across the open yard, and out the front gate we walked.

McCort was waiting outside on a lamp post. He spread his wings when he caught sight of me. I didn't know exactly where we were going, so I told him to follow. He gave a little squeak and crouched, and jumped into the air, circling us until we picked a direction to walk.

There were so many things in my mind now that I could barely concentrate on anything but following Klement. It occurred to me we had walked down two different streets, maybe a quarter of a mile, before I could think clearly again.

I had not been in this part of town before and could not remember the way back to the hotel or The Royal House either. I did detect the leftovers of lunches that had been cooked in the houses as we passed by. The grain storehouse had workers stacking bags and barrels of stores. The thump of dried grain sacks and the dust they put off their own distinctive aroma. Below that, I could sense a cold, musty scent, and pick up the dripping of water into a deep stone place. With another few sniffs, I knew it was where the beer was stored. Much of it was the same beer I had the night before in the hotel restaurant.

"Sir, do we know the runeshift will work with McCort as well? He is the only owl who has imprinted on me, as I was still in possession of full magical abilities when he came to me. I cannot bind to any other owl," I asked with concern.

"We have no reason to suspect otherwise. From our research, the event of runeshifting is identical to dislocating, only on a mechanical level, rather than focusing the spirit and body on a familiar location.

"We are nearing the center of town. There is a narrow, four-story building that is 500 years old. I don't believe you know this bit of our history," Klement began, glancing back at me. "It is built on a small, narrow ridge of stone which sits in the middle of the river. A bridge only wide enough for one carriage extends from each side of the 'island' to the shores. It was originally built for the king to imprison and torture suspected witches and warlocks."

We turned down a couple of streets, speaking quietly, as by now vendors and merchants had their storefronts open and wares out on the roadway for customers. The streets weren't full, but were busy.

"They believed being surrounded by water would isolate the imprisoned and give the inquisitors more power over them. That is the common reason given, as even the literature of the time, as seen in the Malleus Maleficarum, stated their weakness around running water. In truth, the reason it was selected was that the rune wheel carved atop this outcropping of stone was clearly—to them—pagan and should be covered. After the magical accords were reached almost two thousand years ago, most of the ancient runic language documents that would allow for transcription or translation were locked up by the various wizarding ministries, or later, by the Vatican. When the current royal families began consolidating power and isolating magical influences on the world from the ordinary after the Wars of Reformation, we were able to retain this property in the royal registry and protect it. In fact, it is a stop in the fourth year of study for pupils here in Austria studying magical history." Klement paused and approached the locked gate and the guard for the bridge he had spoken of. The bridge had once-elegant arched beam supports from the crag of stone in the center of the river to the bank where we were, set securely into large holes cut into the side of the river's retaining wall.

It was as he described, four-story, pale-white, rough-cut stone carefully built onto a narrow projection of stone in the center of the river. The bridge on our side was no more than five feet wide, made of an oaken timber frame with iron bolts and braces, but the decking looked to be newer ash, held in place with large rosebud spikes. The bridge was possibly thirty feet long and ended at a tall double door with similarly forged iron fittings and annulus door rings. Wood shingles topped the high, peaked roof over the bridge. The sides were solid wood framing, approximately three feet high, with two-inch round wooden bars staved into the lower solid framing, which supported the sides of the roof. The spacing of these was no wider than a man's hand.

The guard unlocked the gate, which was significant, an inch off the stone pavings all the way to the edge of the roof framing. He shut and locked it behind us and sat back down on his bench in the small guard shack.

McCort arrived and roosted on my shoulder. The bridge planking was newer, as were all the spikes. Once on the bridge, looking down its length, I could detect unevenness and a slight tilt, not uncommon for a long timber structure. We walked to the doors at the end of the bridge, Klement turned an annulus, and we entered.

This floor was all open around a central circular structure with one entrance on the side facing us. I could see through it that there was an identical doorway on the other side, surely for the bridge on the other side, leading to the opposite bank of the river. Within were several iron rings along the walls at about eight feet in height, some with chains and shackles still hanging from them. To the left was a high, wooden bench, like a judge or magistrate might use, I suppose. In front of it was a bank of three wrought iron barred cages, with the doors on our side all open and keys still in the lock mechanisms. The stains on the ground—I dared not consider their sources—prompted me to intentionally begin breathing through my mouth only. Klement walked toward the doorway in front of us and began down the spiral stone stairs inside, and I followed.

We stopped at the next lower level, which was still mostly an above-ground space within the building. Exiting the stairwell, I got a better look at the space.

"This is where many tortures and confessions were extracted of those accused of witchcraft," Klement said, waving his hand broadly about. "Please, take a look around."

Cages lined every inch of the walls in this room. About two-thirds of this floor was carved out of the rocky island itself to make the structure. Thin, horizontal rectangular windows lined the top of the walls, spaced about six feet apart. They were simple frames with frosted glass and were not intended to open. With only six inches of glass, they were obviously designed to allow some light to pass through, but not to permit entrance or escape. Tall shelves wound between the cages along the exterior walls and the ones against the circular stairwell in the center. Those shelves held devices and tools designed to cause anguish. That's all I can say. It was terrible. They also held things I had heard of but never seen in person. Hex jars. Mummified cats, toads, dogs, birds, and rats. Maybe evidence against prisoners.

"Sir, why did the witch hunts of the period become so vicious?" I asked. The study of magical persecution is limited in normal schooling to the cases in each nation's history, and I sadly knew none of the cases here.

"It isn't far from where the Protestant revolution began, and in many regions throughout Germany and Austria, the wars of the Holy Roman Empire's church against the Protestants boiled into all-out war. Using witch hunts was a way the

Catholic forces felt their persecution would be less reviled, but many times it simply caused more upheaval," Klement stated somberly.

He walked over to a small stool, dusted it off with his hand, and sat down, looking around at all of it. "In almost every case, this building dealt directly with their enemies, and no magical people were involved or hurt. The fear it caused was no less painful, and it stands as a warning of the effects of our kind interfering in the lives of the ordinary. Even the most change-driven teenage students leave here with a different mindset. It is invaluable, I believe, to solid education and a responsible magical community going forward."

We both tried to remember the things here, I could tell, but we stored it in the part of the mind you hope to never really need. After a few moments, Klement stood. "Now, let us proceed downstairs to the lowest level and start you on your way."

Down a shorter set of stairs, this time to the basement floor, we had to stop long enough to light a lamp, as there were no windows or natural light here at all. We continued to the bottom, and the dim lamp light revealed a storeroom, with cobwebs and a thick layer of dust covering everything piled around. The stone floor, chiseled out of the rock and unfinished, was also uneven, as it was never meant to be used or occupied regularly. Having lived now twenty-four years without magic, it was easy for me to appreciate the innumerable hours spent hammering and chiseling by ordinary people to create this place.

Klement led me to the opposite side of the circular stairwell. Along the path between benches and racks, I noticed five shallow pits, maybe four feet in diameter, with iron cage lids. After everything else I witnessed, I didn't want an explanation of those; I could guess. On the back side, we came to the runewheel. It was also carved from the original rock, and the ground surrounding the four-foot pedestal was smooth and precise, showing a magical creation, not the hammer and chisel work elsewhere. A heavy canvas tarp covered it, with a few broken animal cages on top. Klement set the lamp on top and reached into his coat pocket.

"I almost forgot," He started, "here is some documentation I made for you stating you are an academic working for the Imperial Royal Commission to study indigenous medicines of the Americas. It also states that you are to be afforded all the rights and privileges of a foreign dignitary in the United States. Your name, in case it helps, has been listed as Randall Frog; any magical or Austrian official will be able to cross-reference who you are, but it may still be helpful. I apologize, I wasn't able to add your new title to these documents in time."

He moved the lamp, the cages, and the tarp. It was a magically carved wheel for certain. The inside cuts were made with precision that cannot be matched even today with modern tooling, and it was beautifully crafted.

"If you are ready," Klement said, "take the compass I gave you and open it, cupped in both hands." He used his hands to demonstrate.

I complied, and sure enough, the compass pointed to the runestone wheel, and as I moved around it, the needle selected one rune in particular. I removed my left hand from it, and the needle did indeed point north.

"As soon as you are ready, trace the rune with your right index finger, and you will runeshift," he said, "and yes, your owl will be perfectly fine. His value to you is hardly anyone but me can grasp. You will need him, I guarantee."

"Klement, if you can promise to keep it quiet, any copper or other ores I send you in the coin purse, you know now what to do with it, don't you?" I said, counting on his ability to perceive.

He smiled as widely as I have ever seen, nodding, "Yes, I do."

I closed the watch, tucked it securely inside my vest pocket, took a deep breath, and exhaled. I glanced at McCort, who returned the look but shifted his gaze forward again, unconcerned and wise.

CHAPTER THREE

Runeshifting is a bit different from dislocation. We are taught in school that the runeshift is a tool passed down for a few thousand years. The number dates back as far as the academic literature discusses it. None can pinpoint the magic involved, who invented or discovered it, or why. In fact, the only speculation as to why such a thing would have been invented falls apart with people like me and Klement. We have lost our powers and can normally use them with limited success. And ordinary people cannot use them at all.

Early chroniclers believed it was for non-magical kings to travel, but they were unable to substantiate this in their studies. Nowadays, their mention is but a brief paragraph in Relics class. No one really cares about it in the magical world because they can easily dislocate anywhere, and it is used a thousand times a day. They are quite lucky because in a split second, they can go where they imagine as easily as walking through a shimmerwall.

I always wondered why they were here among us at all. I guess it is no different than a poleaxe on display in a castle now, once important, but now a, well, relic. I won't enjoy this; they warned it would take me time to recover. I sincerely hope it isn't a long delay to reach my parents.

"Thank you, Klement, very much for all of your help. Please tell Monika I will return as soon as possible," I said, reaching to shake his hand.

"Make sure you do, my friend. We care deeply for your parents and you, and we must know the cause of this. Farewell," he said.

One deep breath, a glance up at McCort again, and I trace the rune as instructed...

Ugh! Noo, not like a shimmerwall at all! I felt as if all of my particles were sucked into a rune-shaped hole, all stretched and mashed with my sides scraping along the sharp stone edges I had just finished admiring. Quite nauseous as well. No, I don't like this one bit. It's also taking quite a long time, at least, that's what I perceive...

I detect a storm. No, it is the storm from my childhood, from the trip on the sailing ship, it's below... I can see my father. That means up ahead should be the dragon. I can observe it clearly now, where it was hidden by rain at first, and I couldn't recall many details accurately. I am surveying the events of my dream, not re-experiencing them.

It is an old dragon—its scales thick and rough, its four horns curl around themselves like perhaps an ibex but also curved away from its head, more like a Jacob's Sheep. The thick scales across the top of its head layer down the back of its long neck, and its ridged back spines poke from between the scales. They are green, but not mossy or plant-like, more like old copper. It is a copper dragon! Lightning rips around the clouds and then below us. Its underbelly is smaller, younger scaling, and is indeed copper...

I feel myself tighten, starting at my feet, pained releases of air escape my teeth as I grimace from the pain. My eyes tightly shut, I begin stretching again, but my head starts to feel the scraping like before. I must be coming through now... the scraping zips from head to toe, and I perceive a humming in my ears, then I collapse onto what feels like stone.

"There, there, you should be alright in a minute or two." It was a familiar voice, um, Professor Templeton. Right, I am in London. I push away from him gently, stumbling, and open my eyes enough to view my immediate surroundings. I spot a patch of grass, I think grass, and vomit a little on it.

"McCort! Is he ..."

"Right here, he is fine," Templeton said reassuringly.

Not so happy I had the sauerkraut now, I look around and find myself in a small, basement room that appears to be made of carved, solid sandstone. I lost the contents of my stomach onto what I thought was grass. It wasn't grass. It was straw, but, oh well, better than the professor's feet!

"Here, have some water to wash your mouth clean." He handed me a large glass mug, so I used it. "How was it, considering?"

"Awful if I am honest. I hurt all over, almost as though I had been beaten with clubs through a keyhole by a dozen burly men." Only now did I think about the time that had passed since I tried runeshifting. It had been more than ten years, and I swore it wasn't worth it to try again. I suppose it is true that physical pain doesn't linger in the mind or memory as long as the events that cause it.

"You have some bruising along your neck. We couldn't be sure if it would be discomforting, only that it would work. Feel up to heading to a place to lie down? I have a small room prepared for you through this basement door. You can rest as long as you need. I will bring some brandy, which should help you relax a bit." He helped me up from the runewheel and through the door to the small rope bed with a goose feather mattress. I took another drink of the mug and leaned against the wall, groaning a bit.

"I will take McCort up and let him out while you are resting. I will be right back." Templeton called my owl to his arm and took him up the creaky old stairs.

Reclining, I started to feel better. I turned to look at the small table next to the bed, which genuinely did hurt, due to the bruising he spotted on my neck, most likely. There was a pitcher and basin, so I leaned over and poured some water into the basin and splashed it on my face a few times. The nausea did abate some. A few deep breaths, and I did it again. I wonder if all the stretching I felt made me taller. *Don't be ridiculous.* Still, I would take an inch or two without complaint.

The stairs began creaking again, and the professor came down with a glass of brandy. Trusting his advice, I tried a sip, but liquor never agreed with me. Often, the scent alone would make me ill. This did seem to help, though. Its warmth soothes my sore neck and settles the nervous tension throughout my body.

"I take it that runeshifting was much different than dislocation. It sounds worse than I had hoped."

"Yes, sir, it was." I leaned back to the bed and the wall again. I told him what the experience was like and about the detail in which I was able to view the dragon from when I was injured that day, so long ago.

"A copper dragon! Astonishing! I cannot say the last time one was spotted in the open, near so many ordinary people at that." He sat down in the chair at the table. Adjusting his jacket tails from under his bottom and straightening his shirt as well. Templeton was wearing a nice camel-colored jacket and a black paisley silk vest with bright maroons and yellows. He was not wearing a tie. In fact, his top buttons were undone. I had never seen him relaxed, I guess. "It may explain one part of the tale, though, the lightning which 'enveloped' you, as you stated, could in fact have ricocheted off a copper dragon's scales, whereas another of the dragon family would have been fatally wounded."

"I suppose so."

"I have also brought you some of this powder from a tree bark, which was first brought back when your father visited the Brazilian rainforest. Concentrating on the appropriate compounds in the potions lab should also help alleviate some of the pain. Give it a try."

He handed me a spoonful out of a jar, and I put it in my mouth. Another big drink of water, and it was down. I took another sip of the brandy.

"I remember the trip. In fact, it is the only dislocation I remember before the accident. I had my pet horny toad I had caught in Texas. I would hold him in my hand, slightly sideways, and rub his belly, and he would go to sleep. I had him with me for two years, night and day. When we went to Brazil, I made a small carrying box for him to stay safe while we were in the tent. I didn't want any animals to kill him or to lose him in a strange place."

I stopped, remembering him and how much he meant to me, wincing before I finished telling the professor. "When I woke up after our first night in the rainforest, Brazilian fire ants had gone into his box and killed him. There were hundreds all over him when I woke up. I felt terrible. I had done all I could to care for him, but he had no defense against those ants he'd never lived with before."

"I am sorry to learn that, Raileanu. I sincerely am," he said, looking down at his feet. A sorrowful wave of memories he must have had washed over him, shutting his eyes for an instant, turning his head slightly.

"Sometimes, none of us survives being unprepared in unfamiliar environments, Professor. It was my fault for wanting to take him from his home. He trusted me, and I wanted my friend to join me on my adventure. I have been more cautious since then with such things," I explained.

"It is no conciliation, but I recall your friendship with that little toad, as your parents relayed to me. That's when your mother began to call you her little frog. Surely you comprehend the connection now. She also feared for you each time you ventured forth into lands unknown to you. Especially after you lost the magical abilities our kind has counted on for thousands of years to keep us safe." He sighed when done.

"Well, sir, I did have the advantage of being born a Texan. That makes me the toughest among wizardkind, does it not?" I let a chuckle out.

Laughing a bit himself, Templeton agreed, "I suppose so."

"Sir, does the ole Norse cobbler still have a shop in the alley south of the Thames?" I wondered.

"Indeed, he is my outfitter for each new climate I venture to. Why do you ask?" he wondered.

"Well, it occurs to me now, knowing the violence and disruption the runeshift will cause, it is likely prudent to have a closer representation of local attire before I go. If I am to travel thirty to forty miles south after arriving in this manner, especially if I am unlucky enough to arrive on the runewheel in a heap amongst ordinary folk, I should not also stand out in appearance."

The professor began to nod a bit.

"Take my boots, if you will please, to him and have some American-style boots made of brown leather, and an oilskin duster, similar to the overcoats worn by Norwegian whalers in the North Sea. Only the coat, please. No liner, for God's sake, it's August. He should have one of those on hand, if I remember correctly. My shirt, deerskin waistcoat, and trousers should be acceptable as is." I reached into my coat pocket and opened the coin purse, and sure enough, discovered ten full guldens. I handed the professor all ten, as I was hoping to have the items ready by morning so I could leave then.

"Excellent plan, my friend. I will go right away. Oh, when I was upstairs, Lady Laverne and your mother were waiting at their portraits for word of your arrival. I told them all went well. Your mother said not to worry, all was in hand, and

Arterous had arrived safely to assist. She will dispatch him to the runewheel when you are ready, so you shouldn't be alone when you arrive." Slapping his knee and uncrossing his legs, he set off with my boots up the stairs.

I slowly took off my coat, waistcoat, and trousers, leaving only my long shirt and "longhannles," as we call them back home, and climbed onto the thick mattress, pulling the heavy quilt over myself. I turned the lamp down, lifted the glass, and blew out the flame. I had to sleep.

I slept until morning, and I could detect breakfast being cooked—eggs and ham. Sounded like a cast-iron wood stove on the floor above. I sat up on the bed and put my feet down. The floor was chilly. I dressed, except for my boots, and poured myself a mug of water, which helped alleviate my dry mouth a bit. I picked up my rucksack and headed up the stairs, still quite sore and stiff. My neck turned a bit easier, but not much.

At the top of the stairs, I went through the door, and was, in fact, in the kitchen. Professor Templeton was at the table already eating. His housekeeper, Corrina, was cooking at the wood stove in the corner by the window.

"Professor, I do not recognize this house. Where are we exactly?" I asked and carefully lowered myself into a chair across from him.

"No, you would not recognize it. It belongs to the university, serving as temporary housing for traveling lecturers. I visited a guest speaker here almost twenty years ago, and she brought the runestone to my attention. Apparently, the university and the royal family came to an agreement several hundred years ago to grant ownership of the sites housing such relics, once the proof of indigenous language creation was ruled out." He poured some goat milk into a small glass for me and continued eating his own breakfast.

"I see. The medicine you gave me last night must have worked, at least to some extent. Is there still bruising on my neck?" I stretched my chin up so he could see better.

"No bruising, only some reddish streaks. That's quite good."

"Well, I feel as if the beating was a week ago, but better, I suppose."

Corrina set a plate down for me, with ham and eggs. I offered thanks and ate it swiftly. Manners were not important after I had detected good food nearby. My stomach had begun grumbling as I woke and smelled the meal being prepared.

"Are we far from the cobbler's shop?" I finished chewing and waited until both of us could speak. The habit some have of putting food in their mouth more energetically as they speak has always put me off. Manners or not, it seemed uncivilized.

"No, not too far at all. We're in the Morden Place area, a few blocks from his workshop. He had the coat as you requested already for sale. He said he could have the boots ready by midday today," he said, finishing the last of his meal after answering me.

"Good, I feel I should go as soon as possible. I am not so diminished that I should not proceed as soon as then. Even if I leave then, it will be a two-day ride once I arrive back in Texas, barring unforeseen troubles."

"I will have a courier pick them up and bring them here. It's 10 o'clock now. Why don't you rest in the sitting room after breakfast? In all likelihood, it will rain all day," he suggested.

"Sounds good to me, sir. Will any more of the medicine powder help, or does it last a few days?" I asked, unconscious that I was holding my forehead at the same time.

"No, I am certain it only lasts a few hours. I will acquire some more, and a small vial you can take with you, since it will all begin again by tonight." He rose and went into his satchel to retrieve it, hanging on a hook by the kitchen door to the little back garden. Lilac, marigolds, blue daze, and a few roses were visible, although due to the rain, I couldn't smell them. The small herb pots on the windowsill, however, were filled with dill and oregano, and were some of my favorites.

I thanked him again for the gift and the hearty breakfast and returned to bed, the need for rest and recuperation overtaking me once more. The sitting room had only a lounge seat, and I needed to lie down, so I went to the basement room again.

"Raileanu, Raileanu, wake up." It was the professor. "It is almost two in the afternoon. Did you want to keep resting?"

I blinked hard two or three times and rubbed my eyes. "No, no, thank you. I should be on my way."

I sat up, got another drink of water from the pitcher, and exhaled heavily. "Have you received the delivery of the clothes?" I asked under my breath.

"Yes, it's here at the end of the bed." He reached for it. Wrapped in heavy brown paper and twine, I untied it and opened it. The boots bore a close resemblance to the Texan

63

Vaquero style, being plain with no unnecessary decorative stitching, no extra eyes, a good square toe, and a thick, layered suede and yew wood sole. It should work well enough in the saddle and against rattlesnakes. The oilskin overcoat was underneath the boots. It was a dark, rich brown, with a shoulder cape and underarm straps, a tall collar, and deep outer pockets. Thankfully, it had no liner, which would be standard for European ship coats, because Texas in August is incredibly hot. Rolled up, it can make a great pillow when it's hot, and the oilskin will keep me dry in winter or summer.

"The cobbler said he cast a confusion charm on the shell of the coat. I am curious if it will work or not for you since you can use some magical objects which are enchanted," he pointed out excitedly.

"Oh, one more thing! He had a hat that I remember you describing from home, and I can size it properly for you. It's, in fact, not felt or woven straw. It is magically made. He used a real straw model and, laying it on his basement mushroom boxes, had these rawhide puffballs grow under a charm to shape around the hat. It is so light, as strong as formed rawhide, waterproof, yet naturally breathable. The only indicator of its non-standard manufacture is its dark olive-brown color and texture. Apparently, it is quite the popular item among the upper magical classes to buy and display." Professor picked it up from behind himself and put it on his head as he turned around, grinning at how he imagined he looked in it.

"Now, that is a way of making a hat I had not thought of, sir. Could I inspect it?" I extended my hand towards him, and he dropped his smile and took the hat off.

"Actually, wait a moment, I do want to see it on myself. I will go upstairs for a moment, where there is a mirror. I'll be right back." He walked upstairs, letting himself grin again. At the top of the creaky stairs, his housekeeper let loose a loud 'pssshhh' sound before descending into hilarious laughter.

"I'll have none of that, ma'am! This is a serious piece of kit for our guest!" he dressed her down in his tone. To no avail, she kept laughing at him, and by the sound of it, slapping her leg over and over.

The professor let a grunt out when he reached the mirror, and I could hear him walking back to the basement stairs. He paused at the top, "Corrina, you were right. There is no hope for me in the unsettled lands. It was ridiculous." He came back downstairs, eyes on the floor, hat in hand, extended for me.

I took the hat from him, for he was quite right about how he looked and about its unique fabrication. I could find no fault in the design or creation. I bent the brim quite harshly, and it popped back to its original form.

"This is quite nice. Having your hat bent and losing its shape is the worst." I smiled and did it again.

"Try it on, so I can size it for you."

I flipped it, held the brim with my right index finger and thumb, and my left fingers on the back. It was likely two sizes too large, not surprisingly. Most European men had much more hair than I wear, and often their heads are a bit broader, especially at the front. Besides, if they only display them, sizing is not relevant.

"Here, let me see it," he said, holding his hand out. He took the hat and pulled his wand from the wand-sleeve inside his waistcoat. It was the same one I remembered from school.

About nine inches long of twisted, light-grained wood, with a nickel handle. One circular motion with the wand pointed to the inside of the hatband, and it shrank a bit. He gave it back, and it was as close to perfect as possible.

"It is perfect! Thank you for everything. I'm going to get dressed and head out. Is McCort upstairs? Has he eaten and had a good drink?"

"Yes, he was on the table eating a few pieces of ham and actually wanted some of my tea earlier!"

"Yeah, he can be quite the rascal sometimes. I'm glad he is full."

"I was thinking about your runeshifting trip and the time you experienced—the vision and clarity you had." The Professor took a seat at the end of the bed, put his left hand on his thigh, and his right hand with the pointer finger extended. "When any of us travel across space as we do, it's postulated we are passing into the 'space between spaces,' areas which are not accessible to us but are pervasive—all around us—and we can only pass through them.

"You having a clear vision of the memory may point to an old idea, that the Ether isn't only a place we can pass through, but a place where all our consciousness is also stored. Please record any or all of your experiences in these movements in your notes. They may need to be written in 'the book,' as well as the results of your trip and the question of your father's illness."

I nod my head as I finish dressing, looking down and to the left where the professor is, hoping I can help my family while trying to keep all this in there, too. I pack the coat in my rucksack and pull on the boots. The ole Norse cobbler

66

nailed it. They fit like a glove, and even the spots in my old boots, which had rubbed initially but had been shaped over time, were soft and no trouble. One of the many benefits of magic craftsmanship.

"Can you keep these other boots here, take them home with you?" holding them up to him.

"Of course. Do you feel ready?" He took the old boots from the floor and set them on the bed beside him.

"Yes, I need to go and get it over with. I hope that having a few hours from breakfast until now, I don't have the upset stomach problem again." I whistle for McCort. He comes down the stairs and flies through this room into the one with the runewheel, standing on the edge of it. He appeared to have no painful difficulties from the travel medium. That made one of us.

We walk into the adjoining room as I put the rucksack on, and I take McCort onto my arm and set him on my shoulder.

"Thank you, Professor, for everything you have done to help me return home. I will do my best to keep everything in mind you and Klement have told me thus far." I nod at him, and receive a nod in return. I take a good, long look at the runewheel, trying to discern if any of the symbols match the ones I saw back in Austria. Only one, an 'H' with wavy sides. "Sir, is this the one that would take me back to Austria, the one where I came from?"

"No, I don't believe so. The compass watch Klement gave you would show you, though. Deciphering those is some-thing we can work on together when you return, perhaps." Professor Templeton points to the rune I need. I can see where the drop of my blood is on this one. I look at him, nod, and trace my finger onto it...

This time, it feels as though it's pulling me through the rune by my arm, and strangely, while "stretching," I can tell my body is completely unnaturally bent for an instant. Next, I felt as if my mind was hovering around the runewheel in Texas already, and I witnessed my body squirt out headfirst and end with my mind back where it belongs inside my skull, and I'm standing on the disc. Whew! My disorientation was less this time. I set McCort on the runewheel and sat down, my legs dangling for a moment as the sun was much brighter here, and my eyes were adjusting slowly. Aside from tingling all along my right arm, I don't feel anything out of the ordinary.

I look around since I am out in the open, early afternoon in Texas, and I don't spot Arterous about. The runewheel was carved on an outcropping of bright white limestone near the end of a narrow mesa topped with mesquite trees, spotty broomweed, and bramble. I can not detect any signs of settlement or trail nearby, and that's good. Grasshoppers, small birds, cicadas are all I can hear, well, and the scurrying of the large red harvester ants, which only I can detect. My owl seemed to fare well again but was a little fidgety, so I set McCort off to fly around.

Yeah, it is hot up here, not a cloud in the sky, and the distortion of heat is making anything in the distance appear to wriggle around. So, *where would I be waiting for someone in this area?* The rise I was standing on runs north-south, so I decided to head down the broken ledges of sandstone, which are interspersed in the limestone on the east side. In places, they seem to almost be steps, but brittle enough that it isn't worth the gamble to walk on. Working my way around the east side, being in the shade at this hour, is where I expected I could find him.

As I arrive where shade falls far enough from the crest that I am out of the direct sun, I notice a small draw near the hill's base, and a stand of taller, greener mesquite and good growth of cattail grasses, which is a good sign of water. He is probably thereabouts, the horses having to drink quite a bit this time of year to stay fresh. And they can graze along its bank. It takes a good thirty minutes to make my way down, hearing and smelling horses several times on the way down.

"Ah, good! You have made it in one piece, I see!" Arterous shouted from the shade. His accent was noticeable and heavy, and his pronunciation was crisp.

"Indeed, I have. You are a wise man to stay here while you wait, as distances between safe and potable water are difficult to find with regularity around here," I pointed out. A few yards of loose rock still at a difficult slope later, and I made it down to where the ground leveled out.

"I spent the morning patrolling around, sir. I didn't detect any sign of others nearby." He was speaking loud enough for me to hear, as I was still picking my way through some prickly brush and making racket walking on the loose rock.

"I thought about going north into a small village I spotted, but not knowing the territory, and whether they were friend or foe, I decided to wait here and speak to you first," he said calmly from his seat on an old cedar trunk under some bushes.

"Thank you, my good man. I was going to suggest that at least one of us be armed properly, even for a relatively short trip. I hope you don't mind my vernacular beginning to slip back to territorial, especially in the company of others. It definitely keeps the ordinary folk at ease," I said as I made my way down the different ledges of the bank made by sudden rain storms, which then dry just as fast. "How far are we from the copper mine, do you know?"

"I did fly around last night, as the cover of dark would be good enough protection from curious observers. I believe it is only a mile north. I could be sure I saw its remnants of an open vein of ore from above before it descended into a mine entrance. There was no one around either that I observed, sir." I could detect his shape through the bushes and undergrowth. He had carved another piece of pork and ate it from the tip of his knife.

Coming around the stand of bushes where he was, I could finally see him well. He was at least six feet tall, wearing tall black European riding boots, navy blue riding pants under cowhide chaps with patches of black, white, and brown, an Austrian officer's shirt, and a short riding coat. The chaps looked ridiculous, but he may have bought them to protect his pants and tall boots back in Austria, and the shopkeeper thought he was doing Arterous a service. I imagine there was quite a bit of fun poked at him after he left the outfitters. The chaps will help, regardless of the silly appearance, as hardly anything in central and west Texas exists without thorns of some kind.

He had brought with him two horses, which is a benefit of dislocation, well, for those who can do it. He can bring anything he is touching at the time he chooses, to wherever he is going. They were fit, and by their appearance, it seemed they were part of a group, perhaps having been brought from the Americas to Europe in recent months. It had become a big business in recent years, corralling wild mustangs in the American Southwest, shipping them to Europe and Australia to meet the needs of their growing armies. The saddles and hardware were obviously made in Austria and were practically new, but for our purposes, they would work well.

"Have you also flown our route? Are there any washouts or *arroyos* that will be difficult to ride through?" I asked, untying my horse from the brush and walking it in front of him.

"Yes, sir, I believe if we stay in this valley—if you can call this a valley, more of a dip between some hills—we should be obscured for a couple of miles from either side. From there," he motioned in the direction he was speaking about with his knife, "it is fairly open fields until dark." He stood, standing and brushing himself off, and walked to his horse.

I smiled. He had done well on the reconnoiter. "Well, fields imply cultivation. Out here, they simply call it a prairie." I smiled and said, "Prairies are for riding across and for varmints to live in."

Arterous nodded, and his head tilted side to side a bit in learning the distinction.

"How are my mother and father?"

"I visited with them for about thirty minutes before I left this morning. Your father does not seem any worse than last night. Your mother is strong. She is extremely happy you are almost home."

"Thank you. I am glad they are alright for now." I stopped checking the straps on the saddle and turned to face him. I put my fists on my hips and glared at him. I shook my head side to side. He turned to look at me, nervous at my sudden serious face.

"What, what is it?"

"Now, Arterous, if I may...you will have to trust me on this." I stopped and thought for a moment. For this to be taken properly by someone from an aristocratic family, perhaps leading by example will be more effective. So I step to where the little trickle of water is coming out of the ground, and take a couple of handfuls of mud and rub it all over my rolled-up shirtsleeve and arms; its reddish clay content stains both my skin and sleeves. I rub more on my elbows, knees, and up and down the sides of my boots, and some onto my pants. I glanced up at Arterous, who was giving me a look between shock and disgusted indignation. I found a spot of blacker mud and added some of it on as well.

"What are you doing, sir?" Arterous finally asked, his baffled expression revealing his uncertainty about whether he wanted to know the answer.

"Well, it is three hundred miles in the shortest direction to a riverboat or a seaport where we could have entered the country. Not many people know anything about my family or me at all." I knelt down to wash some of the residue off my hands, shook them off, and stood again, continuing. "If we appear in the middle of central Texas as though we just stepped out of a clothier in Paris, word of strange business will be in California by week's end. We either appear to belong in our surroundings, or those surroundings will attack and betray us. Please, sir, soil yourself as though we have spent hundreds of miles traveling across hostile land in the oven of summer. It may save your life." I said, still applying dirt to the wet mud, and rubbing handfuls of grass on my elbows and knees, using dry grass to scuff my boots and other leather to complete the view for others.

Arterous did so, but seemed pained, especially by the activity when he reached his high, spit-shined boots, as he presumably had spent time working on the expanse of leather himself at times. Anyone who has worked military leather of that size would suffer physical pain while destroying hours of diligent shine work. I advised him to completely remove the chaps, and perhaps, we could trade those in the little village north of here for two pairs of older, well-worn ones more suited to our needs.

The amount of sweat we both exuded, given the almost hundred-degree temperature with thick, heavy humidity and nary a breeze, meant that as soon as we began our trip on horseback, the dust would cake in every fold of skin, completing our look as I wanted.

The village was only three or four miles north of here, if I remember correctly. It was a small Wi-iko village, loosely affiliated with the Wichita tribe to the north. They were excellent farmers, traders, and hunters. Friendly to most, they made unique beehive-shaped huts, roofed with grass. Usually, they had much to trade, including surpluses of buffalo and deer jerky, hides, and vegetables. Before I left for Europe, they had had some skirmishes with the Comanche, as well as with some tribes of Cherokee who had been moving further west as the Americans settled more and more of the land. I suspect that after the struggles with the Mexicans and Texians are mostly over, this group of native Texans will be an important part of the new nation.

"We need to head to the hill near the Brazos River, where the small village you spotted on your reconnaissance is located. They are Wi-iko, and we can buy further provisions before heading to my family's home. Ready to leave?" I said while mounting the horse Arterous had brought for me.

"Yes, sir. I would very much like to see it up close," he said, grabbing his bedroll, which he had been leaning against when I first arrived, tying it to the back of the saddle.

We sent our owls off ahead of us, Arterous ordering his, named Cat, short for Catherine, to return with any news of trouble. After passing out of the shade of the little mesa, the ground continued to slope downhill, it seemed, with the horizontal level of plain grasses lower than the perceived horizon. This time of year, the ground was hard, and although we were fairly near the Brazos, most of the grass was already yellow or outright brown, crunching as the horses walked across it.

There were several deep gullies clogged with dry thorn vines and cactus, but not being certain of their actual path in relation to our destination, I decided we should stay on the path due north according to my compass. Using them as cover would be suitable if we were already being tracked or watched. Neither was true as far as I knew, and with Arterous and my compass combined, with the charmed coat, I was hoping we would pass unobserved to our destination.

It was only two hours, and I could see the rise which marked the outpost, on the south side of the Brazos. A distinct trail appeared now on our right, which in all likelihood followed the river. We were only a mile or so from the Wi–iko village. With the conflict over, I was hoping there might be a Ranger station, or even a real trading post.

Chapter Four

Approaching the crest of the rise, with pines, smaller oaks, and elms on the perimeter, an open plain of about forty acres came into view. There was a new structure to the left, with a newly built palisade fence around it, about eight feet tall. The building was constructed from low, axe-hewn timber, featuring a wide porch and a wood-plank roof covered in sod, with a small chimney located on the south end. The gates of the palisade stood wide open, giving a good view inside. Behind it was the native's village, with distinctive beehive-shaped huts with bound grass exteriors. Within were forty or fifty of those family homes, with racks made for stretching and curing deer and buffalo hides, and my nose could tell all were still done in the traditional way, with cooked brain and oak bark tannins, not the lecherous, hateful, burning chemicals some in Europe had begun using. My sensitive nose despised that. Besides, while those tanning methods may last longer, the leather does not breathe naturally, and here in Texas, they would be usable only two months a year, lest you die of dehydration. By comparison, properly brain-tanned deerskin can be easily worn year-round, as long as a single thin layer of homespun cotton is the only under layer.

The Wi-iko were already in the last weeks of harvesting their crops of corn, squash, and beans. This was the first time I remember them growing tomatoes here. I can also smell a great quantity of muscadine grapes in the far stands of trees. Wild ones grow far up into trees, making them safe from foraging animals but difficult to harvest compared to the meticulously maintained ancient vines of Europe.

We dismounted and walked the horses to the rail and trough inside the little palisade. A man came walking out of the open door and sat in the rocking chair to the left, watching us. He wore a tall, crowned, light-gray felt hat with a wide, round brim and rattlesnake and concho hat band. He had a roomy, natural-colored canvas shirt with a deerskin vest—most likely made here, in fact. His trousers were dark gray wool, with properly designed vaquero boots, spurs still on, so he wasn't some former empresario used to sitting behind a desk.

He had an apple in one hand and a small, wide-bladed skinning knife in the other. As I walked up to him, I observed that his thick mustache and unshaven whiskers were evenly mixed with black and white. He looked up a bit, and the shadow of his hat lifted to reveal a man of Mexican origin.

"Howdy, fellas," the man said with no trace of Spanish predisposition in his voice. "Whatcha need here?" His eyes darted back and forth quickly, surveying the two strangers.

He set to peeling the apple, making a single long, unbroken peel.

"We were looking to pick up a few provisions if there are any here we could buy," I spoke plainly and politely, unsure of his title or purpose.

"Well, whatcha names?" he asked, almost finished with his apple peeling.

"I am Randy Frog. This is Art Metternich. I am heading south, got word my father isn't doing well, got some kinda illness, all alone with my momma. I indeed was looking to buy a couple of pistols, maybe one of Patterson's revolver rifles if you have any about."

The man began nodding a little and cutting small wedges off his apple.

"What is this place, anyhow?"

"Frog, huh? Well, this here place is our little Rangerin' post. Just built a couple months back. Y'all lucky I'm here. We only use it to store things and stay in when we're in the area. My name's Antonio Flores. My cousin rode with Juan Seguin. They brought me on here recent. Seems the Wi-iko injuns here have been having trouble with CO-manches now and again.

"Plus, there's some groups of Cherokee moving through these parts too, causin' trouble on and off. One of them groups attacked a supply cart bring'n supplies in, and we managed to run 'em off." Antonio looked up at us, squinting so much that his mouth opened slightly, revealing why the apple slices were so small. He had only one top tooth I could see.

After a short pause, he went back to his apple and continued. "The owners planned on settin' up shop here 'bouts, and had a mess of them Pattersons. Rangers bought all they could afford but seems the thirty six caliber ball these 'r chambered in ain't all that popular elsewhere. I was told we can sell them here to settlers, but none on credit. You got money, I can sell you what ye need."

"We do. They're Austrian guldens, but gold is gold. We need a rifle and a pistol each. Plus shot, powder, and molds if you have 'em," I said.

"Gold is gold, Mr. Frog, that is true," he let a long, slow nod go. "Come on in," he said, waving his knife towards the doorway, then cutting his apple into slices.

We walked into the door, and with the depth of the porch, even with the two windows uncurtained, it was quite dark. Inside was a desk and chair to the left in front of one window, and stacked all around the walls were crates and barrels. Mr. Flores stood and followed us inside, chomping his apple as he brushed past us, and went to a single crate on the floor at the back with no lid, and straw sticking out of it.

"There they are. Lemme see your gulkens or whatever first," he said, spitting seeds on the floor.

I reached inside my vest and pulled out the coin purse Klement had given me. I pulled out five guldens for him to view. He held out his hand, and after receiving all five, he closed his hand and shook it up and down a bit, likely judging the weight with one eye closed and a one-sided frown. No doubt his concentratin' face.

"Alright, that's enough for a rifle and pistol and whatnot each, I reckon." He shoved another whole slice in his mouth and pocketed the gold. "They're all new'uns, but most of the packing was busted up gettin' here when the wagon wheel fell in a gopher tunnel on the side of a hill, and they all fell out on the ground. We packed 'em with straw after that."

We each took a rifle and a pistol from the straw and ensured that the actions and disassembly for reloading were functioning properly. Looking around, I asked if he had any leatherworks, holsters and belts, and chaps in the little storeroom.

"Yeah, them injuns trade us stuff they make all the time. We got a load of belt buckles in last month. They made some good rigs for all us usin' them Pattersons too. They're up here a'hangin' on the wall."

I turned back towards the front of the small room and found a dozen or more new ones, made specifically for these revolvers, hanging on a series of pegs driven into the wall.

"Did the payment cover those, too?" I asked

"Reckon so. Not many people usin' these Pattersons. They're about the only ones fit in those. Go ahead. There's a stack of leather pants, shirts, chaps, bedroll covers, and such out back on a bench. Give me another two of them lil' bars you got, and y'all can pick out what you want from the stack," he finished his apple in one last big mouthful, crunching it as he spoke.

We went out the front door and around back, to a long foot-wide bench made of a half-log piled high with leather goods. After a few minutes, we each had a fringed pullover shirt made of deerskin and chaps, so we returned inside to show Mr. Flores and ensure he was agreeable with the arrangement. He was sitting behind the desk, making a note in a ledger, I assume, about our transaction.

"That's fine, Mr. Frog. Now, I gotta say, there's a trouble-some band of Comanches round 'abouts who are convinced there is some evil at work, and it's to blame for their mis-fortunes. I'd recommend you git to yer folks and keep 'em safe sooner rather than later. In fact, about everyone 'round here is still riled about one thing or another. Y'all keep safe," he said, starting on another apple, this time a Granny Smith green.

"Yes, sir, and you with your rangerin'. For what it's worth, these Wi-iko have always been good people. I am glad to see you keeping a post here," I said as we turned to walk out.

"Yessir, they are. Be seein' ya fellers." He never looked up from his peeling as though he was involved in a world record apple peeling length contest.

We left after loading our pistols and ensuring the primer caps were set securely on the rifles as well. Arterous had taken off his Austrian jacket and left only his shirt on un-der his new buckskin blouse. Once we passed the edge of the hill and began back towards the path home, I caught him looking down at his garb and giving a silent little head-shaking laugh.

"What is it, Arterous, which you find amusing?" I needed to know.

"After seeing my first American village and indigenous settlement, I would have clearly been an eyesore, which caused trouble. But this, what I have on now, is comical and contrary to everything I have ever seen. I must say," he giggled a little, still shaking his head.

"Comical, maybe, but it can save your life. And Arterous, this is not America, this is Texas," I clarified, looking straight ahead, chin up.

"It certainly is, sir," he agreed. It stood separate from anything he'd heard about the American cities for sure.

Once we reached the point where I arrived on the runewheel earlier, I subordinated myself to him. I let him lead, as he had scouted it, and the bank along this tiny stream was packed with all manner of prickly things, not wide enough for two abreast riding.

The horses were excellent. His was a tall, stout, tan buckskin with a dark brown nose, mine a palomino, not quite as many hands tall but the one I would have chosen had I been the buyer. She's a well-tempered mare, smart, but not independent enough that I should worry about her being startled easily. The saddle and bags were well-worn, but all the tack and hardware were well-oiled, soaped, and cared for. The butt of the Patterson revolver rifle was also worn, so it may have been one that hit the ground when the crates were broken. Its scabbard was fringed, and the leather tooling looked new, though metal stitching tools were used. On the right side of the saddle, the pistol's holster was affixed to the saddle straps.

We followed the meandering trickle of a creek mostly south, turning now and again west a bit before returning southerly. Some of the landscape started to feel familiar when we would each take a side of the hills on either bank to check for activity near us. The last time we edged up to look, the draw was pointing west, so we both went up the south side. Peeking over, we observed that it was pretty flat, and so we dismounted and shuffled up the loose dirt edges to poke our heads through the grasses and take a look. It should not be far to the stretch of trees, which would take us near a little stream called Hoolia Creek, along which is a good stand of cottonwood trees we can stay in for the night, with higher spots on three sides. I checked all around, and short of coyote scat and some groundhogs milling around, I couldn't perceive anything of note.

We came up out of the little trickle dip we'd been following and cantered down due south as the sun softened near the horizon to our right. Not half an hour later, we entered the mesquites and scruffy cedars we had seen earlier, which gave way to a tall growth of white pines. A bit further, and the land sloped down to the Hoolia. I definitely began to recognize the trees, rocks, soils, fragrances, and the appearance of this area.

"This way is a little bend in the creek with good visibility where we can stop for the night," I led us off to the right a bit, and came to it. It was flat and covered in a thick mat of pine needles, just like I remembered as a boy. It may have been used before. There were a few two-foot diameter pine logs, around eight feet long, around the perimeter, perhaps for sitting on at one time. I walked to the far side and tied the horse to the tree by the creek with enough rope so she could drink easily.

Approaching the center of the clearing, I moved some of the pine needles around and, sure enough, I found a small ring of rocks. I used my foot to clear the dry pine needles out of the fire pit, while Arterous tied his horse to another tree so it could drink and reach some of the edge grasses. I took the saddle off, laid it across the log I intended to sleep near, and then brushed more of the debris away from the fire area, kicking most over to where I would sleep. The few dry pine branches lying around, I piled into the fire pit in a teepee shape.

"Would you mind, um..."

"Certainly." Arterous pulled his wand and cast a small fire bolt into the fire pit, getting it started. Then he cast a few protection charms for us, waved them in one great circle above his head, and presto—a cooking pot and stand were over the fire. A table with chairs, set for us. Another two taps on the table, and a hen prepared for the spike, a pitcher of honey ale to drink, and a pile of biscuits and corn on the cob with butter. A ring of three like-new oil lamps, levitating around the table, lit it quite well.

Honestly, the satisfaction of doing all this for myself will never really square with basically wishing things like this into existence. Many find that the magic that ensures long, healthy lives is a gift that sets them apart, making them above the ordinary. I always wondered if it was a way of ensuring that wonder would always exist in the world. But I understand why we had to hide, I guess. The suffering in the ordinary world for food and shelter is so pervasive that even if every wizard spent their lives conjuring food and water for the rest of the world, they would never sleep, and the number of sufferers would never be quenched. There are simply not enough magical people to conceive of trying it. We, or rather they, constitute less than half of one percent of the world's population, by the best estimates. Everyone who received the help would expect it, then demand it, and those who couldn't have it would, in all likelihood, make war on the others. That is the rationale I have heard my whole life, anyway.

"Thank you. I often forget how easy it is. I do appreciate when I can be a part of it," I said gratefully. I speared the hen and put it on the rack and sat down, pouring a drink of the ale. "Ahhh. Very good."

"So, Raileanu," he started.

"Actually, Arterous, the papers I was given by the professor have me listed as Randall Frog to appear more American for our investigation. Not a bad idea, I suppose. My mother called me her little frog as a boy."

"Ah, Randall. Or Randy?" he queried.

"Randy, I guess, at least around strangers."

"How did you come to have the name Raileanu?"

"My father had a friend he served with in the last wizard war named Raileanu. Raileanu Evanescu, I believe. He saved my father's life on more than one occasion. He was from Bucharest, on the shore of Lacul Morii. They were going to visit each other's homes and families, but he passed away before the end of the war. One day, I will visit there, find, meet, and thank them," I explained.

Shaking his head in agreement, he asked, "And my uncle, how did you meet him?"

"He was the only one who had lost their magic from an illness that anyone had ever met. The further back in history they looked, the more they couldn't find one like it. After he graduated, he was allowed to work as an ambassador to the non-magical world. However, in his available time, he worked with the schools of Europe to try to establish a better diagnostic set of tools and training for people like him, especially if they were children. As it turned out, I was the only one who had their loss of "natural" causes. There were others, but their losses came at the hands of magical curses, diabolical actions, and known causes. The professors let us proceed through school, though, testing all parameters to determine what, if any, magic remained. If any abilities lingered, they could try and build on them. I knew, though, I would have none. Wanting to be able to at least identify magic, rare animals, and herbs, and operate at least competently in both worlds, I did my best."

"My uncle," he began, adjusting his weight, "was completely distraught after his loss of power. He spent virtually a whole year in a hunting lodge of the royal family, barely speaking to anyone. We were all worried. I was only five at the time, and I remember him being so happy and playful with all of us little ones. I recall that as a young boy, I didn't understand why he fell into this melancholy. He had used the magic for only a couple of years fully, and was quite good. But as unnerving as the illness was for him, we were all relieved he survived it. As a little boy, I was glad I still had my uncle. He told us that at the end of that year, he started praying regularly. Not for his magic to return, he knew it was gone, but instead for the wisdom to comprehend what it was God may have in store for him. That perhaps, the loss of magic was for a greater purpose. As years passed, and he worked with the few professors who had agreed to help and study the extremely rare cases like his - and later yours - he became excited at the hard work you did, surrounded by those who were still "gifted" with magic. He saw those with magic as benefactors of a "gift". I suppose he is right. My father, who is his brother, would not allow the house help to do tasks for us, as they determined we should learn to manage on our own. For example, at the age of ten, he ordered the stable workers to stop caring for my horse. I had to shovel and re-straw his stall every day. I had to fill his oat bin with a shovel and a handcart. I had to brush him and do all the work a farrier would normally do to care for him. I had to fill his water trough with a bucket from the stream, rather than using the hand pump in the barn. By the time I was twelve, he had me spend a whole month at the tack shop in town to help build a saddle, start to finish. I began to love the work, and the lessons you learn on your own more than those taught to you by another.

"The hen should be about done," leaning forward, I cut into it a bit, and it was. I pushed it off the spike with a fork and onto a plate. "Is that why we must cook the bird, instead of it being ready when you conjure it?"

"Yes, I find they are better cooked to taste than simply conjured." He said as he came to the table.

We dined, and I went to lie down on the pine needle pad I made, laying the overcoat on it. I took off my jacket and rolled it for a pillow, as it was still quite warm, even though the sun had been gone for about an hour now.

Throughout the night, I detected the presence of coyotes, bobcats, raccoons, skunks, gophers, and several frogs and toads. I also heard tunneling crawdads working in the creek and two kingsnakes. The charms must have included animal life as well; none, except the crawdads, were closer than a hundred yards, and their sounds were almost inaudible to me.

Arterous shook his wand once at the table, and it all vanished. A few embers from the fire danced away from it, drawn to the vacuum where the table had been. Another wave towards the log opposite the fire from me, and a quite comfortable cot with nice bedding appeared, under a small canvas shroud striped in his family's crest colors. He then also lay down.

By midnight, the sounds that used to comfort me here had kept waking me up, just the ones from inside our protective bubble. I found some moss on a rock at the creek and plugged my ears. It helped a little. All I was hearing now was the white threads of nearby mushrooms spreading under the carpet droppings of the trees. I found it soothing.

Growling and cooing woke me. McCort was on the ground near my head with a mouse in front of him, and I could smell food cooking, and nasty boiled trail coffee, not the Turkish coffee I had forgotten to pack. There was still a bit of low-lying mist around us. The burnt orange sun was not yet in our little depression of trees. Everything of mine, anyway, was damp. I sat up and looked around. Arterous was already up, frying bacon and eggs, his things all ready to leave, the table set. Cavalry captain, indeed.

"Good morning," I said as I stood, shook off my coat and duster, and began rolling up the overcoat.

"Morning, sir. I rose at the darkest hour and took a quick look ahead to verify our route. It is a gently rolling, um, prairie, with one stream bed that we cross, which has run dry. We should arrive at Wormwell Prison by early afternoon.

I caught sight of some Comanche braves riding away from our path. I don't think they had any notion of us. There were some other riders fumbling around about four miles east - perhaps trying to pursue the Comanche," Arterous said as he finished at the fire and slid the meal onto the plates.

"It smells fantastic, thank you again." As I pulled the seat out and sat down, "I do not want to stop until we reach home, if that is alright."

"I agree, we need to quicken the pace to begin this inquiry," he agreed.

We finished eating, saddled the horses, and checked our equipment, tying it again. He then pointed his wand at the area in a small circle, and everything returned to its original condition. I made sure to wind the watch, providing what protection it could for travel, and we mounted up. We crossed the stream, through the small wood, and up the rise to where the plain opened up. It appeared downhill from here for a long way, not something I remembered as a child when I had been here before. Knowing the tendency of my mind to wander in my youth, ground squirrels, javelinas, and grass spiders possibly distracted me from my concerns about topography. Still, good news if it held.

We alternated between short runs and quick trotting, depending on the ground and whether we were on top of a rise or not, trying to limit our outline to anyone in the distance. We were lucky, and the rest of the ride passed uneventfully. When I spotted the low depression with some outcroppings of rock that marked the boundary of my family's homestead, I pulled my pocket watch out and checked the time: about a quarter after three o'clock. As we reached, and crested over the little craggy rise, I felt the distortion of the shimmerwall, then we wound down about sixty feet in elevation to the depression which was home to a stand of cedar and some live and post oaks with low, long limbs, having been lashed by wind and ice storms when they try every year to venture over the edge of the depression.

Once at the bottom, we wound our way through the trees and came to the tall slabs of iron ore and sandstone mix, which formed the maze in which Wormwell was placed. They were between six and ten feet tall, two to three feet thick, with a reddish-rusty color, and I could tell Arterous was able to read the magical glyphs that marked the path, as he was making all the right turns without asking for my guidance. Mine was from memory now, as seeing those marks was impossible for me. I recall most of them from my youth, but not all of them. The area the homestead covered was twelve to fifteen acres. Most of the rock slabs were covered in sharp edges, and I recall being cut quite often as a boy while horsing around them.

The maze opened to a clearing, my home for so many years. It was the same beautiful log home, built for the previous warden, who served at the prison for the first three years after it was built, before he retired. It was better than new when my father assumed the duties of warden; it was worn smooth in the places where you put your hands, and had additions like the small vegetable garden off to the left, featuring tomatoes, jalapeños, potatoes, corn, okra, and yellow crookneck squash. In boxes along the railing of the front porch, the only area open to the southern sun year-round, small herbs were planted. The round river rock chimney on the front of the house, with a small open hearth on the outside, had smoke lazily wandering up through the tree-tops. The split-plank roofing had the same moss and lichen I remembered, only thicker and more widespread. The home was two stories tall, yet still nestled below the canopy of the trees. The horse stalls were to the far left, facing the open front yard. We passed through the split-rail fencing surrounding the yard, which reached from standing stone to standing stone. The bed sheets and laundry fluttering out back, I can hear on the clothesline, the lye soap rinsed free, but I could still sense it. I came off the saddle, landing with a little bounce and a smile bigger than that. I led the horse and Arterous to the stalls and took the saddle off. Mother had already filled the rail bin with alfalfa hay and the bucket with cool, clear water for both horses.

"If father is resting, I don't want to wake him, so I say we should proceed quietly." We both try to knock as much trail dust off ourselves as we can, Art's bowler cap not as effective as my nice proper hat. Far to the right, between an arch of the natural stone formations, is an iron cage with inscriptions all over it, a large lock housing behind it. About twenty feet through the natural rock tunnel, the door to the actual prison was located.

"Is that the prison over there?" He pointed to it, having followed my glance at it.

"Yes, that's Wormwell," I said.

The steps to the porch were the same, half logs all of twelve feet long, leading up the four steps to the porch. The porch was ten feet deep and allowed for resting in the shade to cool off, which is needed about ten months of the year here. Mother's old tabby cat was curled up in the rocking chair to the right of the door, not bothering to notice my coming home for the first time in three years. I honestly don't care for cats as pets; they're furry, meddlesome, and as likely to pee in your boots as care if you were on fire. As a familiar to magical people, I suppose, they are more useful than a mouser on a farm. I went to the front door, a row of heavy cedar planks held together with mortise and tenon joints and peg locks, hung from ornate wrought iron strap hinges. The handle is a simple sliding plank with a peg on both sides. I open it quietly, and before I can step inside, my mother ambushes me with a great, crushing hug. I returned the hug for a moment, knowing her scent since before I was born.

"Oh, son! I am so pleased that you and the professor were able to find a way for you to arrive so quickly! Please, please, both of you come in." Momma was happy. She let go, briefly waving her hands for us to come in from outside, and hustled around us to shut the door.

"Momma, is Father asleep, or can I go look in on him?" I got right to it.

"Yes, he is asleep now. None of the things we could normally use seem to stop the pain, the coughing, or the problem."

"The problem?" I asked.

"Yes, yes, I will explain, please come sit down at the table. I know the request for some secrecy has made this hard for all of us, but I suppose I understand as well. The professor has sent everything he could think of to help. Lord, sometimes I find a minute to rest here in the middle of the night, and his portrait starts rattling off another list of ingredients I should try. I know he is trying to help, but the time difference is not helping me relax one bit," Momma rattled off, getting things ready for dinner, and mixing something in a pitcher..

We sat at the long table, with benches for seats, the same one that's always been here. As a young'un, I had to put two, two-inch-thick slices from a tree trunk under myself to eat properly. Upon examining the area, it appears to be similar. Father's high back chair still near the fireplace, his bookshelf in arm's reach. His pipe was on the table next to it. I hear him cough. Mother reaches across the table and puts her hand on mine, cocking her head to listen; it only lasts a minute.

"He's still asleep," she says, taking her hand back. "Oh, would you two like some cool lemonade? I made some this morning, it seemed the darn tree's lemons wouldn't ever ripen this year." She jumped up, went to the kitchen, brought back the glasses and pitcher, filled them, and with a tap of her wand, they became frosty with ice slush in them.

"Never had any, madam, please," Arterous said, reaching for his glass. "Oh my, that is very refreshing," making the face of everyone who tries good lemonade for their first time. I waited for him to detect Momma's secret ingredient, a one-to-four ratio of Persian limes to lemons. It showed in the grimace a moment later.

"Darling," mother began, "Arterous came yesterday and early this morning to check on us, even knew a charm or two we didn't, and he double checked everything so we'd be safe."

"It was my pleasure, my lady," he nodded and went back to the lemonade, taking more and letting the limes force another brief anguished look, then a smile, and another sip.

"Mother, please tell me, when and how did this begin with Father?"

"It was, well, honestly, in June, over a month ago. One day, after completing his morning rounds in the prison, he sat down to write his reports. After a few minutes, he dropped his quill and said his left hand was hurting. She waved her hands, wrists down, something she would do in frustration at me and father. "That night, after he had escorted the priest to visit the few prisoners who wanted to meet with him, one of his fingernails on his left hand was blackened. The next morning, two were black, and by the end of the week, all were," she stopped and covered her mouth with her hand, eyebrows inched further down at the corners. "At first, we thought it was a fungus or some slime mold, but after ten days, he couldn't use his hand at all. Well, you know your father; he didn't want to bother anyone. Remember when you were a boy, he had a spot on his shin that was kinda dark and grew; that was just a spider bite. By the time he let me examine it, it was about two inches in diameter. A simple potion of cantaloupe rind fixed it overnight." Momma had said more in the last few minutes than I usually would hear out of her in a month. Her frantic tone worried me. "So, after ten days, that's when he first spoke with the professor, and since then, we have tried everything. Finally, I said I'd had enough, and we had to let you know. The professor agreed. Since then, a dark line under the surface of the skin has proceeded up the arm, down his side, and to his foot as well. He cannot move that foot now. Off the original line, a branch started across his chest, and that's when the coughing began. The only thing that has marginally helped is the honey I give him in his hot tea, the honey made from the blooming jalapeños I grow out back, you know," she sighed and pushed her hands out on the table, exasperated.

"I am sorry he persuaded you to wait. They are concerned that it might be a dark, or possibly ancient magic, which should be investigated. Do you think I could look in on him?" I asked.

"Yes, please do be as quiet as you can. He has only been asleep for a couple of hours now. I would be happy to entertain Arterous for a few minutes," she smiled.

I took another drink of the lemonade and stood up, stepping over the bench. I walked through the sitting area, to the back, and up the stairs, being cautious not to squeak on the stairs, gripping the railing tightly. At the top of the stairs sat my old toy box, my stuffed pegasus still on top. I turned left, and seeing that Mother was watching, nodded that I should go ahead. I went on and opened his door slowly. He was lying on his side, facing away, so I went to his bed. His right arm was out of the blanket, and he wore his short-sleeved summer sleeping gown. All of his fingers were black, his hand mostly black around the veins, and ashy grey in the rest. The line wound its way up the arm, into the sleeve. His breath was shallow and raspy, sounding anything but healthy. I closed my eyes and said a quick prayer for him. A better father I couldn't imagine, always time to play after duties, always supportive of dreams, but never allowing chores to be slackened. I never had to wonder whether he was proud of me; he said so every chance he could. I left the room, upset that we didn't know how to help. Magical people often don't fully recover with time. Their bodies either prevent this kind of crippling disease outright, or spellcraft and potions eliminate it swiftly.

"We will figure this out, Dad. Hang in there," I barely whispered.

I went back downstairs and sat with Mother and Arterous again, refilling my glass.

"Is it as bad as we thought?" Arterous asked.

"Yes, I'm afraid so. It's on his right arm as well." I stated determinately, "Would it be possible to go into the prison, to have a look around?"

"Oh yes. I have the report he filed on the day's work when it started. Not one prisoner has come or gone from their cells since that day, everything is as it was," she said.

"Arterous, you will have to accompany me, as use of magic and perception of magical misuse will fall to you," I said.

"Yes, indeed, my uncle made sure I had this to help." He pulled a beveled glass monocle from his pocket. "It is a goblin-crafted crystal, the same kind they use when appraising goods for their magical heritage. It can determine the type or family of spells and enchantments on objects while using it. We cannot perceive such details with it, but it does show traces of magic, in gradients of white to black depending on strength."

"Looking at the twelve or so bevels making up the lens, you will definitely have to use it. Looking through it might make me ill," I said.

Mother went to Father's desk and retrieved the papers that made up the day's report, handing them to me.

"He went back through every step he made that day, morning and afternoon, the third day after it started. There were only eight prisoners, most of whom had been here for over a year. He could not find anything out of place. Maybe the monocle will help," she said.

"Thank you, anything else we should know?" I kept shuffling through the papers, looking for anything of note. Father was a great note-taker.

"Ah, yes, there is a shapeshifter, a skinwalker shaman who has committed to guarding the prison for two years now; he stays inside and patrols around the halls." Momma rose to collect things from the kitchen. "Take him this for his dinner, he can eat a bit earlier today than usual. He is forever in the form of a grey wolf. His name is Bandos. His family was killed by one of the prisoners. Bandos captured and delivered him here himself." She handed me a whole, cooked rabbit and retrieved the pitcher of lemonade. "This is for him as well. He loves it. He can understand everything we say, but will only be able to speak to Arterous. He said he hasn't seen anything out of the ordinary," she went to the central log post in the center of the house. The post went through the front balcony of the second floor to the main roof beam. "Here are the keys, the large square shafted one is the main gate, the other is for the entrance door. The cell keys are bound to your father; no one else can use them, but the main gate key will work. I will tell Bandos you are coming in so he doesn't attack you."

"That's a good idea!" I said with a chuckle.

Mother went to the central log post in the front room, supporting a main beam for the second floor and roof beams. On it was a silver plaque, with a trumpet flower-shaped copper horn. It was on the back of the post, as viewed from the front door, and I hadn't detected it until she went to it.

She spoke into it, "Bandos, our son and a friend are coming in to look around, to see if they can find anything which could have hurt John. Please be kind and show them around." The voice had a distant echo to it.

"That wasn't there when I left. What is it?" I asked.

"No, when Bandos said he had bound himself to guard that prisoner, John crafted this, and the identical ones you'll find in the prison. It lets us talk to him and each other anytime we want," she explained.

"That's Dad, alright. No problem he can't overcome with his mind and a little elbow grease," I said, shaking my head. As with most people who choose to live on the frontiers or unsettled land, they often create, out of necessity, tools, techniques, or gadgets to suit a need, with no regard to whether the rest of the world could benefit from it. Often, those inventions predate the commercially available ones by many years.

"Alright, mother, thank you. We won't be long." I carried the meal and drink for Bandos, and let Arterous lead with the keys.

CHAPTER FIVE

There was only about an hour or so of sun left, about two until total darkness, so after the long day on the trail, I would sleep better knowing we have looked in on the prison, as it may be the culprit, or at least have clues as to what is ailing my father. We cross the yard, chickens scurrying around us, getting the last few grasshoppers buzzing around before they, too, bed down for the night. Arterous keys the lock, clacks it open, swings the gate, squealing on the hinges, spewing iron oxide dust in little clouds as it moves. The previous warden had always kept the gates well-maintained and oiled, and they were silent when my family first got here. My father decided to care for the gates themselves, so they appeared well-oiled. However, he intentionally did not oil or grease the hinges in any way, making it obvious to anyone in the vicinity when the main gate was even slightly moved. I shut it behind us, cradling the pitcher and bowl in one arm, the lock mechanism springing the latch shut again. As we approach the entrance alcove, the torch in a recess to our left ignites, illuminating the massive door and the copper horn on it. Inscribed by the fiery tip of a wand into the hard stone above it, "WORMWELL WIZARD PRISON" and below it "-1654-". As he switches keys and begins to unlock the mechanism, I say, "This door was brought here from a prison in Ireland almost two hundred years ago. Father said the magic on it is so old that no one really knows its age. But for securing spaces, a stronger door does not exist."

He unlocked and pushed open the door, this one not creaking, but extremely heavy, no less than ten inches of thick oak. Torches along the right side of the hallway light up, leading to the stairs going down and around the corner. I had seen the layout of the prison depicted in drawings before, but having lost my powers at such a young age, I had never been allowed in, not that I wanted to. It is shaped like a descending spiral, with torches positioned on the right, the new communication horns beside each, and the corkscrew and cells hewn magically from the solid rock, beginning thirty feet below on the left. It was only thirty feet below grade here to hard bedrock; above it were smaller striations of various rocks, the iron ore locked in sandstone, some caliche, topped with soils made of stone ground from the movement of ice long ago. It was called Wormwell because the builders knew that over the period of its use, the only life that could enter would be tiny roots and worms. It was magically carved and thereby protected from any outside influences. The prisoners were doomed to exist only on the worms and moisture that ran down the walls. It was so terrible, I couldn't imagine what kind of evil is in a person that would drive them to commit crimes whose punishment could be so harsh. To never see the sun again, or the wind, or the seasons change. Terrible. I never wanted to go inside, nor meet anyone entombed there. The thought of their suffering and the evil that sent them to this place made me ill at the slightest fleeting thought of what was happening in the minds of the people, or the walls of Wormwell.

My father corrected my assumption that evil is a purely innate quality that some people possess and cannot be corrected. He said he believed that all of us are a soul, a brilliant light, with all our thoughts, dreams, and connections to others, bound inside a kind of crystal shell. He felt it was like a golden light inside the shell that we wear here on earth. Some begin early, while others are born into circumstances that immediately cover the transparent shell in thick, opaque grime, like tar, so all they can discern or sense is darkness. They have never seen their light, and if a glimmer manages to shine through, their circumstance instantly covers it in thicker layers. It becomes so dense, they cannot perceive the light of others. When they do, it is frightening, and they react only as they know - by damaging it or blocking it in others. It is possible for some to find redemption. There is one way, as my parents and I believe, to begin to let the behaviors and patterns of life that caused the sludge and decay subside, and not be afraid of one's own light or the light of others. That said, I still don't want to be here.

Inside the door, to the right, was a larger part of the landing above the descending stairs. A large fluffy mattress bag filled with water oak leaves, pine needles, and cedar boughs, by the aromas, with two large steel bowls against the wall near it. I poured the lemonade in one and set the rabbit in the other. Pretty cozy, honestly. I had slept in the granular clots of black prairie dirt of North Texas before, and the impossible sharp rocks which littered everything west of Fort Worth, not to mention the commingled goat's head stickers, blackberry thorns as tiny as hairs, and every other prickly denizen of the wild which find their way into your clothing and bedding. Those places were a thousand times harder to sleep on than Bandos' arrangement here.

We proceeded down the wide, smooth, shallow drop stone stairs, and after about three revolutions of the steps, we had come to the first cell on our left. The cage bars were also carved from the stone itself. An ash leaf-shaped door made of brass, green around the edges, with no lock box, only a tiny slot in its center. A large "1" is carved in the stone above the door. Here, in front of this empty cell by the light of the torch, I check the paperwork. Of the thirty-six cells, the ones occupied are 4, 7, 8, 11, 14, 19, 20, and 21.

"Have you the monocle, Arterous? Can you detect anything yet?" I asked.

He reached into the pocket of his vest, under his leather shirt, retrieving it, and stretching his eye up and down, letting it grasp the rim. "Let me look. Mmmm. Yes, I can identify the carving and binding work spellcraft, a light grayish glow around the whole of the rock structure, the light of the door is a bit brighter, but there's nothing inside the cell," he said.

"Makes sense to me, each warden must place their own secret magic on the doors, but the underground works are original," I said. "Keep it on, please. We should look for anything, even in these empty cells, the stairwell, everywhere. My parents are skilled, and answers have never eluded them before," I said, peering into cell number one. "Perhaps any differences between the seepings in each cell may offer a pharmacological clue." This first cell was smoothly crafted, featuring a flat alcove on one side. I suppose it served as a "bed," and in the back, opposite corner, a clean, dry spot with a slight circular depression. Ew, I know what it is for, that's where they, um, go. Magic, it seems, clears it up for them. Nasty. Within were also many thin, stringy roots with moisture clinging to them, hanging from the ceiling. More than a few worms had found their way in and had died all over the floor.

Arterous peered in, casting a light spell to check more closely. "No, I don't find any traces other than original work," he said.

"Alright, let's continue. Please check the whole prison, if possible, walls, floors, everything," I said quietly.

"Shall I cast silence, so we won't be shouted at by any of the prisoners?" He asked earnestly.

"Probably a good idea, if we come across Bandos, you can ask him if any are worth talking to."

He waved the wand in the appropriate "X" shape, and even the occasional drip sound disappeared. We continued.

We inspected each cell and the pathway we were on, with no obvious discrepancies. We paused at cell number 11 for a moment to switch to a second page of the document.

"JESUS!" Arterous shouted! It was Bandos. Not having been here when he cast silence, the wolf came right up to him while we were focused on the paper, and was completely, well, silent. A quick wave of his wand, and he knelt to speak with him. It was brief. Bandos said the only scent of magic that seemed out of place was on the afternoon of the first day that Dad's fingernail went black. He didn't feel it was related to any specific part of the prison, but perhaps to the air that day. I said I would go back up with Bandos to the top, so he could have dinner, and let Arterous and his monocle check the last half.

I went back up with Bandos and sat on the top two steps of the stairs to wait for Arterous. After eating and drinking his lemonade, he lay in the bed my mother had made for him.

It was only a few moments longer, and Arterous came back up.

"Let's go back inside. I have but one thing that was uncommon." He undid his silence casting, and we went out.

"Goodnight, Bandos," I said as we shut and locked the door.

"He said thanks, you as well," Arterous translated. "I hope your father gets better soon." We went through and locked the outer gate. It was deep dusk now, barely any yellow light left. We walked inside the house to speak with Mother.

We sat at the table, he put his monocle away, and mother brought some coffee to us.

"Well, anything?"

"Only one strange thing, but it does not seem important. A singular, long, tiny root extended from the roof of one cell, 21, all the way to the sleeping cove into a small pile. Through the monocle, it didn't look dark like a root; it looked deep and dark, as if it were revealing some ancient magic, but not like any colors I had ever heard described for the user of this device. I'm not sure what it means. May I speak to the professor's portrait?" Arterous asked Mother.

"Yes, it's to the right of the hearth," she pointed.

"Mother, do you have the files of the prisoners at hand?" I asked. "Can we review the one for cell 21, please?"

"Yes, give me a minute," she said, and went to Father's desk, where she began to shuffle through the papers. In a few minutes, she came back.

"Cell 21, here it is," she laid the book on the table, and opened it, beginning to read. "He is Garivinis Finella. He was brought here twelve years ago, having attacked a nearby convent several times, casting boils and sores on the nuns who lived there over a couple of years. Hmm. He was only nineteen, and he apparently was on probation, having graduated from the school in Yucatan after causing several serious problems during his last year. His family had died in one of the revolutions in central Mexico during that year, and he behaved poorly after they died. The monastery nearby agreed to let him stay and help, but he turned on them for some reason. He hasn't spoken since he came here. He hasn't been any trouble for your father the whole time he's been here. He mumbles nonsense sometimes, but it is indiscernible, and according to father, indiscriminate and harmless. His wand was broken upon his arrest, and the halves were cast one into the Pacific and one into the Atlantic, by order of the jury who sent him here. That is usually due to the magic used by the prisoner, spells no jury wants another to discover in examination of their wand."

"Honestly, mother, if he wouldn't speak to father, in all those years, we likely won't coax much outta him either," I said.

"There's the Texan frog coming out a little," she smiled.

105

"It is in here, it just takes a while to wriggle back to the top," I smiled back at her. "You said a priest had visited, did you not? Is there notation of who he visited, when, or anything?"

She looked through a few pages. I glanced over at Arterous, and he was still talking to the professor through the portrait. He moved his hands around, I'm guessing by the motion, describing the roots he found with the monocle.

"No, he made no note of who or when. It's possible he was asked to keep it private, and he would have. But the chance this Finella would have spoken at all seems slight. Perhaps the priest spoke to him to no avail?" she said. "His name is Father Callious. He has visited roughly once a week or so over the last few years. Your father never had any ill feelings regarding him, or he would have mentioned it. I can give you directions to the monastery. It's only an hour west of here. He was granted permission from the bishop to visit the prisoners. I believe those orders can only come from Rome, as the treaty permits only priests trained in magical counsel to do so. He was never without your father; those were his rules."

"Alright, momma. If father is going to sleep through the night, I guess we will turn in soon so we can head out in the morning to the mission."

Arterous came back to the table and sat down. He looked as tired as I felt, resting his forehead in his hands. Mother and I looked at him, waiting to receive any good news.

"Well, the professor does not have any information on hand that references a poisonous root like we discovered in the cell, but the depth it seemed to show through the monocle was interesting. He is going to look for references in his brace of magical medical texts. He is also going to ask a few others about it. He said the best book is vague on the subject, and even those references are extremely old. I think it's best if we get some sleep," he sighed.

"The files on the prisoner didn't show anything of interest. The only other thing we thought of was the priest who would occasionally visit the prisoners. He came the day father spotted the first sign of a problem," I said. "We can go in the morning, it's not far at all to the mission where he lives." I tried to hold in a yawn, which didn't work, and like its own virus, Mother and Arterous let one go as well.

"I prepared two rooms upstairs for you boys. I will be staying on the bench in the room with John. If he wakes up enough, I will tell him you are here," Mom said.

"Alright, mother, thank you for everything. Tell Father I love him if he does wake. We will turn in," I said, standing to hug her. She went off to the kitchen, took the tea kettle and her jar of honey with the long spoon, and went up to their room.

We, too, went upstairs and into the guest rooms. One used to be mine, but after I started working abroad, they set it up for visiting judges, counsels, and transport guards. The house had six rooms upstairs, including my parents' large suite. We were as quiet as possible, waving goodnight to each other as we quietly shut the doors.

Mom had already put our saddlebags and packs in the rooms, mine on a trunk on the right side of the bed, with the saddlebags hung on the end rail of the log-frame bed. The window was open; she must have brought them in with levitation. Looking in the direction where I remembered the wardrobe being, I noticed a new, small closet structure. I went and looked, and oh my, actual civilized indoor plumbing. I was gobsmacked. Some of the castles and country manors I visit barely have two in fifty rooms. A sink, two taps, and a porcelain throne, even a small round copper tub, the same two taps extending from the wall piping over the tub. So, so nice. Turning around from the bathroom doorway was a wardrobe on the opposite wall. I changed into my pajamas and lay on the bed, exhausted. I guess my mother heard me lie down, because the two lamps flicked out, and it was not long before I was asleep.

"Little frog, little frog, wake up. Hey, it's Mother. Your father is awake, asking for you," Momma said. She was beside the bed, lamp in her hand.

I woke up and looked around, startled. "Is he alright?"

"Yes, he is, please come. He is happy you are here."

"Yes, ok." I flung the blanket off, climbed out of bed, and followed her out of the room. She was still wearing the same thing she had on when we arrived. Again, I wish I could be of more help to her. It was still pitch black outside, so it was the middle of the night. The door to their room was open, with a lamp beside their bed, and my dad was propped up against the headboard, supported by some pillows. The room was the same as I recall from a few years ago. Dad smiled when he saw us come in and raised his right arm, beckoning me to him. I went right over and bent to hug him with both arms. He was so thin, frail. It was easy to observe in his face how gaunt and drawn his skin was across his skeleton earlier, but hugging him now, he was skin and bones. He couldn't weigh more than a hundred and twenty pounds now. It reminded me of those who in the Amazon basin contract dysentery or malaria. I had been around them when traveling as a boy. For a man of six feet, a life of hard work and hearty meals, he had been reduced by sixty pounds in a month. I could feel every rib, the joints in his shoulders poking my arms, his skin loose across them. The private particulars associated with those illnesses would have been detectable by me and my nose from half a mile away, so Mother must have been caring for them in her magical, motherly way.

"So, so glad to be here with you, Dad. I love you," I sat on the bed next to my father, more afraid for him than I had been so far. He could see it in my face, which I tried to hide, but had no hope of doing.

"I love you, too, son. We're lucky our friends could get things together so quickly to bring you here," he managed to force through labored, clinging breaths, clutching his chest, punctuated by coughing now and again.

"Definitely. Thirty miles across the prairie without incident in the summer is a miracle in itself." I took him by the hand, examining the streaks and deep color marks. "Has Professor Templeton shared the information we found yesterday evening with you, since you've been up?" I glanced toward the end of the bed at Mom.

"Some, I can tell you this. It is definitely some type of magic." He paused and drew a few breaths deeply as he could before he continued. "I have never read or heard of something which behaves like this. It is slow, methodical, and it is killing the parts of me it moves through." I could feel the vibration of the obstructions in his airways as he struggled for breath. It hurt me to listen. "It does not feel or behave as a spell, a curse, a potion, or even an ordinary human infection. It almost feels as if it is thinking, deciding where to move each moment. I cannot conceive of what it is." He was winded and descended into coughing as soon as he finished. My father has never had a cough; I fear it's moving to finish consuming his lungs.

"Alright, dad, alright, I am here, and we are going to stay until we figure this out." I paused as he finished coughing again. "Do you have any reason to think the padre from the mission may have an idea what is going on?" He shook his head no, no. Still holding his hand, more tightly now, I could feel his strong heart fighting to push blood through him.

"I spoke with your mother a bit before she went to wake you. I have written a letter for you to take to Father Callious. It will explain that he is authorized to discuss this illness with you. He will not discuss anything about his talks with prisoners, as those are protected confessions under the treaty. I don't know what help he can be, but we should ask." His coughing now was steady, and he waved off any talking for now. A tear squeezed out the corner of each eye, as they were compressed shut while coughing. The veins in his neck bulged from the strain.

"Very good, Dad, I'm so happy to be here with you. I am going to stay here and let Arterous go and speak with him. If nothing else, he would know what is happening, and perhaps some of his parishioners have shared something with him that might be helpful. Just rest. I'm not going anywhere," I assured him.

He lay back, with grumbling sounds in his chest, behaving on their own, and Father wasn't even breathing this time when I heard them. I asked Mom if she had any coffee made, and she shook her head no. I said, "Alright, I will dress and go make some. Then I will stay up here with him so you can rest a while." She had begun wiping her own tears as soon as we began speaking. I could see them, but Dad couldn't. It would hurt him more to see her in pain.

I did just that, and checked the pocket watch, 4:41 A.M.. It will be light in less than an hour. I made the coffee, put it in a kettle, and took three cups up to the bedroom. Dad was asleep again. I set the coffee and mugs down on the dresser and told Mom I was going to wake Arterous and be right back. I got him up and suggested he fly in the moonless dark to the mission with the letter and see what he can learn. I told him my dad is up, sort of, and I want to stay with him. It will be much faster than waiting for me and a trip on horseback as well. He agreed and began preparing to leave, so I went back with Dad. Mom went downstairs, not seeming to want any rest.

About ten minutes or so later, Arterous was ready to go. He stuck his head in to wave goodbye. I motioned to the table by the door, and he found the letter, picked it up, and nodded, then pulled the door shut. Mother was now cooking, and knew she wouldn't let Arterous leave hungry. I heard him say he should hurry, so as not to be seen by anyone, and he waved a couple of pieces of bacon in the air and was out the front door. I could smell it all the way up the stairs, and now I was hungry. I grabbed the pot and cup of coffee and went downstairs. She was scrambling eggs in the pan, the wooden spoon magically stirring them, the wood stove now hot enough. The aroma of biscuits baking in the oven was so good, ole buttermilk biscuits. She stacked another dozen pieces of bacon on a plate and took the coffee pot from me, tapping it and refilling it. The ability to stoke an appetite through real cooking, well, mostly real, is so fulfilling compared to the "poof" and its done method.

"Mom, I am afraid that if we can't figure this out, it may take Dad before long. I am not sure where to start. I hope the professor gets some answers soon. It's not what any of us want to hear, but it seems so bent on spreading in him." I put my head in my hands and leaned on the table.

"Elbows off the table, Raileanu! Manners, boy!" Mom said, frustration being the trigger for it.

"Yes, ma'am. I'm sorry," I put my hands in my lap. "Aren't you going to rest?"

"Here, eat while it's hot." Shoveling the different home-made delicacies onto my pewter plate with her olivewood spoon. She sat down, brushing the flour off her apron as she took her seat. "Whatever we find to do, you will need a full stomach. And no, my boy, I have rested enough."

She was right. One's constitution will be tested one way or the other on hard days; all we can do is be as ready as we can be.

CHAPTER SIX

M onika had spent the last few days unloading and arranging the various plant and animal samples, their tags, notes, drawings, and rock samples that I had gathered during my time near Lake Königssee. She had set up in a small row of four unused officers' quarters on the grounds of the Royal House, along the western wall. She had divided the materials into four groups, the smallest being the rock samples, which she stacked on shelves in the little bungalow where she also stayed. The plant samples, associated drawings, and uses were another group. The insects make up a third, and the mushrooms, molds, slimes, and similar organisms comprise the fourth. The Metternichs had left the day after me, and she was alone, save for the groundskeeper, the cook, and four guards who now resided in the guardhouse at the front of the walled compound in much newer accommodations. She usually ate breakfast with them, sometimes lunch, but always had dinner at the pub across the road, located on the whole first floor of the little hotel.

After the third day of this, she had decided to not only eat supper there, but also to take advantage of the much, much more comfortable bed in the hotel. She mentioned that she might sleep for two days, estimating the weight of the materials to be about two tons, which she had unloaded, sorted, and grouped over the last few days. She closed up the doors to the rooms with materials and locked them. Then she went by the guardhouse to inform them that she would not be staying tonight, and exited through the single-person gate, waving goodbye to the guards. Waiting on a carriage, a horse and cart to pass by, she then crossed the street looking forward to a good meal and a good night's sleep.

She had enjoyed traditional shepherd's pie in England some years ago, which she had kept as a secret, and last year had helped the cook in the magical half of the pub make it quite well. That's what she was hungry for. She went in around the back, where the entrance for magical folks was located. It was behind a bright lamp post which stood in front of a small bay window on the left side of the hotel's lobby, on a wooden panel that looked like it had been painted black a thousand times, and was exactly the size of a door. Over it, on the rock exterior, was the name "Bavarian Baker." Only the magical can spot it. Their bakery skills will be put to use tonight for sure.

She conferred with the baker and the cook, who told her there are quite a few people who have requested it as well, and also enjoy it, even if only when they are here alone. She sat at the small table in the corner, not by coincidence, at the same table she had last shared a private moment with me. She waited not long and had her supper with a glass of red wine. All this time, facing the shimmerwall, back to the rest of the bar, exhaling long and regularly, both from the meal and the thinking of my family's present difficulties. The chair where I had last sat with her was pulled out by the top, dragging the floor, and she looked up at the presumptuous, uh, lady.

She was tall, perhaps two or three inches taller than herself, with long, very straight and very black hair. She was dressed in black, perhaps velvet, with off-white silk ruffled cuffs peeking from underneath her full-length sleeves. Her whole blouse resembled a gaudy, overly elaborate military style, complete with gold epaulets and excessive garnish. Her pantaloons were also completely impractical and tailored to her slim figure out of a similar velvet-like material. Her boots spoke the same way to her, overtly and garishly wealthy, spit-shined, high-laced with silver adornments and a rider's heel. She had obviously not ridden here on horseback, but had dislocated, not a speck of dirt or other dust about her anywhere.

"May I join you, miss..." She said, smiling like a cat clicks at a bird.

"Miss Binder." Monika stared right through her, disdain dripping openly. "I have concluded my dinner and nearly my wine for the evening, so conversation will not distract me, please." Monika gestured to the chair the lady had already pulled out for herself. There was an inch of wine left in her glass, and regardless of what she may want, Monika could easily finish the drink and mark the end of whatever was to come. Monika was not gifted in the art of an empath or divination at all. However, no gifted nature was required to determine that whoever this woman was, there was clearly nothing she couldn't acquire if she wanted to.

"May I have your name?" Monika asked.

"Of course, my dear, my apologies, Countess Runetta Lynchos," she proudly stated, glanced down, and then seated herself. She removed her right glove, snapped her fingers, and her own cut lead crystal wine glass appeared and filled with a whirlpool. She had a strange, almost wooden-looking ring on her second finger, with a small Celtic knot of silver set in its head.

"Impressive, without a wand, no less," Monika remarked plainly. Another display of skill or spending that most could not dream of. Not sure how she did it, and being interested in magical skills and materials, she dared ask. "How is that magic done?"

"Oh, my family is some of the most gifted magical crafts-men in the human world. We are trying this new design." She held out the hand with the ring, picking up the glass and sipping from it with her left hand. "They are caretakers of the oldest enchanted stand of woods and its gifts in all Europe, you know," she withdrew her hand and re-gloved it.

"I have heard of your family. I am pleased to meet you. What brings you to, well, this particular pub, and this partic-ular table, may I ask?" Monika cut to it.

"Well, my dear, (with condescension, as she was no older than Monika was) I am not an exceptional worker of exquisite crafts as you may have guessed. Nor am I content as an exem-plar of royal heritage and duty in all social requirements that entail. I am, however, quite the purveyor of antique crystal balls, and even instruct the gentry whose female companions

116

are requested to learn the discipline, for the benefit of - you know - all." Another drink, which smelled to Monika like port. "That being said, I was able to see visions as a young lady amongst assorted things which made no sense, and seemed to be pointless. Painstaking journaling, and years later, it was revealed that my main gift wasn't only remote seeing with the crystal balls, but seeing things that invariably come to pass up to ten years in the future. They are usually disconnected in a way, and the less in focus they are, it seems, the less relevant to human affairs they turn out to be. Yet, not a month ago, I saw you. You were sitting in that chair, speaking to someone whom I could not see, and even stranger, I couldn't hear anything the two of you were saying. That has never happened to me in all these years. As you might imagine," smiling broadly now, and looking right at Monika with her beautiful green eyes, arms crossed, and elbows on the table leaning forward a bit, "it piqued my interest."

Monika could sense a charm was being attempted on her; she was able to break eye contact for a second, and indeed, Runetta was gently rubbing her ring with her thumb.

"Now, Mrs. Lynchos," Monika began.

"Countess Lynchos," she corrected, and sat back in her chair, both hands flat on the table.

"That is quite rude if I'm honest. Why would you attempt such a thing?" Monika demanded.

"Aw, my, Miss Binder, - Monika, if I may, we cannot know if it works well without giving it a try, can we now?"

"Runetta - now that is impolite indeed. You could have easily begun with your knowledge of me, and I would have enjoyed our discussion more. As it stands, I am not clear of your intentions beyond amusing yourself with testing your divination skills on me as I work on my daily tasks." Monika took the last of her wine, making it clear she did not want to continue this conversation.

"I do apologize, I admit what my class of peers do amongst themselves is not acceptable everywhere," she reached over and touched Monika's glass, and it refilled itself. "I will leave you with your thoughts, deary, do excuse me," she said, and with a sly smile, she stood up and turned away from the table, snapping her fingers, and her drink disappeared; then she too dislocated.

Honestly, it shocked Monika, the arrival, the gall, and to be perfectly honest, the sass of whoever, whatever it was that woman was doing, or wanted. Her mouth may have been partially opened with amazement for a moment or two, after a twist to the left, and Monika swept her glass abruptly up and huffed a bit as she drew a sip. The huff and sip showed it was indeed port, but oh, also magnificent. She happily carried it upstairs to her room. It seemed prudent to report what had just happened to Klement and also to Professor Templeton. So she sat and wrote each of them letters, slipping them into her inside jacket pocket, which hung on the bedpost, then turned in for the night.
****

Back in Texas, dawn brought Arterous back to my house. He had some information, but was unable to make it to the mission to meet the priest. He handed me the letter written by my father, and I assumed that we might have to go together.

"There was a contingent of what looked like Mexican Army marching south, escorted by quite a few armed men, not in uniform, marching through the night. None of the army's prisoners, I'm guessing, were armed, and they were all tied together. Roughly sixty men were guarded by a dozen or so. They spoke about the provisional government paying these men to escort the group to the southern Brazos River, where a barge would take them south to be returned to Mexico. The speed at which they were moving, I couldn't enter without being seen. As I watched, they stopped at the gate, and six of the guards went in, staying for about fifteen minutes. Then, the group started off again, just before dawn was about to break. So I came back," Arterous stated. He sat down at the table, and Mom brought him some breakfast and tapped to refill his coffee. "I used my monocle several times, and other than small flecks that could even be mineral traces of ores used in magic, I did not discern any strange traces between here and there."

Mother cocked her head, listening, and sure enough, Father began slowly, but his coughing increased. Both of us headed upstairs and opened the door. He was sitting upright, so we went on in. I sat at the end of his bed. Mother pulled a chair right up to him. She had her kettle and a cup of her special honey tea, which she gave him right away. He got a couple of timid sips in him, and he sat back to breathe as best he could.

"Son, have you spoken to Father Callious yet?" He forced out.

"No, sir. It was impossible to visit so far, as others were around." I told him. Rather worryingly, he obviously had no measure of time, as it had been only a few hours since we last spoke.

Mother pulled his shirt sleeve up, and his whole arm was now blackened. She immediately pulled the button neck open and looked. The dark branches were up to his collarbones, and all over his sternum. It made me sick and angry at the same time. Mother made a 'tsk' sound and frowned when she realized it was larger than it had been earlier.

"Mother, Raileanu, I have to tell you * rasps * I can feel I do not have long left. This I can tell now is older than anything I have ever heard of." More coughing and exceedingly labored breathing. "It is making it hard now for me to breathe easily. Whatever it is, it is not malevolent. It appears to be functioning as intended. Whatever this is, it is not of the ordinary world, nor, I believe, of ours. It must, however, be our world that solves this riddle." He was very serious in his eyes now. Quite out of breath as well, he closed his eyes, wincing in pain and clutching at his chest, and fell asleep again, still grimacing, exhausted.

"Mother," I whispered. "Can you create an aura jar, now, for Father?" I felt compelled to ask if the time was truly close. I hated to ask after it came out; she was clearly trying to avoid thinking about how bad it was.

"Yes, yes, let me get what I need from out back," she rose and intended to run downstairs for her supplies, but I held her arm, hoping she would stay with Dad.

"No, please stay with him, I remember what is needed, I will retrieve them from the porch cupboard." I ran downstairs, through the kitchen, and out the back door onto the porch. The porch was made of sandstone set in dried clay, with cedar posts and beams, and featured the same split shingle roof as the rest of the house. It was the whole width of the house and maybe twenty feet deep. Mother's little herb boxes are scattered about. To the right as I went out the door, down the whole length to the corner of the house, were her cabinets and workbench where she grafted plants and created new varieties of flowering magical plants. I needed things from practically every cabinet: cloth made from empress flowers, goldfish scales, and sparkling cattails. I found everything, including the cylindrical jar, about ten inches tall, with a cork stopper. I went back upstairs and arranged them on the bed for her. I went back downstairs, as this process is usually undignified, private, and sometimes quite bright. I felt as though it was something which needed to be done to give her a moment of purpose, so she didn't have to concentrate a minute longer on his painful passing.

I found Arterous speaking with Professor Templeton's portrait. As usual, I can only hear his side, and the portrait is a stationary painting as far as I am concerned. He turned to me and asked, "The Professor is asking how your father is."

"Not well, sir, he doesn't feel he has much longer to be honest. I have gathered the things needed for my mother to make an aura jar, so his condition may be studied later by appropriate experts, if we cannot find the cause ourselves." I told him.

After a moment, Arterous relayed to me, "Excellent idea, several I have spoken with are intrigued and disturbed by all of this, and none had the wherewithal to think of it."

"Well, sir, I had good teachers. Mother will relay his aura into the jar regularly, so the progress can be cataloged." I said. "Hopefully, this is not something any of us must deal with again," I sat down with a thud on the bench at the table. Turning my head, I looked at my father's chair for a moment, thinking about sitting in it. That one brief thought nearly broke me into tears, so I shook my head to throw it out.

Arterous said he had some things to discuss regarding his stay here, including the tasks his uncle would be assisting with, and he would call me if anything else came up. So I returned to the backyard, since I couldn't help my mother.

I spent many days here in the back yard with mother and father, ma and pa, as I called them when we were alone, helping build the garden, weeding it - that was my job when I was young, and I, in fact, looked forward to the menial chores they gave me when I was little. I felt important when I witnessed my parents performing a task that seemed complex, one they then entrusted to me.

Sitting there, I saw numerous sprigs of grass and weeds among the squash and corn. I got on my knees and went to work. The beans were tall enough and had wound around the corn, so I knew any new ones that had begun wouldn't make it to maturity before winter, so those went out as well.

I learned a great deal from my task as a little boy weeding the garden. When Momma had made new beds, we had to pitchfork the hard ground and work up all the prairie grasses and weeds, root and all. If we left one, it'd spread and drop seeds, sometimes before we'd notice. The first few times I recall, I would pull with my little hands and fingers, removing only the blades of grass or leaves and stems, leaving the roots intact. It looked good to my young eyes, no weed, it was done, right? I wasn't strong enough to pull the roots out of many of them. But no, Momma told me it wasn't good enough, and was patient enough to wait three or four days to show me they had grown right back. Whereas the ones we had managed to pull the whole thing on were completely gone. From that one lesson, Momma used patience and proof, and I started trying to use the pitchfork to loosen the soil enough for me to pull them up. At that age, I was too small to use it, of course. That is how Momma showed me that I was not strong enough, no matter how hard I tried to do some things. To have a clean bed of soil for a good crop of vegetables, I would need some help. I wrestled with it for some time that day, before finally asking her to do it so I could do a good job pulling the weeds. Her job was pitchforking, mine was pulling weeds. She taught me to worry only about my job, not someone else's.

A month later, she showed me the corner where we had left the weeds, and the plants we put in were much poorer, struggling for light and nutrients against the faster-growing and ground-covering weeds. I understood why it was an important job they had given me. Those plants were made smaller and produced fewer vegetables than the well-worked and weed-free areas.

Some years later, I realized the lesson was also for my whole life. My life was a little patch of earth that would con-stantly—and naturally—have invasive things move in around the edges, which stole energy and vitality from me. I couldn't leave them or push them away when I felt they were a prob-lem; I had to completely remove them from my life. It was as true in my whole life as it was in this little garden I was weeding again.

123

Momma hadn't had time to do any of this, and I was occupied for a good quarter of an hour when the wind changed and I caught the distinct scent of a, no, several goats. We had never had goats before. I stood up and dusted the good soil back into the bed off of my hands and took the weeds to the far corner of the house and sure enough, found three adult pygmy goats - a brown buck, two does, and three adorable little young'uns. They were white with a black saddle mark, and parallel dark lines on their heads, from snout to where the little hairs stand up around their little nubby horn sprouts. The babies, probably four months old, started jumping sideways and making their little cries of excitement. Mom had them in a pen made of woven willow which stretched the whole right side of the house, with a trough for hay and a bucket of water, and a little lean-to. Generally, as long as they can stay in the shade in summer, dry and out of the winter wind, these little guys can make it through all of Texas's weather. They are rascals sometimes, but also very intelligent, caring, and each has their own unique voice and personality. In fact, I haven't come across any goat, wild or domestic, that wasn't its own unique individual. It felt good that Mom had another growing family to care for. Especially now. I grew to all of six feet, stout and broad-shouldered with my dark olive skin shaded by years in the surrounding wilds in the sun, wind, and humidity of this land. And glad for it. The lessons, even in this small homestead, and the hard work my family embraced gave me a strong base that served me well after my accident. I do not recall my parents using magic until all the actual work was done. Making a hearty meal or having the fiddle play

124

music, perhaps, but everything around cultivating, raising, and collecting foodstuffs, we all did by hand together. No doubt some of the grey hairs peeking out above my ears in my brown hair are due to it. Momma used to say every grey hair was a moment that shaped you, that you survived, and that you have a lesson from. She was all strength and lessons now. The lines on her face from a lifetime here, every one, beaten back by the force of her smiles to be at the will of the smile, not the land.

I was back pulling weeds when Arterous came out, looking bewildered at me down in the dirt. "Professor Templeton said Monika met a strange lady who was asking about you. Her name was Runetta Lynchos. Do you know her?"

I stopped and leaned back on my toes, placing my hands on my thighs and taking a moment to think. "No, I don't believe I have heard that name before."

"Professor Templeton said she is from the Glauer family in Bavaria. Obscenely wealthy owners of most of the wand-making wood in Central Europe. Eccentric, but almost certainly a harmless visit, just wanted me to tell you," he said, sitting on the bench at the edge of the porch. "What are you doing?"

"I'm weeding momma's little garden. She clearly has been busy with my dad, and I didn't want it to overgrow while she is occupied. This was my job when I was three and four." I was finished with the big bed, so I dusted off and stood. As I looked at him, I spotted a small plaque above the back door with a large circle carved and burned into it, featuring an "R" in the middle. Huh, wonder what that is. It was on a saw-cut slab of cedar about one foot in diameter and two inches thick.

"Let's go back in and see if Momma is alright," I said.

She was coming down the stairs as we came through the kitchen, the aura jar in hand.

"He is asleep again," she said quietly.

"Alright, glad he's able to rest. Mom, what is the circle R thing above the back door?" I asked.

"Oh, your dad made it when you graduated. He said that, as well as you had done, as hard as it must have been, it was like you circled the wagons and held on to the end. That's the circle of wagons around our little 'R.'"

She then held up the prison keys, which he was strong enough to disenchant, so that was a good sign. She motioned for them to come to me, so I took them and hugged her.

Arterous didn't understand the term "circle the wagons," so I explained it to him, and he nodded, agreeing that it made good sense.

"Actually, since they will move the prison soon, likely much sooner than planned now, we had thought we would call our little homestead the Circle R Ranch," she said, setting everything down on the table.

Suddenly, three loud knocks on the door took us by surprise, and we all looked at the door and at each other. Momma, pursing her lips and shrugging her shoulders, started toward the door, when I motioned her to stop, that I would answer it.

I opened it to find a tall, wiry man with a black hat, a colored canvas shirt, a black unbuttoned vest, a long tan duster, and still wearing his spurs. He had a long, bushy grey and brown handlebar mustache, several days' worth of chin whiskers, and both a Colt pistol slung low with a slot in front of his holster for his wand, and a Henry Rifle in his left hand, muzzle down. He had his big, dirty hat in his hand. It was an old family acquaintance.

"Howdy, pardon the intrusion, my name is Barthow Corden," looking and pointing his hat at Arterous, "Magical Ranger of Central Texas. I believe we received a request from the Warden here a week or more ago to make a visit. May I come in?" He stated plainly in a polite, gruff, territorial tongue.

"Of course, please," I stepped aside as he switched his hat into his left hand and came in. "Here, have a seat," I pointed to the other end of the bench I was on.

"Naw, son, Ima mess. I do apologize for the delay, I had been set to keep an eye on that caravan of Messican prisoners-" motioning to Arterous with his hat - "the ones that you looked in on earlier. We got word in Bexar that one'a them young fellers escorting 'em was the son of one of them men killed in Goliad. He had designs on a'killin' them Messicans first chance he got. That sorta behavior just won't do in current circumstances, what with tensions being so high all around and all. They asked me to see to it no trouble befell them prisoners, with them being so far outta reach once we heard 'bout it. Sure enough, after you flew off this morning, he musta lost his temper and patience for vengeance and set to a shootin' those fellers. I made sure none was hurt, and put the lot of 'em to sleep, and took that boy back to Bexar where he could be kept an eye on by his own. The rest of 'em are back awake and'a marchin' south as we speak, safe n sound. That's kept me occupied since yer letter came in, and I hope my delay wasn't troublesome," he explained. "The fellers in

Bexar were supposed ta reply and ask if that was alright with all y'all, the delay, I mean."

"No, sir, no letter of delay reached us," Mom began, now a bit unsettled.

"Well, shoot. That ain't no good. Apache and Comanche have been shooting owls when they spot them carrying correspondence. I have tried for over a year to get that dern Magical Empresario to stop usin' owls, I told him it's best to use them red-tailed hawks, but I can't seem to shake whatever hooey he learned at that dern Spanish school outta his head. I am sorry about that," he said, shaking his head, looking at the floor. "Is Mr. Tellafrog still poorly, ma'am?"

"Yes, much worse, I don't hold any hope he can beat this ailment." He looked at me, and I refused to offer any hope either.

"And no idea what he mighta got into that caused it?" He said, looking around. "Nothin in the prison or from a prisoner ya think?"

"No, sir, we went in yesterday and looked it over quite well with a goblin worked monocle; we didn't detect anything of note." I looked at Arterous, who was nodding in agreement.

"Ma'am, may I check in on him?" He asked quietly and politely.

"Of course, this way," she beckoned him upstairs.

They proceeded upstairs and pushed the door closed behind them.

"Arterous, I trust him; he has been the Ranger here for over thirty years. I have never known him to be anything but forthright, so we should let him do all he can. He is clever

128

and resourceful, and may, without knowing our purpose, be of great help."

"I trust you and your family. Should we tell him about Father Callious?" He asked.

"My bet is he already knows, he was right there, but the magical rangers are few, I think less than ten in the whole country here. How much he can do may be limited by other priorities." I stopped when I heard the door open again.

They came downstairs, both looking grim. Mother was shaking slightly, he put his arm around her shoulder on the last few steps, saying, "It'll be alright, Mother. Don't fret."

"Well, boys, it don't look good. I reckon he has little of a day left in him. I haven't seen that before, whatever it is. This land is full of old treachery and magic we don't have a handle on yet." He put his hand on his whiskers, stroking them as he thought. "Grandad said one time they'd come across a little Apache medicine woman, not four feet tall, who had sick'd an illness on some Spanish soldados. In those days, the Spaniards weren't careful with the punishment of them they thought was magical folks. She wasn't magical, but worked her people as a natural healer. He'd said she were burnt to a crisp and strung up when they come across her, in that order, hanging over a white rock alcove somewhere up north near Vernon, I believe. The fellas she'd had grey ashy streaks on them, but they were dead in a day, and I don't recall anything about it bein' a drawn-out process, like none of it spread the way it has on your daddy. The only other thing I remember Pawpaw sayin' is that the little cave camp was burned up too, all except a little piece of root that looked like it was made of tar. Grandad never experienced anything magical in any of it as I recall."

Momma poured him a cup of coffee, and we could tell he was trying to remember anything else that might explain things as he sipped some.

"Ma'am, that's some good coffee, thank you very much." He said and set the cup down. "I was authorized before I left to give you as much as one hundred dollars in gold coins to help with the illness, as I see you require. I'm satisfied that you've done all you can, all of you, and it seems there isn't much else to do but love on yer husband and father, best you can. I'm willing to give you that one hundred dollars now if you can make an, uh, uh," Barthow was snapping his fingers and squinting, trying to recall the word he wanted. "AURA JAR, that's it, for him that we can take back to Bexar and keep in the vault, so we can begin building a library here of ailments, and maybe find a source and prevent this in the future. Our records are pitiful as you may imagine, but we gotta start somewhere, and with a better man than your husband, I can't imagine." He drank a few more sips and continued, "It can't be said more plain than that. It's a damn shame. If it's alright, I will set up my little tent in the front of the prison and stay here to look after y'all. I have but one talent in magic that stands out, it is stone carving, and if it suits you, I'd be honored if you let me craft this great man a tomb of the stones that surround your place."

"Of course, Barthow. That would be so kind," I said.

Momma began to well up with tears, shaking more, so I went to her and she sank her head into my chest. I said we should go upstairs, and we did. We sat with Dad, who didn't open his eyes again. It is difficult knowing these are the last days, the last moments with a parent. Trying to absorb all of the person you've loved, and at the same time knowing the mortal body you're watching fail, isn't the man you knew. It is the last of them, showing what many of us face in the end, hurting, losing all you were, weak and frail.

With his occasional wincing, I tried not to think about the pain he must be feeling, and instead let my memories go back to when his father, my pawpaw, passed away. I think I was five or maybe six years old. I didn't understand. I was only confused about why I couldn't see Pawpaw anymore. My dad, the great man he was, bearing his own suffering about his father, sat down with me and told me this. When a horse-drawn carriage is crafted by skilled artisans, it's beautiful, ornate, gleaming with brass and gold, featuring purple velvet curtains, and offering a fine, sprung ride; yet it's just a box. God makes us the same way, with care and unique accents, beautifully individual. But just like a carriage, after time here in this world, it becomes so worn out that it can't be repaired anymore, and it cannot carry people anymore. So, just like a carriage, the joy of life is who we are, not what carries it, but who is in it. When a special person like Pawpaw steps out of his carriage, the carriage may be empty, but Pawpaw is in a new place. We'll see him again.

Pawpaw. I only remember one time with him. We had visited Beaumont to see him when I was even younger, four, I think. He was pretty thick around the middle, and always happy, laughing at everything from finches pooping on his porch to a man falling in a puddle after the rain. He warned me once when I was going out back to the outhouse to keep an eye out for the turd snakes. He said they looove little boy poo. If you think they're nearby, you'd better stay very still and quiet. Darned if that man didn't drag a four foot piece of old rotten hemp rope around the outhouse with a string, which, from the gaps in the boards, looked very much like the infamous turd snake. I stayed in that horrible smelling excrement sauna for an hour terrified of that turd snake. My dad rescued me, admonishing his father, who was so consumed with laughter he couldn't breathe. Later in the day, Pawpaw came to apologize. I was in his backyard, stacking small rocks to make a cave. The day before, I was using the same pile of rocks to make a mountain.

Pawpaw said, "Boy, you'd build a mountain, just to tear it down and move it the next day." I looked at him, confused. I was simply making things I imagined. Then he called me to come sit with him on the back steps. He apologized for the snake joke and said joking around is okay, and good for the soul, as long as it didn't hurt anyone. He hugged me, and I told him it didn't hurt me, but I wasn't sure I'd believe anything else he told me right away, if that was okay. He found it hilarious.

He told me, "None of us get to pick who we come from, but the gifts they give us are in there somewhere," poking at my tummy. "We have to find them all, like a treasure hunt, and figure out how to use them well. However, we CAN choose who else to learn from. I tried hard to make sure that I, your nana, your mom, and your dad are good teachers. Listen to them."

I thought about what he said for a long time while I was building with those rocks. Perhaps he was pointing out how much work I was willing to do that ultimately ended up being pointless. It bothered me forever, like he let slip something he didn't like about me. I didn't change because of it. I think now he was admiring how I would do whatever was needed, regardless of how difficult it may seem, even when I had to then undo it. Regardless, if I decide I need a mountain today, one I shall build. If it gets in the way of what tomorrow needs, then yes, I'll take it apart.

Dad began to reach up with his hand, and Mom grabbed it right away. "Honey, are you there?" She asked nervously.

"My beautiful bride. I love you so much. Is our little frog here?" His voice is very raspy now.

"Yes, Dad, I'm here," dreadfully.

"My little horny toad. Take care of momma, will ya?"

"Of course. Don't worry, Dad." Even at thirty-five, I am not ready.

"Son, don't dwell on any of this. There'll be much to do." He strained and smiled a bit, eyes still closed. "I can tell it's time for my carriage to stop, and me to depart." Now this is too much for me, given all I had thought of, and I give up on holding my tears in. They fall all over me, and I just let go. Head down, I stay only for my mother and fumble over to wrap her up in my arms.

A few moments of breath so low only I can detect it. Mom had his hand so tight she could tell when his heart gave out. We both know now. I only stayed for another minute or two, and I squeezed her, she pats me, saying it is okay, and she stays beside him, crying.

I stood up, using my sleeve now to wipe tears and such, and looked at Momma. She fell on Father's chest, clutching him tightly and breathing more deeply than I had seen in a long time, for the sole purpose of crying harder. "I am gonna step outside, Momma. You call me if you need me." I stop at the door and wipe my whole face with my handkerchief, stuffing it in my back pocket, and heading downstairs.

One look at me, and both our guests stood, nodded, hats in hand, and walked out into the front yard. I sat at the kitchen table. The same table where mom and dad fed me as a baby, where we ate the food we all worked to grow. The earlier wiping was wasted, and it started again. I grabbed my mug and poured some coffee, but my stuttered breathing made me shaky, so I set it down. I spot the five one-ounce twenty-dollar gold coins on the table nearby. I look out the front window, and Arterous is helping Barthow put up his tent and things. This is not at all what I expected to deal with when I received the letter about my father not feeling well. It made me angry, in fact, the intentional lack of information, those stupid coins sitting on the table. I understand their purpose, but right now it looks more like a heinous, hateful stack of metal loosely related to my father dying so fast, and for a cause no one can explain. I swept my hand across the table at them, flinging them across the room, each one making a ding sound, as gold does when struck. It was a childish gesture, one a person with little self-control might let loose. I didn't care. I wasn't going to look at them anymore. When I had finished admonishing myself, I realized I had still been uncontrollably crying, and the whole area below me on the table was wet with tears.

CHAPTER SEVEN

For the whole first half of my life, I suffered from practically uncontrollable fits when traveling through new, uncharted lands, with a wild desire to drop everything of this world's modern facade and run as hard and as fast as possible away from it into the arms of God's unblemished creation. I learned, after one of these events appeared to those in my company to be a seizure, to control it. I treated it like a coydog, always on a leash, its snout brushing my feet as I walked through life, but always right nearby. Urging me to abandon human civilization and run with it. I couldn't rid myself of this feral dog because it was part of me. Maybe a bigger part of me than I wanted to admit. However, with practice in the solitary wildernesses I frequented, I could feel its pestering approaching, and could stomp my boot heel on the rope I had mentally tethered it to, snapping its imaginary head to the ground and controlling myself. But right now, I really desired to let it off the leash and chase it into oblivion, away from the pain welling up inside me over my father.

It wasn't just very close; it was breathing hot, moist breath on my neck. I could almost decipher the sounds as words bidding me to run away. But for my mother, I might have.

I heard a bit of a ruckus upstairs. I could tell mother was moving around, so I went back up and peeked in. She had his blanket off and his nightshirt unbuttoned, with a towel over his particulars, working the jar and her wand over him. She turned slightly, aware that someone was present, and saw me.

"Oh, please, Raileanu, come in! Look at this!" She said nervously, yet quietly. I came the rest of the way through the door and shut it behind me. Coming to Mother's side, there was something different happening to the infection.

The black branches and lines were receding! They were retracting ever so slowly. She was storing all of the motion in her original jar, not a new one, so I asked about it.

"Son, if this is something you were told to look into, it may not be something we need to give the ranger yet. I made his jar a few moments ago, and as I was finishing the final parts of that spell, I watched the branches getting smaller. So I switched to the aura jar for the professor." She completed the task and handed me the jar for the ranger. "Let him know I will prepare for the burial, and let me be, if you don't mind, son," she said.

"Momma, what does it mean?" I asked, watching her and trying to tell if I could discern anything out of the ordinary. Nothing.

"I have never heard of this before, magic or ordinary, cursed or infected. Whatever it is, I may try and extract a bit to cordon off in another jar for you to take with you as well.

When I tried to do it before, it really hurt Daddy. It won't now. I definitely don't want it to go anywhere else. I will stay up here and do this work, son, head down and put some dinner together for our guests."

"Yes, ma'am. Love you, mom."

"Love you too, Dad is with God now, we must carry on." She never stopped working, looking straight at wherever her wand was working, so I went back out into the hallway and closed the door.

I went down and began rustling around in the pantry. Honestly, not much, but I wasn't surprised. It occurred to me that today is a day I would greatly appreciate a magically prepared dinner. I went out front and asked for help, and those turkeys had already set a table and were finishing up a great pot of chili, accompanied by sourdough biscuits, carrots, and green beans on the side. What great people. I said a quick prayer of thanks, asking God to welcome my father. He would want me to tend to the things that must be done. So, I went around and got feed and water for the animals to put out, and took the grey wolf a big bowl of chili, rubbing him on the head. He understood what had happened and stared at me with his big yellow eyes. It was the only time in my life I witnessed a wolf look sad. Mostly, they look at you like they're deciding whether they'll eat better if they let you bring them food, or if they should go ahead and eat you now. I gave him a good rub and headed back outside.

I sat at the table, oh, they also had sweet tea with chipped ice in a pitcher, so I poured myself a glass.

"She alright, son?" Barthow asked.

I nodded. "She is preparing the jar for you and getting him ready for burial. She asked to be alone until it's time."

"Your parents are some of the best, most decent, Christian magical folks in all the country of Texas, son. It has been a great honor to have known them all these years. Perhaps you don't know this but your daddy wrote me a letter sayin' how trustworthy I was back when I was only a hired hand 'round this territory. It's how I ended up goin' into fetchin' rascally wizards. When nobody volunteered to catch a fella who'd cursed a banker after gettin' too much farwater in 'em. I did, and brought him here. After a couple more with no conflagrations arisin', he recommended me be badged, and that was that." He filled a bowl, plopped a biscuit on top, and sat across from me.

Arterous, still amazed and trying to hide his being baffled by everything he sees and tastes, also sits and begins his first bowl of Texas chili. After a few minutes, he gets a big drink of tea, and upright in posture, dabs his mouth properly with his napkin, and asks, "From what native animal is the meat in the chili?"

Barthow chuckles a bit, and I smile and keep eating. I knew when I opened the door what meat it was. I don't know why he likes it so much, but I'll let him explain.

"Armadillo tail," Barthow says and waits, smiling bigger in anticipation.

"What's an armadillo?" Arterous asks.

"Well, son, it's a little critter who is all armored, see, digs around in the dirt and leaves lookin' for worms and grubs." Barthow makes little digging and sniffing impressions with his hands and face. Then he taps the side of his head with

138

his pointy finger. "They ain't too bright, don't see well, don't seem to hear well, and have big strong tails they can whoop you with if'n you ain't careful." Arterous looked bemused at first, but as Barthow continued, he began to show amused disbelief. "They have big ol' claws they dig with, a pointy little snoot they root around with for bugs," the whole time he is imitating the claws and pointy nose with his hands and face again. "The way I see it, there's so many of 'em about, that once in a while if'n I pick real careful, I can get a big ol fella, one who's had lots of lil ones already. No harm in that. Plus, the tail meat is prut-darn good, ain't it?"

Well, about halfway through the thorough explanation, he stopped and stared. The chances he had ever consumed the tail of an armored animal, who is half blind and deaf, who eats grubs, is, well, zero. He thought, chewed a bit, and swallowed.

"It is quite tasty, I will not deny it. But I feel you are amusing yourself with the description of this beast at my expense, sir."

Barthow whipped out his wand, tapped in the air above the table, and a glowing likeness of an armadillo appeared.

"How big are these creatures?" Arterous asked, his eyes large and absorbing the image like a child at a zoo.

"Awe, 'bout two to three feet long, 'bout forty pounds big 'uns get. My daddy found a baby 'un once, raised it up for about five years till it passed on. It would sleep with him, but wernt worth spit for nuthin, dumb as all git out. That'n would leap six feet straight up if you startled it." Bart recalled, chuckling as he shoveled up another big spoonful of chili.

"Those are ordinary creatures, not magical?" Arterous asked, still thinking we were pulling his leg.

"Naw, just ordinary critters. Like possums, skunks, coons and the like." Barthow said, while chewing, which was a habit my mother had forbidden, causing me to tense up. Barthow did not have many opportunities to converse with people in the course of his duties and was very grateful for the company. So, I relented on my teeth gritting and chose instead to watch the enjoyment he had in explaining armadillos to a magical cavalry officer from Austria. After a few more chuckles and exchanges, Barthow had finished his bowl, and wiping his mouth on his sleeve, stood and finished his tea.

"Raileanu, can you tell me if it's alright to git to carvin' your daddy's tomb after dinner?" he asked, taking another bite of biscuit while standing.

"Certainly, sir, it would be a gift for us," I told him. It honestly would. I have attended funerals in Europe, South America, and several in Texas over the last thirty-five years. Too often here, as in any unsettled country, funeral proceedings can be spartan. No fancy dress, no weeping lines of passers-by for an hour. No service in a medieval cathedral. Many times, it is nothing more than one decent person with time and ability who can drag up enough big rocks to keep bears and mountain lions, coyotes and foxes from dismembering the deceased. To have such good friends here, a proper burial will mean a great deal.

We finished eating as Mother came out, clearly taking requisite time to compose herself for company. She looked at the meal, smiling gratefully, having to wipe a couple of squirrely tears that leaked out.

"Only one thing is missing, boys." She waved her wand, and a steaming pan of peach cobbler appeared, accompanied by a blue glass bowl of whipped, heavy, sweet cream.

"A woman's touch is so easily overlooked by hard men, my lady," the Ranger pointed out. "Thank you, ma'am. It has been a coon's age since I enjoyed a peach cobbler." That brought Barthow back down to the bench.

She joined us seated, and we each heaped a mass of its magnificence on our plates, ignoring all mature manners. Often, ladies of the prairie here extract great pleasure from making irresistible food for hard-working men. Nothing wrong with this.

We all enjoyed mother's dessert together, with her great coffee. Barthow took out a crook-neck pipe, by the look of it handmade by himself out of bog oak with an ivory stem. He fired up a bowl of - to my special nose - was southern Tennessee bright broadleaf, gently toasted, then stored in old whiskey barrels. He stoked the bowl a few times, its aroma drifting around the table, and by its path, I assume a bit of an enchantment on it as well, because it circled around us without irritating anyone.

"Ma'am, can I ask if there's anything special I can inscribe on your husband's tomb?" Barthow said, slowly drawing on the pipe.

She didn't hesitate. "John Tellafrog. Veteran. Husband. Father. Warden of Wormwell Territorial Prison for 32 years. There wasn't an animal or plant he didn't love, and he cared for the least of magical folk the best he could."

Barthow nodded as he enjoyed his pipe, eyes down at the table, thinking of what Momma had said about Father.

I held the prison keys up for Barthow to take and put under his protection, which let Momma begin to release another weight. He took them, held the tip of his wand on the big ring that held all of them, and they began to glow blueish, with a crackling sound. Then, a bit of smoke fell off them and dissipated. He put them in his inside coat pocket.

"That he did, ma'am. That he was." Barthow said, nodding. "I will git to it before it gets dark on us, thank you for the fine supper." He said, tipping his hat to her as he set it on his head. He walked over to the right of the house, by the goat pen I saw from around back earlier.

"Momma, are you okay? Is Papa wrapped up where the ranger doesn't see it receding?" I asked.

"Yes, yes, I am alright," that big smile again. "Your father lived 75 years, and I got fifty-two with him. He is wrapped up like a mummy son. I duplicated the original aura jar and wrapped it with him. It is also set to absorb anything that may come off your father. The cheesecloth I have him in is tucked inside the jar. He is wrapped in a thick linen sheet over that. Whatever comes from it will end up in the sealed jar I put in your saddlebag. The unchanging view jar I will give Mr. Corden," she said. "Your father held his smile, I know he is alright."

"Nothing surprises me anymore about you, Momma. You are great at everything." I said, cupping my hand over hers.

We sat sipping our coffee in silence for a few more minutes, and Arterous stood, asking, "May I go check if the professor is available in portrait?"

"Yes, dear."

"May I inform him of all that has happened, or would you like to -"

"Oh, please do, I don't want to try talking more about it yet," Mom said.

He gave his wand a wave, and the dishes and dinner were cleaned up, leaving the cobbler and coffee. Mom smiled. He went into the house.

"Momma, will you be alright if we set off tomorrow to determine what we can find with Father Callious?" I asked, ready to stay here indefinitely if she wants.

"Yes, son, I think I will ask the Ranger to try and convince Bandos to stay with me up here around the house. Barthow said earlier that he plans to have a group from his troop come and move the prisoners tomorrow, probably. He has a day or two to protect our place and guard the prison from up here. I doubt he will stay; his self-imposed curse is strong, and he will go with the prisoners when they leave." She seemed content to stay busy with the tasks that needed to be done. I wouldn't dare ask anything else of her.

It was nearly twilight now; the sun had gone below the horizon, and the west rim of our little ranch was bathed in a deep, reddish-orange glow, as happens in the heat of late summer, with dust rising as the sun passed through it. We finished the cobbler, which was sweet and filling, and Momma cleared up the last few dishes. Barthow's tent fluttered in a bit of a breeze, which always kicks up a bit after the sun's heat leaves the ground at a steep angle as it sets. The same wind rises as the sunlight creeps across the land from the east in the mornings. Though in late summer, that breeze rarely lingers.

Barthow comes bowlegged around the corner and sits back down with us, still toking his pipe. "It's all ready, mother. Whenever you are," he went right up to Momma and put his big coarse hand on her shoulder.

Momma, pursing her lips and trying to be strong, patted him on the hand for an unspoken thanks. "Would you take a minute to speak to Bandos for me, ask him if he would please come stay around the house for a day or two before he decides to leave with the prisoners?"

"Of course, ma'am. Be right back," he said, setting off, fiddling with the keys a bit, and went on in.

She wiped a couple of tears with her kerchief and said, "I am ready, son, as soon as he gets back, as long as you are."

"Yeah, I guess so, Momma," I nodded for a minute.

A wolf cry, yipping and howling, echoed out of the prison, which was incredible, knowing how soundproof it was. Even mother heard it a bit, and had to tend to tears again momentarily, dropping her head back with her mouth open. Bandos hadn't been told until now that Dad was gone. Just as I was easing into this state of dull acceptance, it was now starting for Bandos. He yipped for a whole minute, then it went quiet. A few more minutes, and both Bandos and Barthow came out together. Bandos went straight to Momma and leaned on her, circling back and forth. Mom turned on the bench and set her legs outside, and he sat down facing her, and slowly rose to put his front paws on her shoulders, and they hugged as best as Bandos could manage. I was very relieved he agreed to stay with her.

"I know my friend, I know. Thank you for staying with me a few days, it means everything." She rubbed his neck, and he sat down, whimpered once, and lay at her feet. "Alright, gentlemen, let's lay John to rest. He has earned it," she stood, as did Bandos, and we all went around back.

McCort came and lit on a tree in front of us. Mom and Dad's owls were already there. Beyond the garden, and the grassy area, before the monoliths closed in, Barthow had crafted an obsidian tomb, glistening in the now overhead moonlight. It was six feet tall, eight feet wide, and about six feet deep. It depicted probably a hundred scenes in rows about four inches tall, which wrapped around the whole of it, far too many for me to count right now. The figures were so intricate, so detailed, that even from ten feet away, I could tell the carvings were of my father and his life. The corners were as pillars, wound with ivy leaves. In the center, facing us, was our family crest, surrounded by our family tree. It was breathtaking, and Momma leaned on me when she saw it. I had seen many tombs in incredible monasteries and castles in my day. However, I had never truly seen anything this impressive. Talent sometimes lies in the most peculiar containers.

"Barthow, I, I, my Lord," Momma tried, but tears of joy were mixed with her sad ones.

"Sir, every noble I have ever encountered would pay you whole chests of guldens for such a craftwork," Arterous stood in awe as well.

"Well, folks, that's all real flatterin', but they told me the same thing in school. It disappointed them fierce when I turned 'em down flat. I knew even at fourteen, I wanted no part of spendin' my days meeting with mourning folks who'd

145

lost their family. I only do this fer folks I know deserve it. Your John is one of 'em," Barthow took his hat off.

Momma opened her sweater a bit, took her wand out, stepped away from my one-armed embrace, and looked at the house. She opened the window with a swish and pointed it steadily at the upstairs window. Slowly, my father drifted out the window, above us, and hovered over the tomb's open top, wrapped tightly in white linen sheets.

Barthow began, "Our Father, who art in Heaven, hallowed be His name. His kingdom come, His will be done, on earth as it is in Heaven. Forgive us our tresspasses, as we forgive those who trespass again' us. Give us our daily bread and lead us beside still waters, lead us not inta temptation. Fer thine is tha kingdom, and glory forever, amen."

Good enough, I thought. The help this man has been to us will be forever a gift. What would mother and I have done, had he come not to share sorrow but only to perform professional duties? I was so grateful.

Momma lowered him gently in, her arm shaking as he settled, and stopped, and she started crying again now. I went to her and held her in a big hug.

Barthow waved his wand a bit, and a heavy ornate lid lifted from behind it, adorned with roses, ringed in small horny toads. He glanced at us, I nodded, and he lowered it silently into place. Bandos howled again, and this time, coyotes in the distance answered. We went back inside, and I made sure Momma's bed was made up while she sat downstairs, thanking all three of them for everything. She came in as I finished, and I got her tucked in.

"Love ya, momma. See you in the morning."

"You too, little frog. I'm so glad you were here. All of you."

"Me too, I would have been sick if all this had happened and I wasn't able to make it in time."

"Goodnight, son."

"Goodnight, momma."

The others were waiting downstairs. I nodded, and everyone headed off to bed. Bandos went upstairs, nosed momma's door open, and lay on the floor right next to her bed, and I went to bed as well.

The next morning, I got up late. I had no idea what time it was, so I checked my pocket watch on the nightstand. Half past nine. Good grief, guess I was exhausted, and understandably, I suppose. I could smell that breakfast was already cold. Everyone was out front. I dressed and went downstairs to the kitchen table, where I had scrambled eggs, biscuits, and gravy. I was so hungry, I sat and ate it cold. The coffee was hot and great. I wiped my mouth on my sleeve, since Mom was outside, and went on out with them.

"Mornin' boy, doin' okay?" Barthow asked.

"Yes, sir. And thank you to whoever cooked breakfast and left me a plate."

"Arterous made it, and did pretty well with his first gravy for biscuits, I'd say," Momma said.

"Indeed, he did," I gave him a big smile.

"Son, I have a few rangers, and a few in training gonna show up here any minute so we can git these prisoners outta here today," he said, pointing at Wormwell. "When we head out, y'all go ahead and close that up for good, will ya?"

"Yeah, there's no love lost with that being shut with us." I looked at Momma, who was nodding thoughtfully.

147

"OH, guess what, son!" Momma was excited. "Bandos has decided to stay here permanently!" She gave his big panting head a good rub.

"That's great, that makes me happy for you both," I said. "Father, most of all, will be glad he is staying. I'm sure of that."

A moment later, sixteen fellas appeared, each more scroungy and worn out than the next. Dirty, scrawny, hungry-looking. I couldn't tell which were the rangers from the rest.

Barthow went over to the one on the far left of the group and was handed a small wooden box. He brought it over to Momma and opened it up. Inside was a small revolver, and three more cylinders, set in the cork frame of the box.

"Ma'am, I had them bring this here special from our gunsmith down in Bexar. I want you to keep it with ya, as there ain't nuthin it can't han'l. This here pistol was made fer your hand, light as a feather, and look here at these," he picked up one after the other of the cylinders, pointing to the words engraved on each. "The one in the gun is reg'lar, which'n you might not need. These here are each loaded with sorta, wand cores 'steada shells. They can only be used once each shot, but there ain't no magic it can't defeat. We want you safe as can be here at yer place." Barthow set it gently into Momma's hands and turned to the motley gaggle of fellas. "All you others who've come here, 'memeber this lo-cal. This lady will need checkin' on anytime yer about these parts. That's an order." He surveyed each one's face, making sure they were paying close attention. "Alrighty then." He gave a slight bow and walked over to the front of the prison, unlocking the gate and then the door. "I am gonna git these fellas down there and bound up to the prisoners, then I'll undo the enchantments so's we can dislocate from down there and be off. Y'all take care now. I'll be seein' ya in a couple days when we git them all settled at the new place. Alright." They proceeded down below, Bandos watching intently as the door closed behind them. Barthow was last to go in, waving his hand at us as he walked away.

After about five minutes, Bandos flipped his head up sharply as if he was watching something. I looked at Arterous and Momma, and she said, "Yes, they're gone." We all sighed at the end of so many things.

"Momma, have any idea of how you'd like to close the prison?" I asked.

"Yes. Did you know I never stepped foot inside, not once? I would very much like to open its top and let the light of the sun in, leaving the stairs and cells, but ripping the iron from its place and making something useful of it. Only when green things grow again will I be able to walk where your father had to spend so much of his time," she said, handing me the pistol case Barthow had given her.

A more fitting tribute I couldn't imagine. Let the earth, too, heal from the sourness and labor it had undergone in its duty to those souls it shared space with.

"If we can please, inspect as closely as possible that cell again, maybe leaving everything intact, we will be as quick as possible," I suggested.

"No sunlight, yet?" she asked.

"No, if something in that cell, or anywhere else, can exist only in the dark, we should be able to find it. Only the cell bars and doors, please," I said.

"I suppose that's a good idea," she agreed.

A wave of her wrist, wand in hand, and the gate and door were gone, clinking and losing a bit of rocky rubble also, and the cell gates came out one at a time from the mouth of the prison, stacked neatly standing next to a stone nearby. "You may need to inspect those as well for signs of magic."

She was right. Inscriptions would have been impossible to detect from outside the cells, given the darkness. Arterous snapped his fingers, and the torches lit. Bandos, checking with mother first, got a nod and proceeded down with us. He had never been in any of the cells either, and was more than excited to explore everything.

I followed them in, double-checking what I had seen before and examining areas I had missed more closely, as I had been concerned about the population. Literally nothing other than tally counts, scratched in cells, curses, and scribblings, which made no sense to me. In the cell with the small ball of roots on the sleeping cove, the formation had shrunk somewhat and retracted towards the ceiling, hanging about six inches above the flat surface and blanket. I wondered if my father ever told the prisoners that every one of the pillows and blankets they used to sleep on the mandated stone slab was made by my mother. Each one had been worn through in places, some ruined completely, but some, it seemed, had been cared for as the only comfort they were allowed. Once I reached the bottom and found nothing of significance, I went back up and out.

Mother had finished carrying the last of the breakfast things into the house and was now coming back out.

Bandos emerged first, tail wagging and tongue hanging out the side of his snout, then Arterous, tucking his monocle away in his chest pocket.

"Mother, I think it's alright to go ahead and open it up, and we can maybe go speak with Father Callious today, if you are alright alone here for most of the day," I said loud enough for her to hear.

"I think I am ready. Let me sit at the table here and begin. Oh, and I won't be alone, Bandos will be with me." She sat on the bench closest to the entrance, and, back to the table, sat quite straight, thinking. She drew her wand, eliciting a slight smile from the corner of her mouth, and circled it several times in the air, pointing towards the top capstone that covered the entire winding, cylindrical structure below. The stones and slabs all rose above, slowly rotating as they did, until a great mass was collected in the air. She directed it all to the left of the opening her work had created below and allowed it to settle among the stone plates and columns that made up the labyrinth around our home in our little dell. That created a rise of solid rock and earth on the eastern perimeter of the old prison site. Then she brought in several tons of good dark earth - weathered wear from the stones, mostly - and created a bed high enough to collect the early sun as it rose each morning. Another few conductions of her skilled wand and felled trees lying around our land assembled themselves into a large boxlike structure of framing around the whole plot of new earth.

"I will plant some of the varieties you send me, son, from all your work abroad. Some ivys and honeysuckle on the edge of the 'well' should climb down and bring bees and beauty

151

into the depths, as a start," she smiled at her own work, quite pleased, and began again.

More good earth swirled around the top of the well, drawn from all around us until it, too, was in great quantity, then separated out into individual and equal streams enough for each cell below, to fill the floors of all of them a foot deep. She stopped and set her hands on her knees, smiling and looking around.

"Hmm. How about this?"

She lifted her wand hand again, and speaking a spell I don't remember hearing before, great balls of hot orange glass appeared, brilliant in the sunlight high up. One at a time, each one was drawn out into a square, a rectangle, or a round sheet. They began to have brass bars gather onto their edges and then drop singly into a frame shaped like a dome to cover the garden above, becoming the new top of the 'well'. A beautiful cut-glass and leaded-crystal door with a rounded top assembled itself and sat gently into a frame facing us. Mother grinned, tight-lipped, as big as she could, and glanced at us. There was but one thing we could do. Applaud. As we did, the grin exploded into a smile, and she covered her mouth with her wand in hand as she giggled. It truly was beautiful, brilliant in the light, and a perfect way to let this place heal from the prison, allowing her to enjoy the space. Had Father still been here, even he couldn't have given her something so fantastic in that place.

"That is amazing. It is indeed an incredible structure, and honors both of you quite well, Momma," I told her.

"Indeed, ma'am. Some of the arboretums in Europe are not nearly as grand!" Arterous stated plainly, also surveying it in amazement.

"Is it all right if I begin preparing to go visit Father Callious, Mother?" I asked.

"Yes, yes, I really need him to know about John, but I don't want you boys out after dark, I don't want to be here alone after dark, either," she said.

We went to saddle the horses and fill the canteens, packing a bit of extra alfalfa and oats as well, just in case. It isn't wise to travel any distance away from the protection of our homestead without being ready to survive a couple of days. We checked our pistols and revolvers, giving them a thorough once-over, to ensure all parts were tight, sights were adjusted correctly, and extra balls, powder, caps, and wadding were easily accessible. Momma brought out three round loaves of fresh sourdough, making sure I knew one was for Father Callious. Arterous and I called our owls, and sent them both to fly ahead and wait for us about halfway there. After giving Mother a big hug, making sure she was alright for the day, we started up and out of the rock maze and through the stand of trees that concealed us, passing the shimmerwall of the dome, and out towards the west, where the mission was. It was typically hot for this time of year on the plains ahead of us, and mirages danced among the grasses, standing dead still in the cloudless heat.

Our owls circled back once, and screeched at us, probably decided between them to come check on us, and went on ahead. I had visited this mission before, with my father, but it was many years ago, when a different Priest was in charge;

I don't remember his name. So I rode in front and stopped only occasionally for a drink of water. The ride was a little more than an hour in this heat, staying in the prairies that rolled up and down, with the stands of woods to the north on our right.

After three quarters of an hour or so, I caught the stench of a rattlesnake, which even for me is rare. I had only detected them under two circumstances. If they had just shed their skin, or had dropped scat. I eased up on the reins, and we both came to a stop. I raised my hand so Arterous might stay quiet, and we could hear it in the grass. Not a minute later, I detected it, but he couldn't, as it was close to a hundred feet ahead, going left to right across the path we were riding. Once I knew it was far enough off, I put my hand down and told him what had happened. Not wise to let a horse wander up and startle one; you might be thrown off and right into striking distance of the snake itself. Additionally, there is no way of knowing if anyone is watching us, so using magic to dispatch it or firing on it can both draw unwanted attention.

Not five minutes later, my nose caught something else. From the north, I was pretty sure, hogs, domestic pigs who were unwell, maybe mistreated or underfed, and a very sick human... woman. There had to be a small home or something up in the trees, but since I couldn't detect the odors of any other people, I decided to tell Arterous and investigate. A woman fighting illness alone out here isn't to be abandoned to chance when possible.

Chapter Eight

"Arterous, I can tell there is a lady in some physical distress of some kind, and perhaps livestock also not being tended nearby. I really think we should check on it." I said, as I turned my horse into the stand of wood and off our current path.

"On these matters, sir, I trust you. Right behind you," he followed.

"Can you call the owls? I will try to focus on anything else I can determine as we get closer. We may need to send word about what we find as soon as we can."

"Of course," he whistled several times and then remained quiet, waiting for them to catch up.

We went along a single path, made presumably from foot traffic, as I didn't discern any hoof prints or cart ruts. The dry grass was beaten down, which was clearly visible. The path wound through the sage and brush up against the tree line, and continued into it, with unbroken leaves and pine needles already fallen on the path from the summer heat.

That may have indicated nobody had been down this path in a few days. After a few hundred yards, the trees changed to small ash, elm, some birch, and even a few small water oaks. Off to the left, the ground was better watered, perhaps by a small spring in a layer of rock on higher ground. I knew that to the north of this stand of trees was higher ground, and though I hadn't been in here before, somewhere close was likely a sharp rise to a low bluff.

It was perhaps fifteen to twenty minutes of winding our way up, and I could see the rise beneath the canopy of the trees, then the white, chalky rock edges from ground level up into the height of the branches. I followed my nose off to the right a bit, and the bluff did indeed come into full view, making a semicircle shape in front of us, maybe two hundred feet in width. As we walked into a small clearing, my senses detected a trickle of running water on the left.

In the clearing, was a dugout on the left inside the semicircle, with a sod block front, and a couple chickens walking around. On the right side and slightly downhill from the dugout was a pig pen alongside a small shed with a corn crib on its far right end, which was empty. Two scrawny, filthy pigs in the pen, the ground of which was surprisingly muddy, but also caked in waste. The stench of the sickly woman was coming from inside the dugout.

"Anyone home?! Hello! Two men are coming in, we don't mean anyone trouble! Hello!?" I yelled. Best to announce yourself as a stranger to a small place with only one lady present, I knew.

No response. I looked around again and listened intently. I couldn't determine anything from the ambient odors either. With no breeze outside, the air was dead still here.

"Arterous, would you mind taking the horses off to the left to check if there's a little spring somewhere for the horses to get a drink?"

"Yes, just be careful," He replied.

I climbed down and took my pistol out, handing him the reins. I walked slowly to the opening of the dugout and used my pistol's barrel to push away the old wool blanket they were using as a door so I could look inside. I didn't see any windows or other openings. At the back left-hand side of the little space was a double-wide bed, with what looked like the lady I had detected. She was clothed, had a burlap apron, and was propped up against the chalk rock wall, with one leg on the bed and the other hanging off, touching the floor.

"Ma'am?" I asked, knowing already that what I was looking at was a deceased lady. There's something about the way a corpse rests that is always a bit unnatural, and it was here for certain. I looked around, and there wasn't anything out of the ordinary. A small table and a couple of chairs, a small cabinet, a tiny wood stove, more of a box really, with a chimney pipe that was all crooked and had leaked at the joints. A lantern sat on the table, and a small pile of enameled dishes sat uncleaned in a large iron pot on top of the stove. Not a single thing of value, really, a robber might want. I went to the lady, who was holding a flyswatter in her hand, under a fold of the apron. I went to examine the flyswatter handle because it was as black as tar, which may be due to its continued use, as grease and sweat ground against the wood, but I was

157

drawn to check it. I lifted the single fold of the apron, and her hand was black as well, with tiny strands of it reaching up the wrist. Almost as if it had been burned like the spots on a hen turned on a spit. It was similar to the marks my father had, but less...viscous - maybe. I took the flyswatter and walked back outside. I went to the pig pen and looked in. The pigs were sort of, well, dancing almost, as if it was hurting them to stand on the ground in certain places. Since there was no one to feed them now, and no food for me to give them, they had no reason to stay here at all. I opened the gate, found a piece of a tree branch three or so feet long, and swatted their behinds until they ran out of the gate and into the woods. They'd be fine out there; this freshwater runoff from around here somewhere will keep them healthy and happy with acorns to fill their stomachs nicely. I went over to where Arterous was with the horses and told him what I found.

"Here, take a look at this with your monocle," I said, handing him the flyswatter. "The lady inside is deceased. I am going to try and block off that doorway and close her inside so the pigs and coyotes don't abuse her until we can return this evening and bury her properly."

"I left the monocle with your mother, in case she had an opportunity to examine those gates from the prison or anything else she wanted to have a better look at," he said, sticking the flyswatter into his saddlebag.

"Alright. I'll close it up, we can handle this on the way home." So I went and found a bench to cover the doorway, and stacked a few heavy chunks of the white rock and a wheelbarrow to try and keep varmints out for a few more hours.

We were in and out in less than thirty minutes, back on the road to the mission with no further incidents. The route from there to the mission became more well-worn by cart and foot traffic as we approached the flat, open location where the mission was situated. There were a few trees around the outside, especially on the western side of the wall. Those few pines were tall and probably allowed to grow to block the afternoon sun from entering the compound.

It had an eight-foot-high brick wall covered in adobe mud, but most of it had worn off over time and weather, exposing brick and the straw used to make them. We viewed the top of the old sanctuary, and it looked the same as I remembered. There was a bell in the wooden frame tower, and I could see the odd timbers sticking up along the walls, likely from small buildings or lean-tos built against the interior wall that circled the whole perimeter. The main entrance facing us was an arched doorway ten feet tall, with the post oak framing a foot square holding the double doors. The doors were in poor shape, very old and worn, originally a two-inch-thick plank, but now splayed and cracked, held together with flat iron bars. We stopped at the hitching post to the right of the doors, checking to see if the water trough had any water in it. There was only a few inches of water, and it was relatively clean, so we tied up the horses and went to the front door.

McCort and Cat came and lit on the wall in front of the horses, then jumped down into the trough and also got a drink.

"Why are the doors closed in the middle of the day, I wonder?" Arterous asked.

"I'm not sure, perhaps not a good sign," I confirmed. We both drew our pistols in anticipation of trouble. Arterous went to the left side of the double doors, and I stayed on the right side.

A round iron bar extended from the doorframe out about shoulder height, with a rope hanging from it, tied off with a knot at the end. I looked, and it was pinned to the wall; on the inside, at the end of the bar, was a small bell. I peered through the poorly maintained wood slats of the door and tried to see anything I could. There was nothing and no one. I reached for the rope and rang the bell, keeping my eye between the boards, watching to see if anyone was stirring. Waiting a polite amount of time, I gave it another, longer ring. I also couldn't smell anyone, but the lack of wind wasn't helping; the only breeze was blowing from us into the compound.

Now I heard some shuffling which seemed to be coming from behind the chapel's left side. I spotted small animal sheds, hay storage areas, and a couple of small garden plots scattered around the courtyard. The tomatoes and jalapenos, as well as the okra and beans, were also dry and yellow, likely too far gone to bring back now. Puffs of dust began drifting from the back of the chapel now, and a priest appeared, shuffling slowly towards the gate. He had dark brown hair, unkempt, had dust on his black robes, and was shielding his eyes from the bright sun.

He approached the gate, placing one hand on the horizontal bar latch, the other still blocking the sun. "How can I help you, men?" He asked.

"Father Callious?" I asked.

"Yes."

"I am Raileanu Tellafrog. This is Arterous. May we come in?"

He lowered his head thinking for a moment, "Tella, Tella - oh, John's son! Yes, yes please," he fumbled weakly with the latch, trying to unbolt the door, finally succeeding, holding the door open for us, and closing and latching it again behind us.

"Please, follow me inside out of the sun," he said, and went into the chapel with the same strange gait he had come to the gate with. We entered the chapel, which I remembered had a few windows and stained glass, but all were gone. The frames still clung to shards of glass, some of which lay broken on the ground, both outside and inside. Dust and leaves had blown in and lay everywhere inside. That was strange; I know that none of the children who live around here ever wore shoes. No one would leave all the broken plate glass lying around. The priest went in and sat down in about two rows of pews, slumped over. We both stood at the back of the room, near the entrance.

"Please, I apologize for not visiting your parents in the last couple of weeks," he appeared quite out of breath, and he was beginning to appear weaker and weaker. He wasn't much older than I was, and all of the priests in these missions are always sturdy, hard-working, self-sufficient men.

"Father, where is everyone? Why are the gates locked in the middle of the day?" Father Callious seemed to fall asleep as I finished asking. Being midday, the direct sunlight was overhead, none coming in the windows, and it was quite dark inside. My eyes might not adjust for a few more minutes, but he was acting like he had some physical problems.

He just shook his head. "No, no, no. Is there something I can do for you?" His eyes were still closed.

"Father, we came to check on you and see if everything was alright. My father was very ill and has just passed away. Mother mentioned you had not visited in a couple of weeks, so we wanted to see if you were sick as well." I walked over to him, knelt beside him, trying to look at his face. He had dark, bruised patches that were swollen, and one eye was swollen almost shut, with black discoloration surrounding it. He wasn't falling asleep; he was having trouble keeping his eyes open from swelling. "We also came across a lady about halfway here in some woods; she, too, had passed on."

"Oh my God, oh my God, I have failed everyone!" He began wailing, crying uncontrollably, rocking back and forth, his puffy, bruised hands alternating between his face and his knees.

I looked at Arterous, stood, and put my hand on Father Callious' shoulder. He kept rocking and crying aloud, now in Spanish. While I waited for him to calm himself, I looked around the room more closely. Several of the front pews were broken and knocked over. The doors on the confessional were ripped off the hinges with splinters still hanging on. Something had obviously happened here.

"Please, gentlemen, I must lie down. Please, can you help me to my quarters behind the chapel?" He stood feebly, grasping my arm and walking down the center aisle towards a door to the front left of the pulpit. As soon as we stepped outside the door near the back of the chapel, I caught the scent of dead people, buried, but the outgassing of dead bodies was distinct. We made our way out of the doorway, then to the right, and around to a small structure attached to the back of the chapel. We took him inside and sat him on the small bed.

"I am so sorry I couldn't be there for your parents, Raileanu. I am so sorry. Your father was one of my best friends," he managed to say, while wiping tears and such with a handkerchief from his nightstand.

"Father, where are the other priests? Why are the gates closed? What happened here?" I tried again.

He sniffled a couple of times, clearing his face again and again, trying to muster the courage to tell me. Arterous and I found some chairs and sat down to wait for him to compose himself. Whatever it was, it was severe. This land was unforgiving; it would be so hot that even ants would seek shade in the heat of August. Every few winters crippling ice storms would coat everything in ice, like a layer of glass. The weight of the ice disfigures every tree it touches. Sometimes, even wells whose surface was thirty feet below grade would freeze a foot thick in winters. The Apache, Comanche, the Mexican Army's defeat, bandits, dust storms, crop failure, all of it makes for hard folk, and something has clearly broken this man.

"Bandits came. A couple of weeks ago. They were renegade Mexican soldiers. They demanded we give them everything we had. We did. They left for a day, but returned, having found cases of alcohol on a wagon somewhere; all of them were drunk and furious." Father Callious was weeping, suffering through the ragged, stuttering that happens when you try to take a deep breath during a hard cry. "They tried to blame us for having lost the war, saying we took the side of the Texians and helped them. We told them we help every one of God's children, and Jesus said to respect the government, whoever they may be. I said that to them. I did this. It's all my fault." He fell across the bed, with unbearable physical and emotional pain, moaning. "I tried to help, but just saying that enraged them. They tore apart the church. They threw a dead dog into our well. They beat all of us with boards. Then their leader decided the best way to punish me was to kill all the other priests, ALL FOUR!" He pushed his face deep into the pillow, screaming. The pressure in his face from the beating, the crying, and the screaming was hard to look at.

After a few minutes of deep breathing, his attitude changed somewhat, from sorrow and pain to anger. He sat back up, distorted face now wanting to say more. "He cut their throats and made me watch while I was tied to a tree right outside," he pointed vaguely out the little window in his room. "They all died because of me! Even Digger and Mary Loggins now also! That's who you came across, I am sure, on the way here! Oohh!"

"You mean the lady we found in the woods in the dugout? Was there a man also? We didn't find him, maybe he..." I tried to ask.

"No, no, I'm sure they're both dead, I did that! Oh no, no, no," he cried. "Digger came here ten days ago. He told me the bandits had been at his house and stole his money, most of his pigs, tied his wife up on a bench outside, and tied Digger in the pigpen. They made him watch them all violate her. I tried to counsel him, but the horror, I don't know how either survived." Father Callious was in pain, from the stretched skin in places all over his body, cracked and broken bones, and through the misshapen face, his eyes showed resolute anger. "The soldados were drunk and left both of them tied up, probably thinking they'd die. Digger got free and freed his wife, and came here demanding I send for help to catch these monsters. "His lower lip was shaking uncontrollably between sentences. "I did send word with a local orphan boy. But they caught him, and finding the message, they came back with rage and did all this. Beaten, and I am sure my right hand is broken, several ribs, and a couple of bones in my left foot. It took me three days to bury my brother priests here. When I went outside the walls on the front of our mission, I found the orphan boy messenger tied to the big pine, dead also. Then I had one more grave to dig. And now I learn your father has also died. Oh, I am so low, so low," he adjusted on the bed in a somewhat normal posture, breathing deeply as he cried, and still shuddering from the images we all create in our minds, retelling terrible events.

"Oh Father, I am so sorry." That was about the most terrible series of events I had ever heard. He covered his face with his hands, and one was indeed quite swollen compared to the other, seeing them close together now. "Is there anything we can do to help?"

"I don't know, there is no mission here, nothing but me, and I caused all of this," he moaned.

"Father, that is not true. You gave to those in need. You spoke the truth, as God commands us all to do. We are never responsible for the actions of evil men, regardless of our proximity to them. He allows free will, and these evils are ones those men must contend with God over, not you." I went and knelt in front of him. I wanted him to understand I meant what I was saying to him. "Your brothers in service, the young boy, all are with Him now, and you know that. I find no fault in what you have done here. The only other courses of action you imagine would not have swayed men in such a state of mind any other way, surely, you know this. Please, our God IS forgiveness, and this land needs their priest. Isn't there a mission east of here that we can contact to promptly send you aid and help?" I attempted to comfort him with things that are hard to grasp through pain and broken bones.

He thought for a minute, lowered his hands from his face, and said, "Yes. In fact, you might send an owl. There is a priest who can take confession from magical people. He arrived from Portugal last year. His name is, uh, Lorenzo. I would let you use a pigeon, but they killed all of ours after they found the boy carrying my message about them. That is a large mission, fifteen miles due east. He can receive your owl, and will understand." His breathing had calmed a bit, his tears had slowed. He wanted to come out from behind his grief, but the reflections of what he had lived through were still clouding his view of the world.

"Alright, I will write to him now. I'll get you some water, and Momma made you some bread, too. You rest and eat when you can. We will do what we can around here and help, but I don't want Momma to be left all alone at night, so we won't stay too long." I told him.

We stepped outside, and I asked Arterous to give the bread from Momma to him, and if he was certain no one was looking, to use his wand to clean the dog carcass out of the well and make sure it was drinkable again. He agreed and set off to attend to those things.

From outside the door, I asked loud enough for the priest to hear, "Do you have some paper, a pen, and ink?"

"Yes, yes, the door to your right on the back of the chapel building, it goes to the basement where the scriptorium is, where we do our writing, you will find some on the big desk," he explained.

"Alright, I'll be right back," I said, and I found the door and went downstairs.

It was indeed right below the floor of the sanctuary; the big wood beams on this room's ceiling were the floor framing for the area above. The wall to the left was lined with a desktop covered in writing materials, and a small wooden rack, extending from that surface to the ceiling, held manuscripts and rolls of paper. Directly across from the stairway were floor-to-ceiling, wardrobe-like cabinets that ran along the right-hand wall as well. They were not all the same; some were old, some were new, and they had different styles. Likely gifts from locals over the decades, or maybe new parish leaders had ones they brought with them. They fit fairly tightly against each other, except that the last one on the right side was slightly too wide and sat at a slight diagonal, which was probably the best way it could fit. I am guilty of making things that don't fit from time to time, so judgment withheld with a smile. I found the necessary writing materials and wrote a brief letter explaining the events as politely as possible, emphasizing that Father Callious needed help as soon as they could manage. I addressed it to Father Lorenzo and went back upstairs to call McCort. Arterous was coming back in the front gate, and brought all the canteens as well with him. I called my owl, wound the message tight to the leg, tied it with a burlap string, and sent him off. He wouldn't make it back until nightfall from that far away.

"Here, you take this to the Father, I'll start on the well if that's alright." Arterous handed me everything, I nodded, and we went to our tasks.

"Father, do you have any jugs I can put this clean water in for you? I have also sent the message out to Father Lorenzo. He will have it tonight." I sat down in the chair and unwrapped the cheesecloth from the sourdough loaf, breaking off a piece and handing it to him.

"I do, in the shed by the well." He ate from the handful of bread and took a big drink of the canteen water. "A family came for mass the day after I finished burying everyone. They saw what had happened and returned the next day with a full barrel of water. It's all I have had."

"None of us are meant to live this life alone, Father. We will return and assist in getting your mission back up and running. Don't try to do too much, rest and heal up, I bet there will be help from Father Lorenzo's parish in a week or so." The bread and as much water as he wanted were well received. He must have been rationing the water he had, and he was eating one bite of bread and a long drink of water as fast as his sore face would allow. "Also, you should know that those bandits were seen arrested and being escorted by Texian Rangers a couple of days ago. They aren't going to be causing any more trouble." I stayed with him for about fifteen minutes, just in quiet company. When he had eaten half of the

168

large round of sourdough, he gently let his body relax onto the bed.

"Thank you for the food, Raileanu. God is good." Smiling, I stood up and went outside with Arterous. He had finished clearing the filth out of the well and had also filled the barrel again with new water. He was near a mimosa tree at the front of the compound, squatting down and looking at the ground around its base.

"You all done?" I hollered.

"Yes. Are we alright to leave now?" He asked, standing still, looking at the ground, and then walking towards me to the entrance.

"He should be okay. I told him about you spotting the bandits having been apprehended and escorted out of the region."

"Raileanu!" Father Callious yelled for me. He was standing in the doorway, leaning against it, and seemed to be standing a bit more erect than I had seen him before, even smiling a bit. "Leave the front gates open if you would."

Smiling back, I gave him a wave and we untied the horses and turned to leave, knowing he already felt better knowing none of those troublemakers would be around.

We proceeded to the Loggins' place, and I went to remove the barricade I had erected to keep trouble away from her. Arterous went into the flat area west of the indentation where their dugout was located. The water runoff fed the ground, and with the shade of the trees and an abundance of beautiful green ryegrass, it was a peaceful scene. There wasn't any scrubby underbrush or thorn vines, so he began to dig a proper grave for her with his wand.

I went inside to wrap her up and try to find anything personal I could place with her to rest. She was quite stiff and foul, from the heat, I'm sure. Her passing had left waste on her clothes and bedsheets, so I used them to wrap her, and went across the yard to fetch the wheelbarrow. I set her in it gently and went back inside to check for personal items that should be buried with her. Sadly, there was but one folding picture frame of a man and a woman painted in it, but I didn't know if it was them, or one of their parents, or even siblings. I couldn't tell. But it was the only thing I found. I set it on her and went to where Arterous had finished his work.

"Would you, please, lower her in? It would be undignified if I did it." I asked him.

"Of course." He directed her up with his wand, and slowly over and down into her grave. He looked all around again and began letting the dirt fill the hole. He had also removed a stack of the white rock from the bluff's edge and stacked it nearby.

"Wait, Father Callious told me their names, let me fetch a few bits of wood and make them a proper marker." So I went back to the collection of crates and things near the house, but couldn't find any boards big enough for me to carve legibly on. Well, I thought, those split rails around the pig pen have no further use, so I'll use those. So I forced apart a few pieces and was searching through the junk outside for a saw. I was in front of the dugout's door and turned to look at the corn crib - maybe it, being roofed to keep the corn dry, has saws and other tools to keep them out of the rain. That's when, in my periphery, I spotted something bright white in the pig pen. It had been mainly under the muck, but when I pulled down one of the fence posts, it must have revealed it. I went straight to it, afraid of what it presumably was. It was the bare top of a human skull.

"Arterous! Can you come here?" I yelled loudly, and I couldn't take my eyes off it.

He calmly walked over and stopped dead in his tracks when it came into view.

"Is that..."

"Yes. And it may be her husband. Can you - lift that, him, from the pigpen so we can see if it is?"

"Yes, stand back a bit, please." He made a small cross shape and a small circle with his wand, and the body began to rise. It was all in the same place, but not all in one piece. Clothes colored with pig filth clung to what was left of him, and most of the meat rotted and was trampled. The bare top of the skull was the only part exposed. Right away, I wondered why I couldn't smell him before now. Far bigger things to consider than this, though, so we took him also slowly, along with the rails I had to the side of the first grave.

"Let me do both the grave and the markers. I don't want to linger here any longer than needed." Arterous stated firmly. I wasn't about to argue. He set about making the matching hole, lowered the remains of the man in, and I used the wool blanket from the doorway to cover him. Arterous filled it in, placed the stones, and in a hurry had the markers made and placed. Setting another layer of large, heavy stones on top, we finished, washed up in the trickle from the rocks, and got back on the horses.

"Remember when the hogs were in the pen? I think that's why they were dancing, or stepping carefully, or whatever I observed earlier, they didn't want to step on him. You may not know this, but even domestic pigs, especially scrawny ones, won't blink twice to find a meal wherever they can. They didn't. They didn't even want to step on him. Also, I couldn't smell him. I only mention it so that when you are able to speak to the professor, you should mention it. And have a good look at the lady's flyswatter before you speak with him."

"This is a wild place. It is also vast. I can barely understand how people from European nations would want to come here. In this place are dangers that I can not fully comprehend." He said.

"You honestly don't understand?" I asked

"No, sir, I do not."

"This small cove, in that stand of young trees," I pointed back to them, "far from anywhere, was THEIRS. They shared none of the fruits of their labors with any noble. Every single thing they bought, or built, repaired, or reused belonged to no one else. They had to ask no one for permission to plant a field, raise pigs, hunt a rabbit or a deer, and no one had a legal right to take it from them. They had a right to the firearms to try and prevent that atrocity we witnessed. They lived according to their own priorities, guided by what they could do. They would thrive or perish based solely on their ability to generate food and income through free trade and contracts with others, and to use whatever force they deemed fit to protect the fruits of their own hands. Every one of these little homesteads we cross owes allegiance to no one but each other, and the religion of their choice. I must say, for everyone raised in two-thousand-year-old cities, whose entire life is ruled by nobles and royals, what Europeans term 'commoners', the freedom in all arenas here probably seems like a fantasy. But all men and women who know they are in the image of God, and refuse to settle for being called 'common' by other humans stained with the same sins, are the ones unafraid to come here," I explained.

"I suppose so. The industriousness and hearty nature I have seen in my short time surprises me," he said, motioning to me for my special flask.

After the work we had done here, it was a fantastic idea. It was so hot that a tar-pitched roof might slide off into a pile. So we enjoyed our fill of glacial runoff water, and it was divine. It took another hour, and we were able to make it back into the homestead just as the sun was settling in amongst the trees now, bright orange, and scorching less of the land every minute.

CHAPTER NINE

We put the horses in the stalls, filled their water buckets and hay bins for the night. Momma was inside cooking, and we went on towards the house, knocking all the dust and dry grass fibers from our boots and clothes as we got onto the porch.

"I'm going to try not to trouble Momma with all we discovered until tomorrow, if that's alright. Maybe wait until she heads to bed before you speak with the professor," I said, as hushed as I could.

"Yes, agreed," he whispered as Momma came to us at the doorway, wiping her hands on her apron.

"I have dinner ready, boys!" She came and hugged us as we came in and sat down at the table, already set. Ol Catherine the Great flew in and sat atop a high-back chair near the fireplace.

"How was Father Callious?" She asked busily, wanding food onto the plates and serving bowls.

We looked at each other, and I said, "He is doing alright, a bit under the weather is all." Hoping it would satisfy for now, not wanting to spoil her good mood.

"That's good. I hope he gets better! Here we are!" She levitated everything to its place on the table and came and sat down by me. "Give us a blessing for the meal, son."

"Alright. Lord bless us and this food. Thank you for all your kindness and for holding us up when we need it. Please find the hearts of all those who need peace, and bring your justice to those who are lawless. Amen."

"Okay, everyone, dig in! It's steak and baked potato with collard greens and hominy. Oh, and I have a nice chocolate pudding for dessert," she smiled and began to work on her steak.

We didn't bring it up at dinner or afterward. We were genuinely a bit worn out and emotionally drained. Momma knew we hadn't said everything, but trusted us to do so when it made sense. Besides, I was very relieved to see her in such high spirits. I didn't expect her to mope around and be in doldrums about father. We knew where he was. I was quite glad she hadn't let a hint of grief sneak in. The good meal helped, and after dark, once the animals were taken care of, we retired to bed. Tonight, I thought, I am going to actually use that hot water bath. And I did. I don't remember the last time I slept so well; I was clean, sore, and physically and emotionally exhausted.

****

Monika had spent the last few days diligently working through the plants, rocks, minerals, drawings, notes, and samples I had collected, but was growing tired of being confined to the Royal House. She hadn't been back across the street to the pub or hotel since her meeting with Runetta. Tonight, though, she thought, she would at least walk the few hundred yards of rampart surrounding the high walls of the courtyard, as the nights were already cooling a bit, and autumn would begin here soon.

When she had put all the collections away and locked them up in the old barracks, she walked to the dining hall, about fifty feet long and twenty wide, made for a time when far more soldiers were garrisoned in these smaller royal residences. They had prepared turkey and some black sea fish tonight, along with cabbage and mushrooms. She had some fish and cheese, along with a glass of red wine, because the cask they had opened recently was very good. Afterwards, she walked to the front of the yard and entered one of the guardhouses, which had a spiral stone staircase leading up to the ramparts. It was dark now, and she walked all the way to the perimeter wall on the west, where it met the taller and separate city wall. Then, she went back towards the front gate, where there was a bench, which she sat on for some time. By now, the street lamps had been lit for two hours, and most foot traffic outside had come to an end. She could see that the four-story buildings and homes within sight had most of their lights out, the residents asleep. She let out a polite yawn, barely audible to even herself, and leaned her head back to look at the stars.

"Oh, darling Monika, you need some rest." Monika's blood went cold and almost stopped, as she heard a voice. How could anyone have heard a tiny yawn?? How could anyone have known it was me?? Runetta. She obviously knew Monika was there, so she stood and took a look over the rampart wall. Click, click, click. Runetta's form was moving a few steps closer to the street, and she stopped. Was it her? Surely, the size and outline indicated it was. The lady brought something to her face and struck a match. She lit a small cigar, or something like it. The light of the match and the slow draw on it did indeed show her face. It was Runetta. She looked right at Monika, who by now could tell it was some expensive clove-tobacco cigarillo by the aroma. Monika stood quietly defiant, saying nothing. Why was this woman here again?

Runetta took another draw on her tobacco and then turned and walked back around the corner of the pub with her high boots clicking as if they had metal plates on the heels snapping on the stone cobbles as she walked. She must have dislocated in the darkness because the sound of her boots stopped.

That was enough of this. Monika went straight down to the guards and asked them to inform her if they caught that woman loitering around again. She went inside to the great room where the professor's portrait was, but alas, he wasn't available. Well, in that case, I will just spend the night here and speak with him as soon as possible. She fetched a serving tray with cream and sugar, a small pot of coffee, and a cup. She retrieved some paper and made essentially a sign which read, "Wake me when Professor Templeton is available. She placed it so that if the butler, and the professor himself, who happened to pass into view, would not miss it. She grabbed a light blanket, a footstool, and positioned herself about six feet from the portrait. She didn't finish her small pot of coffee before it went cold, and she fell asleep.

It was daylight, and the light touch of the butler woke her the next morning. He had seen her note, passed word along through the night shift, and the morning man was here, alerting her that the professor was indeed waiting. She shook herself more awake, thanked the butler with a light touch on his hand with hers, and stood, blanket still around her shoulders.

"Professor, I apologize for being asleep. I hope I didn't keep you waiting," she began, still rubbing her eyes clear of crusties.

"No, no, my dear. I have been here but a few moments. How are you?" He said whilst pouring himself a morning cup of tea.

"I am fine. Is there anything you know further about this lady, Runetta Lynchos? She was here again last night, right outside the gate, more or less toying with me," Monika stated firmly.

"I'm afraid, nothing more. However, I believe Klement has also been looking into it, and he should be arriving this evening with you. He has a meeting with someone on an unrelated matter, but I believe he mentioned this person may have helpful knowledge about her, nonetheless. Please do not speak with her again until we know more about her intentions. When Klement arrives, it may be prudent for you to return to Vienna with him, if he is also concerned," the professor said.

"I won't speak with her again. I think it may be better to finish this work in Vienna as well, although I will be away from Raileanu's source materials if I need additional samples or drawings from this area. I'm sure he will understand, though," Monika said.

"Yes, he will care more about your peace of mind than your access to nearby plant life while working on his texts. You are right. Please do not worry anymore; it is time to pack up those things and move your studies to the safety of the Metternich home in Vienna. I'm sure the staff can help if you require it."

"No, I have it well organized, I can manage. I want to ensure that everything is delivered intact and with the best possible reduction in the risk of damage. Thank you, professor, please let me know if anything else changes with Raileanu."

"I will, of course. Goodbye for now."

She finished, laid the blanket on the chair, and went to eat some breakfast. There's a lot of packing to do, she thought. It was a bit comforting to know she'd most likely be gone by nightfall, hopefully.

****

The next morning, back in Texas, I rose as dawn broke and headed down for breakfast, where Mother and Arterous were already nearly finished eating.

"A nice hot bath does help you relax and sleep better, doesn't it, dear?" Mom said, already preparing a plate for me. My affinity for shredded potatoes with a fried egg and about a dozen pieces of thick, crispy bacon hadn't eluded her memory, and it was almost ready.

Living in the ordinary world, I had learned to enjoy the simple making of my own food, precisely the way I liked it, but honestly, having someone who could produce it exactly right was, well, special. And so delicious. No denying that fact.

"Have you begun decorating the new arboretum? Do you have any requests from overseas I might offer?" I asked after a few satisfying mouthfuls.

"I did some yesterday, yes. I decided to ring the interior of the opening and down the walls with moon vine, which should illuminate the interior at night. I also changed the upper fixed glass panels to hinged panels that I can open. This way, lightning bugs and other night critters can come in and enjoy pollinating at will," she said, proud of those brilliant changes.

"Outstanding, Momma, I had considered none of those things myself." Pausing now for MORE of my favorite breakfast.

"So, boys, are you going to tell me about Father Callious, and what is going on at the mission, or are you going to leave me guessing the worst?" She stopped and stared at me.

"I promise, Momma, the Father is fine, but he is not feeling well enough to travel right now. He was very upset about Dad's passing, and very grateful for the sourdough you made him." I hoped to assure her. "I honestly am not ready to talk about the other unrelated things that occurred on the trip. Please, Momma."

She reached over the table and put her hand on my wrist. "It's really okay. I didn't want you sparing me anything I could help with. I understand, and some things don't help anyone to keep in, or let out."

After breakfast, we attended to the tasks that had been left undone at the place while Dad was sick. I weeded the back garden again, and watered it for her, Arterous restocked (magically of course) the hay and grain supplies for the horses, and took momma and papa's horses out for a run, as they hadn't been out for several weeks other than a canter up and around the perimeter. He cleaned their hooves, checked their shoes, restocked the coal bin, and soaped all their saddles, bridles, and leads. He made sure the cans of lamp oil were full and even crawled around on the roof of the stable to make sure it wasn't in need of repair. He asked mother about firewood for fall and winter, and she informed him that father only allowed deadfall and storm damage from the wood surrounding our little enclave to be used for firewood, so he went up and found several large branches of live oak and water oak that had fallen, along with a whole foot-diameter branch of broken, likely in an earlier spring storm, which was rich pine. Rich pine variety has a rich red streak of essentially natural kerosene in it. They burn vigorously and easily, so we decided to let him splinter the whole thing into kindling. It was an uneventful morning, but productive.

When we stopped at midday, I remembered the stick we had found at the Digger family's dugout and asked Arterous to fetch it so he could look at it with the monocle still in his room.

When he came back out of the house with it, in direct sun, what had looked almost like tar in the shade of the dugout and trees, in reality, had no sheen to it in any angle or light. It was a flat color, almost like a wooden version of cast iron. He took a few minutes and said he perceived no sign of a troublesome magical quality. He let Mother examine it also, who made no discoveries either. She went into the house for a moment and came out with a pitcher of lemonade and glasses.

"I am not convinced that's a natural stick, however, it doesn't look artificial either. Boys, it may only be a weird stick she found and fancied so she made a flyswatter out of it," she said as she poured the drinks for us. "Hang on to it, long enough to show it to the professor this evening is my advice."

"Good idea, Momma. We will do that." I said as we relaxed on the front porch in the shade. "How about showing me around in your new work when we're done here?"

"Yes, I do believe it's best before the hottest part of the day. I may even open the center up a bit to the water table while we are down there to keep humidity up and moderate the temperature a bit. The well water is a very comfortable fifty degrees around here, it should help," she said.

"Did you ever have a chance to look at the cell gates from below, while we were gone yesterday?"

"No, I wasn't sure if you boys took the monocle with you, so I didn't bother," she said. "I did save the old main door, in case they want it at another prison. I moved it out back under the porch roof."

Arterous splayed his fingers out and upturned his wrist, I guess indicating he had left it out, but maybe he forgot to tell her why.

"Arterous, would you mind terribly?" I looked at him, feet propped on the rail, and leaned back in the rocking chair.

"No, I suppose it is a good idea before we forget. Plus, if there's nothing of interest, you," leaning his glass of lemonade towards momma, "can use them as railing or grates or something in the arboretum."

"Exactly the plan, sir," Momma said back to him. We finished our cool drinks and headed out.

I went to and held the door for Momma, allowing her to enter her glass dome for my first look. The section she added for the honeysuckle and similar plants was about ten feet tall, domed to match the main cap dome, and of the same total height and construction. Two-foot-tall windings of them, and some orange trumpet vine, were already springing up. She had arranged the center spire of solid rock into a low handrail wall that snaked down the inside of the stairs, about a foot wide and three feet high. That was good, I didn't need her falling into a hundred-foot pit! The cells, which had been carved from solid rock, had rectangular indentations, not very impressive, she had arched the ceilings of, and put niches all the way around each one. Each of those had a bowl-shaped basin full of dirt waiting for her selections. The cut of the glass on the dome allowed ample light to reflect down into the spaces better than I had imagined, both in summer and winter. I glanced up and marveled at what wasn't visible from ground level outside. The center of the glass roof was essentially a gigantic Fresnel lens. Some of the rooms at the top quarter had long wooden tables in their centers, with pots and baskets of rich soil waiting to be filled with plants. When we were about half of the way down, she drew her wand, and waved it at the west side, and moonvine was planted, transplanted actually, from wherever she already had some, because it was about six feet long. That plant will remain dull, dark green in the light of day, and at night, it will emit a pale blue light as it processes nutrients from the soil. We continued down to the bottom, which was a twenty-five-foot diameter circle of flat stone. We stayed at the bottom of the stairs, where she waved her wand again in a tight little circle, and the stone, ten feet from the very center, resorted itself into a fish-shaped fountain, pointing up, with water all around it. The fish let loose a hundred-foot column of water about a foot wide, going all the way up to the ground surface, before falling against its own sides and back into the pool around the fish statue. That instantly caused cool air to circulate in the whole of Wormwell, and also carried light from the sun, or I suppose, the moon, all the way to the bottom. Magic or not, my momma has a great imagination.

Arterous called down from the rim at the top, "The gates don't have anything of interest; if you need them, they are all clear."

"Okay, thanks!" I hollered back up.

"Ready?" Mom asked, already holding up her wand.

"Yeah, sure." I stood back against the wall, smiling.

She raised it high and brought each of the twenty-one gates down to us, collecting them into a ball of swirling, white-hot iron. One by one, dozens of small and large balls of molten iron fell away and formed into small frogs, falling to the floor in front of us. They began leaping to the edges of the pool, making charming poses and groups, and some were even horny toads. Several large toads then assembled themselves into bench ends, holding iron bars woven into lattice seats that crossed between the toads, bending up at the back to form beautiful seating areas. There were six evenly spaced large toads, looking upward with their mouths open, and a small series of holes appeared on their necks. Another swish, and large drops of water, randomly timed, began falling into their mouths from the great pillar of water, making little creeps and ribbits as the water drained out through the holes. Genuinely beautiful, what an imagination! We stayed at the bottom, in the cool air, until evening, talking about all our time here with Daddy, telling her about all the things I had found in my time in Austria on my last visit. It occurred to me that she was likely in a good enough mood, and that it was safe to show her the locket and tell her about how I was feeling recently about Monika. I handed the locket to her, and while she had seen her through a portrait, and suspected our fondness for each other, she was brought to tears of happiness as I explained.

"Look, honey," Mom held the locket open back at me. "She is looking right at me; she had to have been looking at your painting. Oh! She says she is! She says she misses you! Ooooh my, oh, I am so happy!" She looked at me and hugged my neck hard. "That's from her! Oh, she says to make sure and have Arterous talk with the professor this evening."

"Tell her I will. Tell her I miss her, too." I said, smiling.

"May I stay here and speak with her for a while, son?" she asked with her fingertips together over her mouth, smiling.

"Yeah, yeah alright momma," I said, smiling, and I started back up. I guess at thirty-five years old, she has waited long enough for me to consider a possible courtship. Additionally, it actually ached a little knowing I could not speak with her, or see her form a smile.

I went all the way back up to the top, and out the door into the front yard, and caught a whiff of distant rain. A cold rain from the north. I walked up to the rim and yelled down to Momma that rain was coming. She stood and started up the stairs, still talking through a wide smile to Monika, so I went back out in the yard. Now I could also detect a distinct whine sound in the distance. I looked to the west, where the wind was whipping up grass and dust in the air, and the dark gray cloud bank towered as high as I could see. The mid to bottom levels were still obscured, but the whine only comes from one thing - a tornado. The wall of clouds stretched from north to south as far as was visible; it was a massive storm.

"Momma! I can hear a tornado somewhere in that storm! Please come up! Arterous! Where are you? A tornado is coming!" I shouted down to Momma, then around to wherever Arterous might be.

"It's okay!" Momma shouted, about halfway up now. "Calm down, this place has weathered a dozen of them in our years here, we are well protected."

Oh, right. This place is fine. Lord, that is a relief, but EVERYWHERE else, EVERY OTHER time in my life, that is a terrifying prospect, and painful for me because I can perceive them long before any other person, and I have failed to convince some in the past. No, I think I will hold onto my fear and apprehension regarding this terrifying force of the natural world.

"What?" Arterous came from inside the house, looking confused. "What is happening?"

"A thunderstorm," of which I can feel the thunder approaching now, "one that has a tornado hidden in it somewhere. I can hear it."

"What is that, a tor- tornado?" He asked, still confused.

Momma had finally come up and out the front, "Not to worry, boys, this place is quite well protected, has been for decades."

Regardless of my mother's lack of fear, I relayed mine to Arterous: "It is the single most powerful storm that forms unpredictably on the face of the earth. Its powerful winds rip the strongest trees to shreds, obliterates any man-made structure in its path, and can even rip the sod from the earth in severe cases." I laid out, still nervous. "Not for us, but for every living thing in its path."

"Really? These are common here?" he queried, looking now nervously at the sky.

"More common than most think, I'm afraid."

Momma had made her way to the front porch from inside the house by now and was setting the rocking chairs up to face outwards, and pouring lemonade, almost comically calm with her little grin.

Now, the clouds at the front did indeed begin to boil, rolling like millions of huge balls in the sky, thick black swirling shells with an eerie green glow inside them. That was a sign I had seen in every tornado in north, central, and eastern Texas I had ever encountered. I pointed the feature out to Arterous, explaining it was a sign to find shelter no matter what anyone else might think, if caught out in the open.

We walked to the house and sat down with her, each holding a glass of ice-cold drink, dripping with condensation, as we watched the clouds swirl and lumber closer and closer. Momma took her wand and did a little circle wave up in the air.

"What was that for?" I asked

"Your father and I were, after much practice, mind you, able to modify the protection spells so that we let just enough rain and wind in from storms, while keeping everything else out. You will enjoy this. Previously, it allowed the wind and rain to continue uninterrupted, and things would become terribly muddy. Now it is gentle and just enough that it gets through, the rest runs off to the perimeter of the property, and seeps into our water table," she kept rocking back and forth peacefully.

"Mother, I am glad you and Dad were safe all these years. I know you have heard what happens to ordinary people and animals who experience a tornado; it is heartbreaking." I said, as heavy raindrops, about the size of glass marbles, began striking the layer overhead, each making a blueish, glowing outline. Only a small drop of much lower velocity came through and fell to the ground. Each one made a "donk" sound, which was very faint, even for me. Thousands began to fall, and the noise grew to the point where it was all-consuming. The light show it produced as they danced around plonking on the magical shell was beautiful, I have to admit. However, then the hail started, and even through the light emitted and the sound, and the heavy blowing sheets of rain combined, we could see tree branches and so much long dead grass from the prairie outside the wood we were in, I knew one of the deadly twisters was nearby. Larger pieces of trees had been ripped from their trunks and began crossing our view, seemingly opposite the direction the sheets of rain moved. A few struck the shell, creating a rippling wave of blue light, but no more than a gentle breeze, and steady, small drips evenly coated the ground and in little streams from the roof edges. Then, huge chunks of ice hail struck with tremendous force, some as large as my fist, dozens, and built to hundreds. At the edges of our yard, to the west, the pea-sized hail and these larger balls collected and sat pinned between the arc of our dome and the walls of rock pillars that surrounded our place. A whirring sound grew, almost deafening, seeming to come from all directions.

"That is the sound of a tornado. It comes from the debris combined with the compression of winds moving more rapidly than anything else on earth, aside from volcanoes." I said, pointing to the sky. Lightning in the leading edges began striking the ground ahead of the storm with far greater frequency, accompanied by huge, thunderous cracks, followed by its remnants rumbling and rolling towards us.

"How big are they?" Arterous asked.

"There can be many more than one, sometimes they split from a large one into many smaller ones. They can move across lakes, and they can hide inside heavy rain, so we can't spot them. Sometimes they come with no rain. Sometimes one will destroy every blade of grass, every cow, and every tree, but then lift and pass right over a house or barn. Some are as wide as you can view in either direction, some leave a trail five feet wide. They are genuinely terrifying forces." I laid out in a monotone voice, scanning the sky above. The blinding white of lightning increased, making everything appear monochrome, and the cracks of sound they made were virtually unbearable. The whirring and whine of the winds in the twister was so intense now, Momma gave the air a tap with her wand and made it practically silent, thank goodness.

Suddenly and sadly, we watched as several squirrels, impaled with a thousand shards of splintered wood, slid across the dome, as did a jackrabbit, broken and twisted in unnatural ways. The bright flashes made it even more macabre. Several dozen mockingbirds, blue jays, crows, and grackles also had misfortune. The blurred edge of the funnel then leapt across the eastern edge of the protective shell, moving so fast that it was impossible to watch as rain, ice, or debris fell from it. The power of the funnel began to force lightning itself to wind round it. Its edge continued to lift up and across and stayed for a moment, long enough for us to even glimpse blue sky at the end of the funnel. Arterous' mouth was wide open now, staring essentially through a hole in the worst storm he had ever seen.

For that brief moment, the edge of the center was near us, then it vanished, heading off in what direction was not clear, thankfully, not over us. A moment later, on the back side of the event where winds were less powerful, more and more debris and small animals clonked onto the layer above us, each one in its time being blown to one edge or the other, where all the hail had gone. Now, only thick blankets of rain fell mixed with leaves and pine needles, washing off above us in waves. A few minutes later, it was nothing more than a drizzle, and a few more minutes after that, the sky began to clear to the west, until finally, the setting sun emerged from behind the towering monster of a storm. I was still able to pick up the rumbling of thunder as it rode further away from us; the speed with which something so large could move across the land was fascinating.

"That is the most amazing and terrifying thing I have ever seen," Arterous said, swallowing dryly. "I do not know of any magic producing that kind of power; it was truly awesome."

"There is no magic which can equal the power of God's creation, dear boy. None at all." Mother said without looking up.

"I believe you. Certainly not." Arterous said, now surveying the carnage of trees and hapless fauna strewn about the perimeters. Only then did Bandos finally appear, having been in the house, likely under the table. Mother gave a wave of her wand, and we heard all the debris falling around us, in and around the maze of stones. Bandos lit off in a hurry, wanting to smell-check every critter that was around and explore all the things that had blown in from afar.

"Mother, what about Father Callious?" It occurred to me that he might be in serious danger from something that strong.

"His mission is pretty well built. If he is indoors, or underneath in his basement, he should be fine," she responded with confidence.

I looked at Arterous, who was already looking back at me, knowing he was diminished and alone. We had to check on him.

"How fast do you think that storm is going, Momma? Do you think it will be over Father Callious in less than an hour? It seemed pretty quick to me, from when I first detected it to when it began destroying things here." I asked her.

"Oh, yes, probably under an hour," she stopped and looked at me, concerned. "You aren't going, my boy, it's only a couple of hours until dark, you'll never be back before dark."

"No, but Arterous can dislocate, only long enough to determine if the Father is alright, but not be seen," I said, looking at him then. "If you are alright with doing so?"

"Well, I think I will wait the time needed to make sure I don't show up right in the middle of that beast! Barring that, I don't mind," he said wisely.

"I think he should check, Momma, it's possible some travelers, or a family who took shelter at the mission, may need help," I said to her.

"Okay, okay, that may be true," she conceded. "But you, Little Frog, are NOT going."

We all agreed, and I went to retrieve the boxes of my extra ball and powder to give him, and spent a few minutes making sure he knew the hazards of even letting locals SEE his wand, or his interactions with his owl. Many of the tribes in the new Republic of Texas fear owls, and go right past not trusting anyone who consorts with them, to seeing it as a sign they are evil. I made him a sling out of rope for the rifle, so he could easily take that with him. Arterous took one look at the crude rope, recognized its usefulness, but shook his head, no. He took his wand and waved it the length of the sling, and it changed to a beautifully tooled leather sling. He smiled and gave me a nod. I agreed it was much better, and he lifted the rifle up and rested it across his back, his left arm outstretched through the sling. We agreed it was probably a good idea for him to first go to that spot where we turned off to the Loggins homestead and determine where the storm was, before going all the way to the mission. I also made him take Cat, in case of a problem, again, reminding him not to have her with him. She had returned and rested last night. When he was set, with his wand secured inside his vest, he shut his eyes and dislocated. All I could do was pray and hope for the best, for both him and Father Callious. I went back inside and helped Mother prepare dinner. She had decided enough with the easy way; she was ready to cook properly for her guests. When Arterous returned, she would have an authentic homegrown meal for him. So she set me to collecting vegetables out back.

CHAPTER TEN

Late in the evening, two hours after nightfall, Klement and his family arrived at the residence. By this time, Monika had packed everything and relabeled the crates according to her inventory and the additional work she had done. She had eaten and checked the portraits several times to see if there was any news about Raileanu, Runetta, or indeed anything at all, to no avail. She had retired to the same chair she had waited in before and fallen asleep. Klement woke her and sat across from her in another chair.

"Well, I must apologize for our late arrival. The meeting I had earlier in the day took longer than I would have liked on official business, and then we began discussing your friend."

"You mean Runetta, he knows of her?" Monika sat upright from her slouched position, waking as swiftly as she could to converse intelligently.

"Yes, he did. She, like most aristocrats of her stature, wandered from one formal occasion to the next, living lavishly and fomenting discord in her wake. Her companions at

194

each event seem to differ, each as polished and reviled as the next. Her family's fortune being built on the largest stand of ancient wand quality timber in the world affords whatever distractions pop into her pretty little head, honestly."Monika scowled at this, affirming her guess at the kind of woman she was. "Many of her family stay in these circles, but it is reported she had spent many a summer with an uncle, the brother of her mother, who illegally trained her in black magic even before she began school. This man, Dolphus Tangleweed, never married, but fathered children with several witches who spent time in prisons across the world after they gave birth, each one more driven towards madness than the last." He paused long enough to pour himself and Monika a cup of coffee that the butler had brought on a tray. Handing her the cup, he continued. "It is rumored by some that he is possibly her father. He has been a hermit in one of the many small castle ruins that litter their family holdings, and has not been seen in something like twenty years. He is technically still under an arrest warrant in Bulgaria, having killed a woman who rejected his advances in full view of assembled revelers on New Year's Eve, 1818. She is not known for her criminality, nor is she wanted anywhere, but no one can recall her being a positive influence at any gathering. I'm afraid we don't know much more than that."

"None of this explains why she has such an interest in me," Monika said firmly. "I refuse to cower to her, or anyone. I request to stay with you in Vienna to complete my work on Raileanu's collections of this year, and if possible, to have someone in authority alert one of us if she is in our proximity again."

"I understand. I can have you stay at our townhouse in Vienna, which will have my private security, not royal guards. I'd rather not encroach on my employment with the royal family in these matters, and it's much safer there. My people can be more informed and alert of such things, and I feel they will do a fine job in this." Klement stated.

"Have you spoken with Professor Templeton recently?" she asked.

"I have, earlier today. He told me about Raileanu and Arterous's trip to a nearby Spanish mission, which had suffered recent calamity at the hands of some roving bandits. Everyone was alright." Klement held his hand up, signaling they were fine.

"Yes, I did speak to Raileanu's mother today at some length. She is doing wonderful, considering the loss of her husband. They are hearty people, Klement. She also told me they were alright after that trip. She is holding up well, as is Raileanu with his father's passing, busying herself with the renovation of the Wormwell Prison," she said and smiled proudly.

"Good. That is good to know. I am glad for all three of you. Is everything packed, or should I arrange..." he began.

"No, sir, I have already packed it and it is loaded into two wagons, ready for us to depart, as soon as you give the word." She finished for him.

"Well, would you grace my wife and eldest son with a short visit before we retire for the night, so we may begin in the morning?"

"Of course, I'm so happy to see them again. Let us." She stood and waited for her host to motion towards his spouse's location.

The next morning, they loaded into carriages, one for the governess and the two youngest children, and Klement's son rode with them. Two carriages of his personal soldiers and equipment, and two with the cargo and luggage at the rear. Three men in Klement's personal service rode their own horses, in front of the column first thing in the morning, but had moved around several times before midday, speaking with all of them at one time or another. It was nearly 200 miles from Lake Königssee to Vienna; they would take several days to reach their destination, even with the excellently maintained roads on their route. Displacing would be easiest for Monika, but he could not, and he was expected to travel ordinarily to visit each district governor in his position en route. This trip would be safe and relaxing, to be honest, for Monika, and give her the opportunity to enjoy the things that travel often overlooks, which are magical to people.

The Professor had spent his time since speaking with Arterous, scouring his books and papers, and trying again to see if his new reports of chaos in relation to the mission and its hardships, even that strange stick-handled flyswatter, had any connections. So late into the night that he fell asleep, after finding nothing of note to reference, he finished by inscribing the stated facts in the special book.

After acquiring the copy he had sent to Klement to show Raileanu to inscribe the events surrounding John Tellafrog's illness and now his passing, he had begun locking himself into the secure study room in his London home. It was on the third floor, at the back with only two tiny windows which had been long painted shut and couldn't be opened from the outside, if they did budge at all. He had been warned of its rarity and importance, and took all of it, as well as the weight of this inquiry, very seriously. Even his housekeeper had no key to this room, but she was used to him locking himself in there for long periods over the years anyway. She had no reason to suspect that this instance was any different from previous scholarly work in which he had behaved this way. A single potbelly stove had replaced the fireplace some years back, and its crooked stovepipe had never been cleaned. It would sweat and leak coal dust, leaving a mess on the floor, which his house-keeper constantly complained about. Sometimes, the wind blowing across the rooftops, or perhaps children scaling the building and playing around on the roof, would cause it to wiggle, making it squeak and creak.

He thought he began to hear that sound, and roused from his slumped position across the desk just a little. He fumbled, eyes half open, for his glasses on the desk. Then he did detect rain falling outside, occasionally a gust would blow some drops against the tiny panes of glass and make a 'tink tink' sound. So he relented, overcome by sleepiness, in the search for his glasses. But then he heard the unmistakable sound of softly clad footsteps, and he shot back in his seat, flung his arms forward to the desk, and rummaged around for his glasses so he could see. It was a very tall figure by the small windows; the combined factors of barely waking, no glasses, and the glare of outside light behind it made it impossible for him to tell who it could be.

When he got his spectacles properly mounted to his ears and nose, and he adjusted to the light, he was sure he had no idea who this was. They were at least seven feet tall! They had pure white hair hanging down the sides of their face to mid-chest, with a hood on their floor-length overcoat. The clothing was all very dark grey, very soft in appearance, almost out of focus.

"Who are you? How did you break into my home?" The professor demanded.

"I am Kleet. You have inscribed some strange occurrences in the book, sir." The figure slowly approached the Professor. Kleet then lowered his hood, letting his hair fall around his shoulders, and his face came into focus. He had very sharp features, flawless skin, electric blue eyes - not glowing but definitely self-luminescent, and tall, POINTED EARS. It was without doubt a High Elf.

"Sir, um, Kleet, you are, um uh, are you...." he tried to ask.

"A High Elf, yes. I am. As I said, I am here because of your writings in the book. It is curious to us, and anything that catches our attention is important. You must assist your companions to compel their efforts to collect information regarding Mr. Tellafrog's illness and record it for us." He stood perfectly still, penetrating the professor with the seriousness in his eyes.

"You have a copy of the book?" The professor asked.

"Of course. We created the books for our own purposes, and the magical world has corresponded with the events of the world and its complexities to us, and we have used the books for thousands of years. It is usually the only communication we concern ourselves with from what you call the

199

mortal world. You are now one of three living persons who know we still exist. For the sake of yourself and your friends, it must remain that way. Not even your friends may know of our meeting. I am here only to impress the importance of their search on you and the dire consequences of revealing our meeting. Nothing more." Kleet slowly bowed his head, and then was simply gone. No whoosh, no slight vacuum in the space we would dislocate from, were that a wizard or sorceress, no light, no distortion, nothing.

The High Elves are, of course, in our magical histories, but in the last three or four hundred years, they have fallen from former fact into myth, even in our circles, he thought. Not twenty years prior, the great libraries in Europe, which held our magical history, had agreed to move the tomes regarding interactions with the High Elves to the same sections as those on Fey and other nature nymphs of legend. Many magical creatures are under our protection, and far too many go uncared for at all. Without research, I would wager it was over two thousand years since any direct interaction with High Elves was recorded, and even that may be spurious. This was serious, and the professor decided to determine if anyone was available to discuss this new urgency. He straightened himself up, and went to unlock the door and nearly knocked his housekeeper over to the ground floor where the portrait of the Tellafrogs was. No one was visible, so he went quickly to the two he had of Klement, and neither was occupied. What to do?

****

Arterous did indeed arrive at the junction going to the Loggins' homestead and paused to inspect the area. The skies above were shrouded in wispy grey clouds that barely covered the sun from this place, making it hot and dreary even after such a cooling rain. No one was in sight, and the wind made the trees nearby fling water off the leaves now and again. There was no damage like he observed at the Tellafrogs. That was good. It looked as though the heavy rain was fairly far off now, and didn't appear to be storming in the direction of the mission. He didn't see any lightning striking this side of the storm either. It was going somewhat north of his current route. He felt safe going on to the mission, keeping Cat on his shoulder, since no one was around. He was wrong, however. Someone was around. A single Comanche scout was in the trees to the north, and although it was a quarter mile off, this lone observer could tell that a large bird of some sort was sitting on that lone man's shoulder. Then, the Comanche witnessed the strange man vanish.

This time, he appeared right outside the front gate to the mission, with doors wide open, hanging from the hinges, which had been blown around in the storm. The latch must have been broken off and was lying on the ground near the wall. He had a good look around in all directions, trying to see if anyone was nearby. When he had satisfied himself he was alone, he loosed Cat and started inside. Everything was still wet and dripping, pans or buckets left outside had filled with rainwater. There was close to four inches of rain in that hour-long storm, and this time the trough outside the front gate was full. Inside the walls, he didn't see much damage either, but it was obvious some strong winds had hurled things around. The dust of late summer that was here before had washed away, and aside from the blown-in debris like leaves, it in fact looked better than before.

"Father Callious! Are you here? It's Arterous Metternich!" he yelled while looking around. At first, there was no answer, but then he did perceive a muffled voice from behind the chapel.

"Yes, down here!" It was Father Callious.

Arterous went around the left side of the chapel and to the back, where there was a thick, well-built door to the right he hadn't seen before. Father Callious' quarters were to the left of this door, probably concealed earlier by a rack of barrels between the two.

"Down here, my son!" he could hear the father was behind this new door easily now. "The rain has swollen this door, it is a bit stuck, could you help me? It opens out, you will have to grip the rod to pull it out, I'm afraid."

"Yes, let me get a good grip on it..." Arterous grabbed the round wooden dowel of the latch, which was in the open position, and pulled as hard as he could. It creaked and scratched as it inched past the stone doorframe, then, pop, it opened. Father Callious fell onto Arterous as he was pushing from the inside. He helped the Father up and steadied him.

"Thank you, thank you. I went down there when I saw the storm coming, somewhat needlessly, I fear. It didn't sound as bad as I had feared it might. Things look remarkably good around here, I must say," as he surveyed the area. "We tried ourselves to build a new door for that basement, we were not very good carpenters, I fear. It is obviously too tight. So, what brings you back here, my son? Is everyone alright at the

Tellafrogs?" he asked as he kept trying to brush the dust off his black priest's robes.

"There was a tornado at the Tellafrogs. We were concerned about you here alone, especially if it had come this way."

"It was a violent storm, no doubt, buckets of rain and wind, incessant lightning and thunder the whole time, but I don't believe I heard anything like a tornado here. Is everyone alright?"

"Yes, yes, we are all fine," Arterous assured him.

"That is good. God is good. God is good." Father patted him on the shoulder. Then, both of them heard the sound of horses approaching, and it sounded like quite a few. Arterous called Cat with a whistle, peeking around the end of the chapel to try and determine who it might be, looking out the open front gate. He could see a good five hundred yards down the path he had come.

"Are you expecting anyone, Father?" he asked nervously, putting his hand on his pistol.

"No, but there may be some people coming to check on the mission also." Father posited, also straining to see. The angle of the late afternoon sun had slipped below the remaining wispy clouds, and it was bright again.

With the benefit of rainfall, there was virtually no dust in the air of the setting sun. It was now clear that it was Indians, Comanches, at least six or seven, who could be heard now, their shrill cries echoing through the air. "Those are Comanche cries." Father Callious said, his voice trembling with fear. Their horses' hooves were stamping through the wet topsoil into the dry layer beneath, making dust as they galloped towards the mission. They were coming straight for the front gate as fast as they could ride. Arterous took Cat on his arm, corralled Father Callious back to the doorway, and ushered him downstairs. He launched Cat downstairs as well once the Father had cleared the narrow stairwell, and followed them. He gently shut the door so it wouldn't make a loud sound and give away their position. From the back of the chapel, they were concealed from view of the front gate. It was possible, as Arterous knew from his time in the cavalry, to have escaped their view, riding that fast.

"Father, it's Indians, the front gate is open, and the latch is broken and lying on the ground. I could not reach it in time anyway. I need a board or something I can wedge against the latch on this door so they cannot open it," he shouted down.

He could tell Father Callious was rummaging around, then he staggered up the stairs with a small chair, whose back was wide enough to put between the sliding latch and the wall. He had to kick it in place, but it worked. They both went to the small room below and tried to listen to what was happening. Arterous took the Patterson revolver rifle off his shoulder and set it against the wall; the lamp the Father had been using before was still lit, illuminating the little room.

"I need to send word to Raileanu that we are trapped here. Can you write a note I can send out with my owl?" he asked the father.

"It's all my fault! All of this is my fault! I caused it all! I was just trying to help everyone!" Father Callious began sobbing and fell into the chair at the desk, slumping over it.

Arterous went and grabbed him firmly by the shoulder and shook him. "Father! Compose yourself. You must stay quiet or they will find us." He spotted the loose papers and pen. He grabbed a piece and wrote "Mission under attack from Indians. We are trapped in the basement." He tore the small part off that he had written on, called Cat, and wrapped it around her leg. Looking around for some string, he couldn't find it, so he pulls his wand and points it at her leg; now it's tied tightly with a cotton string.

Father Callious sees this and says, "No, you cannot show them you're a wizard, my son. They will kill you. Magic may have caused all of this." Then he stopped and stared blankly at Arterous, having let something slip he didn't want to.

"None of that matters now, sir. We must survive this first." Arterous was gathering the few preloaded cylinders for his pistol and rifle, as they were the same. He pulled another chair next to the wall by the stairs, set the three cylinders on it, ball side down, so the caps would have no chance of falling off.

Now they can tell by the sounds that the fighters were inside the chapel above, banging, breaking, just destroying everything. They both froze, scanning the ceiling and tracking their movements as best they could. Arterous looked at Father Callious, who had resorted to covering his mouth with his less swollen hand. He was so nervous that Arterous could hear the nervous breath passing through his nostrils, making a faint whistle sound, but not loud enough to give them away.

They listened intently, and when the Comanche went out the front of the chapel, and towards the sheds at the front gate, Arterous went up the stairs, with Cat on his right forearm. He whispered to her, "Cat, fly over the top of the building right away, and then go to Raileanu as fast as you can." He approached the door, moved the chair away as quietly as he could. He listened intently one more time, and the intruders were not audible anywhere close. Maybe they had even gone. Arterous pulled his pistol with his right hand, cocked the hammer, and slid the latch to the open position. Then he remembered how he had jammed it shut. Maybe he could do it slowly. He tried. No, it would take swift and decisive action to get it unstuck. He would have to open it as fast as possible, let Cat out, and pull it shut again, so he holstered the pistol. Then he heard someone speaking, but couldn't understand it, of course. He pulled his wand out, slid it up his right sleeve, and put the tip behind his right ear. Now, thanks to magic, he could understand them speaking.

"I know that priest is here. He is hiding somewhere. We must just keep looking. He is working with sorcerers, and they are the ones who sent that storm among our people today. I caught sight of one in alliance with an owl. They have owl magic! None of us are untouched by the devastation today. This evil comes from here. Stay quiet and keep looking." They spoke amongst themselves in low, calm voices, but then Arterous heard them walk back into the chapel, located above the basement. However, the path to this door was far enough away that he felt he could open it, let Cat out, and shut it before they could reach him.

He took a deep breath, exhaled, and looked at Father Callious, who was holding his hands clasped together over his mouth and was very nervous. He put his wand between his teeth. Grasping the peg handle with his right hand, he stepped back and hit the door as hard as he could with his shoulder. The door did spring open, Cat immediately left his arm, but the force of opening was such that Arterous's foot caught on the threshold as his body weight went over the center of his boots, and he fell forward onto the muddy ground. His wand flung out of his mouth, probably four feet away from him. He looked up and around, and there were four fighters to his left near the front of the chapel, fifty feet away. Then he looked straight ahead, and there was one on top of the surrounding wall, who spotted him instantly, and drew his bow instinctively fast, but held it as Arterous scrambled back towards the doorway. The door had flung all the way flat against the wall, so reaching the opening, he reached for the latch peg handle now three feet from the doorway, when he was hit with what felt like a white-hot poker having been punched through his back, below the ribs on the right side. He spun around, trying to essentially fall back with his body weight to slam the door shut again. Another arrow slapped his right arm off the latch, so it didn't slam, but it did close. His arm was pinned to the door now, and he reflexively tried to pull it free, but it just broke the shaft off, leaving the arrowhead in the door, and he realized now the arrow had missed any serious blood vessels somehow, but his arm bone was cracked, if not broken. It was excruciating, already swelling and stretching at the adrenaline-filled skin. Arterous was sitting now, couldn't lean against the wall because of the one in his back, and one had pierced between the bones of his right arm. So he reached up with his foot, pushed the latch shut, and pushed the chair in its spot to hold it the best he could.

"Father, please, come help me to get down there!" he shouted. No sense in being quiet now. He could hear them talking and shouting at the door, but had no way to know what they were saying, as he had lost his wand outside.

Father Callious was still crying, still near crippled from the beating he had taken from before our first visit, made his way up the stairs and helped Arterous to stand and go back down the stairs. They collapsed into a pile at the bottom of the stairs on each other, Arterous's back slapping the wall and breaking the arrow's feathered end off and pressing it further out the front of his abdomen. Blood was running down his front and back, pooling around his waist and down to the ground in large volumes now. He was feeling quite faint now.

"Father! Please try to pull this one out of my arm. Tie it tight with a cloth. I will try and keep them away from us by firing up the stairway, if you can help me use a chair to rest my rifle on. Please! " Arterous labored out.

Father Callious was still weeping, crying, and saying that it was all his fault. He took his handkerchief out and went to Arterous. He shakily grabbed the long feathered end of the arrow shaft, and went to pulling on it, twisting back and forth. Arterous let out a loud cry, and as the broken end passed through the hole in his arm, he passed out for a few seconds. By the time he had come around, the arm was tied up. His head flopping around in a circle for a moment, he saw the arm and watched the father trying to dab at the arrow in his stomach, sobbing.

"Stop, father, that one must stay. If I take that out, I will be dead much sooner, but I am going to die today. Arterous also knew that with these injuries, there was no way he could dislocate. Even if he could, who could help? Raileanu cannot dislocate at all; there was no one to get help from. "Go and say whatever prayers you need to for a dying man, but in the process, bring me that chair and put me at the bottom of the stairs." The fighters above were hitting the door with something, maybe the splitting axe the priests used for firewood. It was hard to tell. They stopped striking the door for a moment, as Father Callious and Arterous got the chair and rifle set up in their path in the narrow opening at the bottom of the stairs. Arterous heard the unmistakable sound of his wand being broken, and then their talking turned to whoops and war cries.

"Father Callious, move away from this stairway, and say prayers for yourself as well. They found my wand. I dropped it when I got hit, and I am pretty sure they are blaming me for the tornado hitting their homes, based on what I heard earlier. They will surely kill us both." He pulled the pistol out of the holster and laid it on the chair's seat, motioned for the father to hand him the rifle, which he also laid on the chair seat, barrel through the bars on its back. He then dug the extra bags of ball and powder out of his trail coat's pockets and set them on the ground by the chair. Looking around the room, he really wished he could move one of those big wardrobes over here in front of the entrance to this room. Neither of them could budge those things in the shape they were in. Oh well.

"This is not your fault, my son. It is all my fault; I did all this. I will make my confession to you, so that someone can know what happened here that led to all this." He was still suffering from his bout of crying, but was speaking more clearly.

"Father, telling me would be fine if we had time. But that will not help anyone going forward. You must write and hide, or secure somewhere, the facts of what has happened here. Raileanu, or the Rangers, will find it and know what to do. But we don't have time." Arterous was certain that even just blood loss was going to be a problem very soon.

"I will tell you as I write, you are correct." Father Callious agreed.

The crashing at the door upstairs was intensifying, and Arterous was happy they were trying to push in, as the door opened out. He heard a loud crack; the best he could figure was that it came from the peg handle on the outside of the door. They were screaming and chopping at it with their tomahawks. He was hoping he could last long enough to get shots off before he passed out. He was honestly unable to concentrate on the father's words and stay focused on the job. He was really wondering if he would have consciousness when they broke through the door. Arterous really didn't know which would give out first, the door or him. Father Callious was writing and talking, but the throbbing that started in his gut had gone cold now. The arm was swelling, still leaking, but not badly, but it was throbbing badly, and the skin was burning from the tearing action of removing the arrow and its stretching under the force of swelling. So he concentrated and forced himself to watch the door.

A small corner of the plank on the latch side at the top was being broken off, and the hole then became large enough so one of them decided to reach in with their whole forearm. Arterous let a rifle round go into the side of that fighter, who was knocked clear to the ground. He tried to cock the hammer again, which was really difficult, as his arm was starting to straighten out from the swelling so he couldn't bend it very well. Their furious cries heightened, and the chopping continued. They worked on the third plank from the left, at the top, with the axes now. Knowing his time was limited to be effective at all, Arterous decided to fire anytime he thought shadows indicated a person may be near. He kept adjusting to be effective. After a few more shots, his finger was swollen so much that he had to force it into the trigger guard. A couple more shots, and he couldn't get anything more than his fingertip into the trigger. The board they were chopping was not as large a hole as the first, but he saw a hand come through, and decided to take a shot. He missed, it was to the right, against the wall, but even that sliding ricochet seemed to hit that person, and the hand disappeared, matched with screams of pain.

Arterous noticed now that the throbbing was in his eyes and made it hard to hold his head still. Another hand came through, and he worked the trigger, only to hear a 'click'. The rifle was out. He laid it on the chair and picked up the pistol with his unswollen left hand. By the time he switched firearms and looked back up, they had run a rope between the two holes around the full-height board between the broken ones. Oh, they figured out the door opens out. They were presumably going to pull it open with a horse.

"Father, they will have this door open in a minute." Arterous fired two quick shots, trying to hit the rope, fruitlessly. "Hide that letter right now. RIGHT NOW!" He heard the horse being brought to the left side of the door, and he figured he wouldn't get a shot at the horse.

Arterous heard the father scrambling around behind him to his left, stretched out on the floor, pushing something under that cockeyed large wardrobe, and then crawling on his hands and knees over to the wall by Arterous.

"I put it all in the letter, and wrapped it in deerskin, and put that inside a rawhide map case. It should survive whatever they do to us." Father Callious said. "Thank you for hearing everything, and I am sorry for what I have done. I thought I was doing good."

"It's alright, Father, God gives us all forgiveness if we beg in humility in Jesus' name." Arterous had no idea what he was talking about. He fired twice more at the rope on the door.

With a slow, ripping, cracking sound, the latch gave way, and the door flew open. The screaming and war cries were from maybe a dozen men. More than he had thought were there. As this last minute approached, Arterous's vision was coming and going with each heartbeat. He decided to fire as soon as he heard footsteps, which came but a moment later. One shot, two shots, click, and a tomahawk crashed into his forehead. Father Callious was grabbed, and they cut his throat and threw him down, pointlessly hitting him in the back with their tomahawks as well.

CHAPTER ELEVEN

I t was dark, and Arterous should have been back by now. I went out to the front porch after helping Momma with dinner. We were waiting for him to eat. He had been gone for over an hour. Even if the circumstances were bad at the mission, he should have come back for help. I was beginning to seriously worry. As I turned to go back inside, I heard a bird in distress, but barely. I went out to the center of the front yard and strained to listen. It was an owl, injured. It is true that the time I had spent with Catherine and hearing her voice was limited, but it could be her.

"Mother! I think Catherine is around here, hurt. I need to go out and check." I yelled over my shoulder.

"Are you sure?" she asked, coming out rubbing her hands with a cup towel.

"I can be sure it is an owl; it may be her. If Arterous is in trouble, I have to know."

"Oh, just a moment," Momma grabbed my arm, then turned back into the house. "I think I hear the professor calling."

"I'm going before it gets any darker. I'll take a lamp and my pistol." I stepped in the front door, grabbed my gun belt, took the pistol, and made sure it still had percussion caps on all 6. I took a match, lit the lamp, and headed up the trail. It took me about twenty minutes to make my way out on foot. I had to go around the left side to follow the sound of the cries, which were definitely in pain. I didn't detect anything else out of the ordinary. I arrived at a small group of large cedars, which were located on the edge of the woods that protected our home. She was somewhere in the lower branches. I set the lamp on the ground beneath the low limbs and stooped underneath to take a better look. She was on a limb next to the trunk, dripping blood from her right wing. It didn't look broken or held in an unusual way, so maybe it was just a cut. I held my arm up, and called her by name, and she stepped onto it. I grabbed the lamp and went back through the woods and the rock maze into the front yard.

I went straight into the dining area and set her on the table. Momma was standing in the front room, talking to Professor Templeton. I found an old rag that was clean, and Catherine let me lift her wing and extend it, looking underneath for the injury. It was but a small nick under the arm, but it was a nick that had to have come from something man-made.

Momma asked the professor to wait a moment, and she came over and held the wing, and pulled her wand. As she did then, I found the note on her leg. I took it off and read it silently. Momma had her fixed up instantly, with a short, warm, yellow glow on her wand tip touched to the cut.

"What does it say?" she asked as she cleaned and pet Catherine, telling her it was all done.

"They are trapped by Indian warriors, likely Comanche, in the basement of the chapel." That's what it says. "Mom, if he were okay, he would have been here by now. I genuinely have a bad feeling."

"What did the professor want?" I asked.

"Wait, let me tell him about this letter while he is still available." She went back to the portrait. It always looked silly to me, since I had no ability to use those portraits, like a crazy person talking to a picture. The humor helped me learn to be okay with this, but I had also found out that laughing at them doing it was, sadly, frowned upon. So I went and sat down, trying to think about what could have happened to Arterous.

Momma finished in a few minutes and sat down. She sighed and began to tell me what had been said. "The professor wants me to take a closer look at the flyswatter handle you boys found, with the old examination tube that your father had made in his last year of school, the one that lets us view very small things and examine them more closely, looking for anything. It is in his old trunk, stacked up on the back porch with other ones we use for storage. He is alarmed by the events with Arterous and advises us to wait until morning. He said we should send both of our owls out to try to contact Barthow for help, and send them tonight. I told him Arterous' owl, Catherine, was injured and couldn't fly tonight, but maybe in the morning. Oh, and McCort came back while you were out looking for Cat."

"Yes, do you know where Barthow might be now?" I asked.

"No, but your father's owl has found him before in the wilderness, we should try that too. That makes three," she said.

"I want to go, but I will wait until morning. I will not wait any longer than that, Mother." I said definitively.

"Alright, let's get that scope and see what we can find. Also, did he have his monocle on his person when he left?"

"Yes, he never took it off after we got home the day before yesterday, since we could have really used it that day," I said.

"Oh, well, we will make do," she said. We got up and went out back, dug out the chests in the way, and got his old school trunk. I set it on my mother's planting table and dug around until I found it. We set up on the dining room table, and Momma made the lamps all as bright as they would go. I went upstairs, found the stick in Arterous's saddlebag, and brought it down. Momma took it and began examining it, inch by inch. After reaching the end with the wire-wound frame of the flyswatter end, she flipped it over and then jerked the metal end off. The wood of the stick looked the same, smooth, ripples running in spirals around it, and flat color, no light could reflect off it. She made adjustments to the knobs and dials several times. "It looks in the valleys of the grain to have nodules, almost like chicken skin, with a tiny filament protruding from the nodules' centers, as a hair would from a pore. They were worn down below the peaks of the woodgrain. She paused and sat straight up. "They aren't hairs, son. They are remnants of root sprouts. This was the root of a tree, but I have no way of knowing what kind of tree." She went back to the eyepiece, now looking at the handle

216

end more closely. "Yes, the very center of the handle of this is more fibrous in a linear fashion than the center of a tree's branch wood normally is, but it is common from a tree root."

She then looked at the end that had been covered by the swatter apparatus, and pointed the tip of the stick at the bottom of the scope tool she was using, fiddling with the wheels and knobs again.

"Yes, there is a single hole here, in the center, but no fibrous section at all. It is not much bigger than a human hair, but it is artificial..." I honestly don't know how this even came to look like this. I haven't seen any normal, natural, magical, or ordinary process that would produce this visual result. I don't know what this is," she said with incredulity.

While she worked on that, I penned three letters to Ranger Barthow, explaining as much as I could about the circumstances surrounding Arterous. I wound them tightly around, and with momma's special stationery, it was practically invisible on their legs. Tied with her dark hemp string, it looked like little more than a bit of straw on its leg or foot. I sent McCort out and asked Mother to come speak to hers and Father's - maybe it would help. She whispered to them and sent them off as well. It was all the help I could be, and it didn't feel like much. No amount of time in the territory, magic, or strength could overcome some of the many perils that populate our land, especially at night.

She turned and looked at the portrait. "He is still there, let me speak to him for a moment." She went to the painting and explained to him what she found.

I got a pot of coffee ready, along with cups, and waited for Momma to come and work her magic on it. After ten minutes of their discussion, back and forth, she said goodnight and came over to me, sat down. She tapped it, and within a minute, the aroma of perfectly brewed coffee emanated from the spout. It's a lot easier than doing it over a campfire, over-boiling it, and cleaning out the egg white; it's the simple things, really.

"What did he say?" I asked as I poured the coffee for us.

"Son, he isn't sure, but he said he might know someone who could help. He should know by the time the sun comes up. Honestly, I don't know when he has slept in the last two weeks. He's doing his best," she was saying, and almost sipped black coffee. She sat it down and gave it a quick fix up, cream and sugar instantly swirled into it.

"So that's it. All we can do for the night, huh?"

"Yes, but I did instruct our two owls to come wake me if they found him, so it is everything we can do."

She was right. So we finished our coffee, finished the work around the place, and I even took time before bed to brush the horses again. When it became clear that I was overtired and the owls weren't going to be this lucky, I went ahead and washed up from chores and went to bed.

****

Their small convoy had traveled without incident or notable event that first day from Königssee to Pitten and had stayed in a small villa slightly east of the town, a residence of the regional minister who was in Italy on official business. The staff were very happy to welcome them, and even before daylight, had all the horses tended to, drivers and soldiers fed, and they were all waiting on Monika and Klement's family to be ready to depart.

Traveling in the heat of summer, most places are quite uncomfortable, but the cool breezes that made their way down past snow-filled crevices made this trip more pleasant than most. They left at about eight o'clock in the morning, hoping to reach Kottingbrunn, where Klement's mother still lived. They would hopefully arrive in the early afternoon, as the roads were relatively manageable from here on to Vienna. He was also looking forward to spending the whole evening with his mother, visiting his eldest brother and his wife. His boy was also very excited to see his grandmother.

The carriages stopped at midday, at a small meadow next to a beautiful stream, after crossing the bridge over it. There, they set up a picnic, and while they set up to eat, Monika went down to the stream. The rock bed was carved down by the stream, and the very fertile soil was built up nearly four or five feet, then beveled away from the rock bed at a forty-five-degree angle. Large gray rocks littered the stream bed, and Monika went to one as large as a couch, took her boots off, pulled up her slacks, and walked to the stone and sat on it, feet in the water. This was fantastic. The sun was on the hotter side of warm, but with her feet in the crystal clear stream of cold water, it couldn't be more perfect.

As Monika realized the picnic was almost ready, a little green frog came jumping up the side of the rock she was on, and then onto her leg. She put her delicate hand down, and it walked sideways onto it. She raised it up to her face, smiling, and could have sworn the little frog smiled back. It closed its little eyes, soaking up the sun. Just then, she really hoped Raileanu was okay, and was glad she was going to a safer place. She gave it a little kiss and set it back down, as

219

they were waving at her to come eat. Maybe there would be a portrait she could use at the overnight halt so she could check on her own little frog.

Professor Templeton had worked into the night, even before hearing the several messages from Mrs. Tellafrog about Arterous and the descriptions of the stick he had asked them to inspect closely. He recorded them in the book and decided to research further in the morning. Again, it was not to be. This time, Kleet shook him by the shoulder to wake him. Grabbing his glasses from the chain around his neck, which he had attached after his first encounter with this incredible man, and fumbling them on, he gave a shocked look of terror to Kleet.

"Oh my God, Kleet, you are making a habit of terrifying me!" he gasped at him, clutching his chest.

"Two incidents cannot accurately graph a habit. Besides, sir, there are important matters to discuss. May I sit?" Kleet stated

"Oh, yes, yes, please do." The professor waved his hand around to the seating area, which consisted of two chairs.

Kleet sat bolt upright, staring intently at the professor. "What your friend has found that was disguised as a flyswatter is in fact a root wand. It is a very old technique, dating back to our time. You have not found any helpful reference on the subject because it is one of the crafts we removed from the world when magical people were just pawns of the most brutal humans. They can not be fashioned by any living creature from a knowledge base we are aware of. It is not something that is practical for anyone. It is imperative that they return it to you, whereby I will take possession and properly destroy it. Moreover, if it is possible to determine its origin, it is our responsibility to resolve that as well. We will stay in contact, Professor. While I know you may have many questions, your service to the world in these matters will demonstrate your worth in any further endeavors. You know we refuse to spend time among your people, which does not benefit us. I can say, this may benefit your people as well."

The Professor sat straight and attentive as a student, eyes wide, intentionally refusing to even blink until Kleet was finished speaking. So when he did finish, the professor blinked, and Kleet was gone. The chair where he had been sitting was still turned slightly toward the professor. He spotted something on the red fabric of the chair, so he went and leaned over, adjusting his glasses for focus, and there it was. A pure white hair, maybe a foot long, perhaps fallen from Kleet's coat. Well, at least, the professor thought, I'm not going mad. He had begun to worry that some of it may have been imagined due to the long hours. He had also felt as though he was letting everyone down by not finding any useful information, so it was good to learn he hadn't missed anything. He cleared his head, went and unlocked the door, and called his housekeeper. He would need to eat and wait at the portraits for anyone who could get word to the Tellafrogs as soon as possible.

****

As the first orange rays of light streaked over our home, I had been lying awake for an hour already. I heard a strange whooshing sound in the front yard, followed by boots on the front porch and the front door opening downstairs. I pulled

221

on my pants, stepped into my boots, grabbed my pistol, and opened the door to my room sharply, pointing it towards the stairs, and waited to determine if it was trouble coming.

"Hello!" I shouted. "I have a pistol aimed at you, who are you?!"

"Well, boy, it's good you have a pistol on me, but you definitely ain't lookin at me, or you'd know who it was." It was Barthow.

"I'll be right down," I said loudly. I could also hear Momma moving around now, and we were happy it was Barthow, and that he had arrived this quickly.

Momma and I were dressed about the same time and went downstairs, where Barthow had conjured breakfast already for us. Bacon, biscuits and pork sausage gravy, and coffee.

"You got the message?" I asked as I sat down to eat.

"Yeah, don't you eat without blessin' that boy," he said gruffly.

I bowed my head, closed my eyes, "God, bless this food, our family and friends, and show us your will each day." Momma patted my hand after I was done.

"Good," Barthow said. "Let's eat this grub and go to your friend, buddy."

"Where were you when you received it? Were y'all done with getting the new prison set up?" Momma wondered.

"Yes, ma'am. It's called Schism, and it's in the craggy stone at the south end of the Rocky Mountains. There's a good feller there, names Binti Rudebar, who'd come over from India. He worked with us fer 'bout a year, then went off to work'n one in Europe somewhere to learn how to make'n manage a good

222

prison. You'll be happy to know he decided after a'talkin' to us to let preachers in thar to work with them inmates, iffin they wanna."

"That's great news, Barthow. Father would be happy." Momma was happy to learn that, as there was consternation among the authorities when Dad decided to try it, but it worked out well for everyone, and their fears were unfounded. She smiled a bit to herself, no doubt remarking to dad's memory how he was right and justified, in that important choice.

"We need to load up on this here meal, Raileanu. I checked that you had the horse still here, and one for me as well. I can take Arterous's horse, and make our way over as quick as we can. We'd heard 'bout that twister that'd come through here yesterday. It went through a spot in a secluded creek bed where some Comanche had hid out. Kill't a bunch of em. That whole creek bed was ruint. All them cottonwood trees that lined it, just twisted in a giant knot about twenty feet tall and couple hundred yards long. Ain't nobody can even git through it to try and save anybody. Terrible. Just awful." he shook his head, having seen carnage of tornados many times. "We ain't been over yonder yet, the rest of my guys are busy tryin' to help in other places where lil' towns got tore up, and without magic, it's slow a'goin. Ain't no way to untangle that mess without magic, so if some folks is still around, we definitely can't do that."

Momma looked over my shoulder towards the portraits, and she excused herself and went to Professor Templeton's.

Barthow and I finished up, and he scraped all the leftovers onto a plate, and whistled, and Bandos came running from somewhere out in the rock maze. Barthow set the plate down for him, and Bandos' tail was swinging wildly in thankfulness.

Momma came back over, and said that the Professor told her that the stick was an important clue, it was a root wand, which is ancient, harmful magic, and he needs that to be secured and returned to him. "I told him I would seal it in a hex jar, and that you two were going to go check on Father Callious and Arterous. He asked if the root wand would fit in that bag Klement gave you, but I explained it was only for copper. Which reminds me, Lil' Frog, your father has a small pile of raw copper he has found out back, not much, but it may help you, it's always been in my way really, so please use it."

"Lil' Frog," Barthow started, "let's git them horses ready and git goin. I want to git there as soon as we can, but I am riding so we can check along the way for any other damages from that storm."

"You boys go on, I'll get this cleaned up and will spend most of the day in my new gardens," Mom said.

"By the way, mother, it was John's owl that found me." Barthow leaned back, still chewing. "That's a good bird, you might find out how to teach that to other 'uns. All three birds got fed this mornin' too, before I set out. They out front." Barthow and I walked out to the stables and got ready to leave in about twenty minutes.

I wound the watch, clicked it, and we headed out, waving to Momma as we walked into the passage in the rocks. When we cleared the woods and turned towards the mission, Barthow said, "I have a charm we learned from an Apache medicine woman to let us ride these horses at gallop for a whole hour without it causing trouble for them. We should wait and use it at the halfway mark on the road."

"How does it work?" I asked.

"Well, we take these little branches of green sage, cast a charm on them that makes em smell like chocolate - well - smell like that to me - and it also makes em swell with spring water once a horse gits them into their belly. Pretty good idear. Could have used that about a thousand times I can recall." He said. "I call it Sagerush."

"That's incredible, I need to put that in my collection of research that I can publish next year."

"Well, maybe as long as it's only goin' into Europe, least a couple more years, so's troublemakers out here don't git wind of it, making things harder on us rangers. If'n you don't mind." He suggested.

"I will wait until I confirm with you before I include it in published versions, yes." I looked around the landscape, and honestly didn't observe any damage that couldn't be attributed to a big thunderstorm. "I don't think that tornado came this way, I think it may have eased by here, or gone further north than west."

"Yeah, that place where the woods were twisted onto the Comanches is about ten miles east of the mission, so I'm guessing you're right."

After an hour, Barthow stopped, came out of his saddle, holding the reins, reached into his saddlebag, and got the sage out. He handed me a branch of it, thick with leaves. Tapping them both with his wand, he went to the front and took the hackamores off both horses, and we let them eat it. When it was all chewed up and they stopped drooling, he refitted the hackamores, and we mounted and began gallop-ing. Standing in the stirrups, things were going by so fast, we really weren't surveying damage anymore. For the record, there is a big difference between a horse being comfortable at full gallop for an hour and my legs being able to sustain it. After fifteen minutes of it, we slowed down enough to sit for a few minutes, then began again.

We did that maybe four times, and as we neared the mission, we could see smoke rising, not from a fireplace or burning leaves. There was a big fire, and my heart sank. I could tell by the scent that it was a destructive fire. We then rode at full speed for the last leg, and it was the mission itself that had been set ablaze. Most of the flames had gone out, but smoke was still pouring out from inside the walls. The gates were gone; the remains of them were smoldering charcoal strewn about. We rode straight in, pulling our pistols right before we went through the gateway. Barthow leapt out of the saddle before the horse even stopped, and ran to the front of the chapel. I kept going to the back of the chapel, where I knew the basement doorway was, and then I dis-mounted.

The door for the basement was pulled out and broken apart on the ground. An arrowhead was still visible on the INSIDE of the door, draped in dry blood, so I headed for the doorway.

"Arterous! Father Callious! Where are you?!" I fast-stepped down the stairs, practically sliding on the last few steps and falling. I braced my forearms on the walls of the stairway as it opened into the room. Both men were there. Stripped to underclothes. They were both dead, blood covering them in several areas, but obviously, the priest's throat had been cut, and Arterous had a clear tomahawk wound in his forehead. The shafts of two arrows were broken off in him, one in his back, the other in his forearm. Fire ants had already found them and were swarming in the fresh hot meat.

I turned and went back up the steps to the courtyard, trying not to vomit, scream, or cry. "Barthow! I found them! They're down here!"

He came out of the back doorway of the chapel just around the corner to my left.

"And?"

"They're both dead."

CHAPTER TWELVE

Barthow went to the door, inspected the arrowhead, and then went down. After close examination, he stood. "Yep, that's Comanche." I wandered away to the far end of the yard, leaned my back against a mimosa tree trunk, slid down, and sat on the ground. I know coming last night I would have died as well. My mind was whipping from should've to could've to why didn't I. I should have known; the smell of their bodies was so heavy now, but everything in the mission was burning, I suppose, which had distracted me. I suggested Arterous go and try to help or protect Father Callious. Is this my fault? Oh, God, I will have to tell Klement. Now, I did vomit. A big breakfast seemed like a good idea, but ugh, not now. I didn't want to sit next to it, so I pushed up and away from the tree. I realized what I'd done was in a small depression that had been dug out around the base of the tree. Whoever did that had broken a fairly substantial root. I know that isn't good for the tree's health. To get away from the stench of the vomit, I decided to go back to Father Callious' little room, pull a chair out, sit at the top of the stairwell, and wait for Barthow. I didn't want to go back downstairs.

Barthow was down there for quite a long time, so, feeling useless, I went and tied up the horses, and found a bucket, and filled the water trough for them, and found some hay to put on the ground for them as well. When I got back to the chair, he was finally coming up and out. He went into the quarters and got himself a chair, sat down, put his head in his hands, and took his hat off, throwing it on the ground.

"Son, this is bad. We are gonna ta have to clean this here place up and send word to Father Lorenzo. He will have to decide whether to keep this place open, or if'n just leave it abandoned. Y'all told me you'd sent word, and some other priests or workers are on their way here already. I can find em, and turn them around, maybe. They can't witness all this mess here, regardless." he just rubbed his forehead.

"Arterous. I can bury him at home, for now, but he can't stay here." I said, staring off into the distance. "He only had one magical item on him, a goblin worked monocle. It's beautifully made, but of no use to ordinary people. It allows magical people to detect traces of magic work. Just so you know, if you come across it. They took everything else, didn't they?"

"Yeah. There's nothing of value left on them. He had a revolver rifle and a Patterson Colt, didn't he?"

"Yeah. We bought them when I arrived here in Texas, a set of each for both of us." I told him.

"Well, he was obviously hit with at least two arrows, went down thar to try and hold them off, and emptied both. I see lots of blood up here, on and around the door and doorway, he might'a killed as many as three or four, and hurt a mess more. They'da carried off their kilt and hurt, though, no way of knowing fer sure. Thar's a little puddle of dry blood up against the wall, and a bigger one at the bottom of the stairs. I reckon he set up that busted chair in the doorway at the bottom, and tried to keep em out long as he could. I don't know why in that extreme circumstance, he didn't try some magic least to fix himself up."

That was curious. Holed up down there out of sight, he could have at least tried that.

"Well, it ain't gittin' any cooler son. They will git to a'swellin and such if'n I don't git movin' on takin' care of them right now. You want Arterous to go to your place?" He stood and reset his hat on his head.

"Please. I think it's important he is at the home of a friend, not here in the wild of this abandoned, ravaged place."

"Alrighty. I'll git the priest up, then I'll take Arterous to your place, and make sure mother is going to be okay before I head back." he walked into Father Callious' room, came out with the bedsheets, and went downstairs. A moment later, both came out, floating waist-height, wrapped neatly in the sheets, and came to rest on the ground. It was easy to know which was which, as Arterous was a foot taller.

"You'll be alright for a little while, then?" He directed Arterous up and over his shoulder with his wand.

"Yes, thank you, sir, again for being here when we needed help. I will bury Father Callious next to his brothers over there, and try and clean up what I can." I said, still sitting in the chair.

Barthow took a look in that direction and made several looping ovals in the air; the grave was then excavated. "Alrighty, son. I'll be back soon as I can," and he wisped away into a single spot with Arterous, and was gone.

He was right; the longer I waited, the worse it would be on the priest. I found a handcart and got him in it, then used some rope around the mimosa tree limb to lower him in. I started shoveling the dirt back in, taking several breaks in the heat, and was thankful again for my magical flask. Ugh, I was not ready to think about telling Klement. It took half an hour in the heat to finish. With the amount of destruction wreaked by the fighters on this place, it wasn't hard to find suitable wood for a cross marker. The best wood I remembered seeing was from the door they had broken to gain access to the basement. When I went to collect good pieces, I picked up the longest, sturdiest piece. Under that, I found the reason he couldn't have healed himself. Arterous' wand was broken, mostly buried in the dirt, a good six feet from the entrance to the basement. It must have happened before he went down the stairs. I put the pieces in my inside vest pocket and proceeded to make the marker for Father Callious.

When it was finished and set, I went to my saddlebag and got some sourdough and jerky. I was starting to feel hungry and more focused on the work at hand, and I knew the next stop would be downstairs, where I could clean up. The news of what happened here was going to be hard enough. Seeing evidence of it would be a hardship for any new men of God, making them useless to anyone. After finishing my meal and having a few more drinks from my flask, I was ready to head down.

First, I went and found their bucket of lye and an old, worn horse brush. I got another bucket half full of water and took them downstairs. I set them down on the floor and had a good look around. Strangely, they didn't seem to care about the books, papers, and scrolls. They were messed up, not destroyed. I guess their anger was satisfied, or they would have burned all this too. Turning around to where they had been killed, I saw where the blood had pooled, but also the smearing that had happened when they came down and attacked them. Bloody moccasin footprints were all over the front half of the room. With the amount of dust and dirt on the ground, my time would be better spent on the spots that had pooled, but the rest would have to be swept up.

At the end of their writing workbench was a broom. I swept the areas that I could clean, then got down on my knees, dipped the brush in the lye water, and started scrubbing. The caustic fumes were unpleasant, but it was coming up. I got the area at the bottom of the stairs done, and spun on my knees to face that whompyjawed wardrobe, and started that area. As I reached the end of the spot, I spotted something like a tube under that wardrobe. I grabbed the broom, fished it out from under the cabinet, and brought it to me with the broom handle. It was about two feet long, made of hard leather with a strap and cap, resembling a map case. I chucked it over by the door and finished cleaning.

I continued up the stairway, scrubbing with lye water, blood off the walls, and some off the flagstone steps where it would work, coming upstairs after about an hour. The air up here was so much nicer. I decided to walk around the whole compound and see what else had been damaged that I could fix, which is pathetic compared to what Barthow can do when he returns. I decided to check for a ladder or something to climb up to the bell tower for a better look. The open entrance to the back of the chapel was black from the soot of things they tried to burn in there, and I went in.

They had burned about half of the pews, the lectern, and some of the decorations; different paraphernalia were scattered about and broken. More of it might have burned, had the rain not drenched everything just prior to their arrival. To my left was a small closet door at the back of the raised pulpit area, so I went back for a closer inspection. It appeared that they had thrown lamp oil on the wooden floor here and lit it on fire, but it was mostly just charred on top, with a few gaps burnt into the spaces between the boards, in all likelihood where the oil had run down between them and dripped through. As I walked on them, which I had never been to before, the hollow sound beneath the floorboards sounded 'deep'. I assumed this was built on a pier and beam floor, which isn't usually more than a foot or two off the ground. This sounded to my ear more like ten or twelve feet. I went to the little door, and it led to a closet for the roof ladder. It was actually part of the framing of the back wall of the chapel.

When I reached the top, I opened the small hatch, made of cedar with a tar waterproofing coating on its entire outer surface, and stepped up onto the small platform. There wasn't more than two feet around the sides of the bell, but it was easy to observe out and around. I couldn't detect anyone nearby by sight or sound. Smoke still rose from the damaged wood structures around, but it was only the chapel and the courtyard where the damage was relevant to the attackers. Clearly, they only wanted the people dead. They could have stayed, taken this as a little fort, even, but often when their anger boils over, it is taken out against people. After all, it is the invading people who are changing their world, not the stones and wood. It all felt so sad that all people do this, it is worth noting that even before we arrived, or the Spanish, or now the Mexicans and Texians, the Comanche fought every other tribe, including the Apache. They killed and took land and slaves from each other. I'm sure there are tribes that no longer exist because of the evils men force on others. For whatever reason. That cycle cannot be what God intended for us. For any of us. The worst, at least in European history, is when violence is 'justified' because of what they perceive God, or a god, wants. In the end, it is always the ambition and thirst for power of one group over another, and God plays no part in that conceit. Free will is either totally free, to decide what to do and how to justify it, or it is limited and manipulated by the Almighty. I see no evidence that anything other than the same impulse that led to expulsion from the Garden is to blame for any atrocity.

Survey complete, I climbed back down the ladder. I decided to pry up one of the damaged boards of the burned area on the floor of the chapel and have a look. They were so badly ruined, they would all have to come up anyway, if they wanted to rebuild. I found an old rock bar at the back of the small horse stable area and took it back to the chapel to figure out what was beneath it.

It took quite a bit of wrenching back and forth to pry those old square nails loose, but the board was maybe two inches thick by ten inches wide, and a four-foot section broke loose. Enough room to lower a lantern and look. I found one that wasn't broken back in the basement where I was before, and it turned out to be the only unbroken one. I picked up the map case and laid it on the table before I went back upstairs.

Striking a match and getting it on the wick under the glass, it lit up fine. Trimming it down, I lay on my belly and lowered it down. It was deep. It was a mortared stone room, maybe twelve feet square. There was nothing visible, no furniture, and no crates; it was pretty empty. It did look like a door, maybe in the corner, towards the room where Arterous and Father Callious had died. I brought the lamp up and set it down. I stood up, dusted myself off, picked up the lamp, and blew it out.

"Raileanu! You around?" It was Barthow. I was glad and went out to see him.

"I got the blood downstairs cleaned up. Father Callious is buried, too."

"Good. Your mother said she suspected somethin' bad happened when he didn't return last night. She is alright. She's telling the professor now and will tell Mr. Metternich when he arrives in Vienna. They're travelin' there now, and should arrive in a couple days. Your Monika is with 'em, she had another unsettlin' encounter with that Runetta woman. Is it alright if'n I try to find that other mission sent some people on route here, talk with them? I shouldn't be more than an hour or two." Barthow was clearly in a hurry to get all this in a better place; if he had other pressing business, he might not tell me.

"Sure, yes. Thanks for taking him to Momma and checking on her for me. It is greatly appreciated by everyone." I said, comforting him to go.

"Alright, son. I'm sorry 'bout all this. I'll be quick as I can," and with that, he was gone again.

I went over to the front gate to figure out if it was remotely salvageable. It wasn't. I took apart some of the sides of the small sheds along the wall and created a makeshift fence that allowed me to close the front of the compound if needed. I went ahead and closed it up, after considering I was alone for an indeterminate amount of time, and even if someone wanted to come to the church, there was really nothing they would want to see here now. I spent the next few hours cleaning up what I could and trying to put the chapel into a presentable state.

Barthow came walking into the sanctuary about three in the afternoon, sat in a pew at the back, took his hat off, and took a drink from his little flask.

I went over to him and handed him the flask I got from Klement. "Try this."

"Whatcha got here, son?" he asked, "look purdy fancy."

"As much as you want," I said, smiling. He lifted it to his nose, sniffed it, gave a "hmm," and tilted it back. After a few long seconds, he stopped and let out a satisfied breath. "That, is, incredible. So good. Oh, that's good," and he went back to another big drink.

"I git it, where's the water from?" he paused only long enough to say.

"From a silver basin behind a waterfall in Switzerland. Good, huh?"

"That may be the best flask I have ever seen in my life, son." Barthow handed it back to me, quite satisfied.

"It was given to me by Arterous's uncle, right before I came back home," I said, putting it away in my vest. "I also figured out why he couldn't survive the attack here." I pulled the broken wand out of my pocket and showed it to him.

He looked at it for a second, then up at me. "I'm sorry, son. He seemed like a really good fellar. Tell his uncle I'm sorry this is such a harsh place." Looking back at his boots. "You neither should feel guilt, son. I know youd'a died as well. None of us know God's plan, and don't never let anyone convince you of guilt, if'n yer sure you'd done everything best you coulda, with the siteation and knowin' ye had at the time of troubles. Besides, I know what Arterous know'd too. You, yer ma, Father Callious, yer all good folks, and fer a true soldier, standing between danger and those ye care fer is all that matters. The big JC said it, too. No greater love is thar than to give yer life fer yer friends."

"Well, break is over. I found 'em on the trail, after speaking with Father Lorenzo to start with. They're only a couple hours out, planning on showing up here tonight. Father Lorenzo got all the details, thought for a moment, and said to go'on 'n clean it up. He had told them that Father Callious was very ill before they left. They were going to be ready for him to have passed. So we'll spiff the place up for them, I told them we'd come across him already passed away and buried him. They don't need to know all this grizzly business, as I also looked in briefly on the Comanches who were involved here, they had lost all but one baby girl and one squaw, I saw only four braves, and they've already gone approximately forty miles due west. They ain't comin' back here." he slapped his knees as he stood up, and walked out the front door of the chapel. Once out front, he crossed his arms and looked around. He tipped his hat back on his head, wiped his forehead with his sleeve, and raised his wand.

I could hear the sound of lumber flipping, hissing, smoke, and dust puffing out the side windows. He walked around the right side, which had only about twelve feet clearance to the wall, and even new windows popped into place from inside. He then went around the left side and did those windows as well. He paused, took a few steps back, looked up, shielded his eyes, and squinted. Then, he pointed his wand at the bell and replaced the pull rope from its arm, which I had failed to notice when I was up there. He pointed to the back door we'd used earlier, and it got a brand new door.

He went to the quarters around back, put new bedding and sheets on the padre's bed, then went around to the bunkhouse, which we hadn't been into. The windows, again, hinged to open in, fell into place, and provided them with new bedding as well. Barthow continued around the perimeter, repairing, cleaning, and replacing necessities as he came to them. I decided to head down to the scriptorium and get the map case off the tabletop that I had left. I wanted to examine what was in it. It didn't look like anything, down in the dark, so I went upstairs in the afternoon light. There was a piece of leather stuck down at the bottom, so I pulled that out, and then I thought I saw something else. Angling it so the sunlight went all the way down, there was only a single sheet of paper rolled at the bottom. I reached in and slung the case on my shoulder, and unrolled the page.

****

The time with Klement's mother, while a lovely experience being with a tight-knit and loving family, was extended by a whole day before Monika and the troupe were back on the road. Truthfully, she welcomed the extra day off riding in the carriage, as it is so much more difficult on one's body than dislocating. They would be in Laxenburg tonight, and the hotel was already preparing for their arrival. Klement would give a small speech at the town hall tonight, followed by a reception to which Monika would attend. However, his wife and children would retire to the hotel for dinner. The meeting was intended to discuss increased seed stock for local farmers and the government's plan to build a grain mill on the river, which would operate at no cost to the farmers, except for a ten percent claim on the milled product.

Monika was looking forward to the midday halt, as it would be near a location known for truffles. Raileanu had shown her something the time before their last visit that may help find them using magic. He had discovered it while someone was using a spell to show where a plant was healthy, glowing red, and not healthy, glowing blue. He noticed, while this was happening, that he could use his keen hearing to verify the movement of white threads of mushrooms through the soil, thanks to their speed. He perceived the ones he was observing were glowing green. She was keen to try it. Nothing else of note occurred on the pleasant ride to that spot.

The slope of the ground away from the roadway led downward into a huge stand of old, old oaks on the left side of the roadway. Some of them were four and five feet in diameter, their canopies stretching sixty or seventy feet high, overlapping each other, entangling their branches to be one huge interlocked wall, impervious to any normal storm. Their limb's breadth was conceivably a hundred feet around. Monika couldn't see a single blade of grass or shrub inside the dripline of those woods. The perfect place for a long-standing mat of truffle growth. Stepping out of the carriage, she stretched in a most unladylike fashion, not caring how it looked. She tugged at the bottom of her hip-length jacket, grabbed a woven willow basket from the supply carriage, and marched off into the woods to see what she could find.

She spent about an hour walking half a mile into the woods, enjoying their shade and the beauty of these massive, wise, living things as her soothing companions. She knelt here and there, using the spell on the mat of the forest floor, and by now she had half a dozen fragrant marbled truffles, maybe the size of peaches. The system worked well. She decided that was enough and sat down on a huge fallen trunk for a few minutes. She set the basket down and knelt facing the trunk to test the spell on the place where the forest floor met the trunk, to see what kind of mushrooms might be growing in that area or in the trunk of the fallen tree.

"Mmmm. Delicious." That voice said from the other side of the log.

Monika stood straight up and pointed her wand all in one motion, aiming it at the location of the sound as she stood. It was Runetta, lazily leaned against the opposite side of the log with her back to Monika. She was biting small pieces off a truffle. She leaned her head back and to the left, not really trying to look at Monika.

"Do you mind? I do love a good mushroom, dear."

"Explain what you want right now, or I will incapacitate you and have you arrested for stalking and threatening me. Don't forget who I travel with either, deary!" Monika mocked her civility.

"Tsk, tsk, tsk." Runetta taunted her, letting her wand slip into view across her left shoulder, clearly indicating her preparedness. "I have posed no threat to you, dear, merely curiosity. Anyone can see that. Only one of us has drawn down on the other." She turned around slinkily, facing Monika with a broad smile. She then dislocated without motion or blinking, letting the half-eaten truffle fall into the basket. Monika did not waste a second; she snatched the basket and dislocated herself right to the carriages, basket in hand. It was a risk, but hopefully worth it; perhaps the sheer number of travelers in their group would allow such an act to be unclear to any observer.

She arrived on the far side of the carriages from the road and immediately looked around for Klement, who was at the front of the row of carts of cargo.

"Klement!" she said quietly but seriously. He excused himself from the conversation he was involved in and walked calmly over to her.

"Yes, Monika, what is it?" he approached, smiling.

She lifted the basket, picked up the eaten truffle, and showed it to him. "Runetta appeared to me, more than half a mile deep, alone in the woods. She ate this, taunted me, and dislocated. Just now, I also dislocated here, so I could tell you straight away."

Klement looked displeased by this, looked front and back of the line, spotted one of his soldiers, and whistled at him, swinging his arm for that person to come to him, who swiftly ran to him.

"Sir, how can I help?" the guard said.

"This is Wenzel Prog. He is your personal bodyguard now. Wenzel, you are not allowed to let this woman out of your sight, save for private matters she must attend to. Her safety, honor, and protection are your sworn responsibility now. Do you understand?" Klement was dead serious, and this man knew it. "This is Monika Binder, she is one of my very best friends in the world. Make no mistakes."

"Nice to meet you, I am sorry for the circumstances, however," Monika said.

"He is one of the best discreet guards in Austria, and one of the few who are also of magical heritage. He will be able to serve in that capacity, where none of these other guards are of that ability. Until Raileanu returns, he will protect you. And one more thing, no more unescorted jaunts into the wilderness, please." Then Klement smiled and went back to the conversation he had left before.

"Fear not, madam, I will ride on the top of the carriage, and never be further than a room away. I will always be able to see you, no matter what. Quite seriously, make no changes to your behavior. I will be nearby, but never close." He went to the carriage he had been on, retrieved his bag, put it in Monika's carriage, and stayed there.

Klement walked back over to her, made sure no one was in earshot, and whispered to Monika, "The next time you encounter Runetta, you should immediately bind her, and we will sort out what is happening with no more delay. She has chosen only to visit when you're alone, so it should be safe to plan on that action." He touched her on the shoulder lightly, and was about to walk past her, when he stopped and looked at a carriage approaching to pass them on the road. They both looked at it to see who it might be. Monika grabbed Klement's arm, and it was Runetta! She was calmly smiling and waving from the window.

"That's her!" Monika said sharply, pointing at her. "That. Is. Her. Right there."

"I know that carriage. This mystery may be solved as soon as we arrive in Vienna. I don't feel you will see her again before then." Klement said calmly.

"What do you mean?"

"That is the carriage of the Glauer Family. Occultists. If what Raileanu and his family are dealing with is some kind of forbidden magical knowledge, they will be interested in it, no doubt. They, and some other ancient family lines, secretly seek the power of demons, or more accurately, the fallen angels from the beginning of human time."Klement stopped, scoffed, and shook his head. " Mostly, what they obsess over is sad old, dark magic that causes more harm than good, but they collect harmful knowledge, artifacts, and spells. If they are sniffing around, they suspect it is more than an illness, and what we know so far is that it was not some unknown mortal illness. We may be able to gather enough evidence to convince them it is nothing of interest to them, and she may just stop looking." Klement looked hopeful now, maybe.

The remainder of the trip was uneventful, and that woman, Runetta, didn't appear again. After an hour's rest at the last hotel of the trip, Monika left with Klement to the other side of the town, and into the church building for the meeting. There were already fifty or sixty townsfolk inside, including the Bürgermeister and his Chief of Police. Upon seeing Klement enter, they both walked briskly to the entrance where Klement was shaking hands, and interrupted the greetings. Monika overheard them speaking, as she had already sat down, and they stopped abruptly and looked at her. They were portly men, with wide, waxed mustaches and great, round cheeks. Both dressed for the occasion, the Bürgermeister in his best suit, hair combed-over with some kind of oil to hide his large balding spot on top of his head. The police chief, in his uniform, with a cross-chest patent leather harness for his pistol belt, and a dark blue jacket and pants, along with new shoes. Briefly, it struck her as comical, the first moment of levity of the day, but neither looked to have put those clothes on in some time, perhaps fifty pounds' worth of time. The police chief hustled everyone away from their little conclave, then pointed at Monika.

"Do you know this woman?" the police chief tried to say with force, but whispering, and Monika could see he was profusely sweating now as he asked in earnest.

"Yes, she is my assistant." Klement came up with quickly.

"Can she be trusted to be discreet?" The mayor then asked, looking at her, wiping his own head with a handkerchief to control sweat.

"Sir, would she be my assistant if she were not capable of discretion?" He responded, staring him down sternly.

The Bürgermeister glanced back at her, and then shook his head as if to say, oh, of course. Yes. yes.

"Now, what is it that has you two behaving like this?" Klement demanded, feeling his already long day stretching further out.

The police chief pulled a small rag out of his pocket, unfolded it, and showed it to Klement. It was a black and oozy potato. Once Klement had seen it, he wrapped it back up and put it back in his pocket.

"The whole store of potatoes that were stored in the warehouse barn you passed as you came into town was fine this morning, then late this afternoon, a porter was storing some sacks of barley in it and found them all like this! People are already saying witchcraft! Something must be done, Counsel!" The Bürgermeister was dead serious, and the chief was nodding as fast as he could, his cheeks flopping around like fish hung on the side of his head.

"Of course. May I ask you to go to the barn with some workers, take those potatoes out to a safe place, and burn them? They have a black slime mold, I have seen it before this very week in another town." Klement cleverly refused to give a name, so questions and rumors would have no path to follow. "Since encountering this earlier, I have already ordered Imperial stores to be sent to replace those affected by this blight. Just let me know how many crates, and I will have them here before the first snows, you have my word." Klement grabbed the Bürgermeister's shoulder tightly and gave it a little shake, then held out his right hand for a firm

245

handshake to seal the arrangement, which was reciprocated. "Now, let us speak to the people about their new grain mill."

Both men were reassured and walked to the stage of the church, where chairs had been set up, talking and nodding to each other as they congratulated one another on how they had handled it.

"Runetta, do you think?" Monika asked, leaning toward Klement, who was still in the center aisle.

"Yes. Presumably just for fun as she passed by." He said, shaking his head in disbelief at her disregard for their kind in every way possible.

CHAPTER THIRTEEN

This is what the letter said that I found in the map case:

Dear Tellafrogs,

After the troubles with the former Mexican army, the bandits, the rape and torture of the locals, and several other nearby families, I prayed to God for some way to help. I prayed for a week and fasted every day of that week. I was kneeling in the fountain stone room behind the scriptorium, praying, when I felt a shock in my hand, as you might feel on a cold, dry day. In that moment, I felt that God was guiding me on how to help those in my flock. I put my hand back on that mossy spot next to the fountain stone, and it told me to dig up a tree's root and bring it to the fountain. I did. The next day, I went to pray, and it had changed the stick somehow. I thought it was God who had done it. When Mr. Loggins came with his terrible story, I gave it to him to use against the bandits if they came back. I knew when you told me about what happened to them, it had to have been that stick. I knew I shouldn't have trusted that. Leviticus 19:31, I turned to sorcery, and it defiled me. That mark *spread up my arm and across my chest, just like it did John. Just like John and Mary Loggins. Whatever that was, it's in the room behind the big wardrobe. I covered the fountain stone with a cloth to hide it. That stone in the fountain was brought here in 1812 when a nearby farmer found it. No one knew what it was, but it didn't seem natural, so they hid it there. I used the room for solitude. I was a fool; all of this is my fault for not trusting God, but instead looking for signs and retribution. I am so sorry. Please forgive me.*

Father Callious

I was about to call Barthow over, but then I remembered what Professor Templeton said. If it were possible to solve this problem without allowing knowledge of this - now obviously some dark power - to spread, I should.

I decided to tell Barthow that I'd like to head back home, if he'd be alright with staying and explaining about Father Callious to the new arrivals. He agreed, so I saddled up and went on out, headed home as promptly as I could. I didn't have any way to make more Sagerush, but I could still make it before dark if I didn't get sidetracked.

Maybe due to the previous day's storm, I heard dozens of animals feverishly running around in the distance as I made my way home. Gophers, coachwhip snakes, rattlers, and even some coyotes are rustling around, rounding up the remains of other small animals from the storm-damaged area. All were too busy to concern themselves with my trip, and without incident, I made it home after the sun had set, but before it was dark.

Mother was very happy to see me, and went on about how she was sorry we couldn't do more to help Arterous and Father Callious. She reminded me, correctly, that had I been with them, I would have died as well. Maybe so, but that never really helps. No one can know what level of fighting and resistance they were able to tolerate. Knowing all that had happened to lead to their anger, that fury was uncontrollable for the Comanche. They had lost so much more in that terrible storm than anyone else in a hundred miles.

Mother had already spoken to Professor Templeton after Barthow brought Arterous here. He said that Klement and Monika had not arrived in Vienna yet, but he would let us know as soon as they did. She said the professor was very adamant that the stick be preserved, which she showed him was in a hex jar already. I finished getting the horse put up and doing the chores for the other horse as well. I also spent a few minutes telling Arterous's horse that he was gone, brushing and comforting him, before heading inside right after darkness had fallen completely.

"Mother, is the professor there?" I asked, as I went to wash up.

She looked that way and said, "No, it doesn't look like it."

"Okay, do you have a minute to read this? I found it hidden where Arterous and Father Callious died. Father Callious, I think, wrote it while Arterous fought off the attack by himself, then he hid it under a wardrobe in that basement room they were in." I pulled it out of the map case and handed it to her. When she saw the heading, she sat down to finish reading.

By the end of the letter, her hand was covering her mouth, and the corners of her eyes were downturned, feeling the sadness and desperation Father Callious had leading to all of this. She looked back at the portrait, and I guess the professor still wasn't there. "He will need to see this. We will stay awake until we see him, and I will hold it up so he can read it. This is not the kind of thing we need to let go of, I mean, to pass by owl or any other means to anyone." She was very serious about it. The maternal concerns about what had happened to our friends had drained away, replaced with somber intellectual fortitude.

"Put this with that root wand, and son, protect that satchel with your life. The professor has seemed more and more anxious about these reports, and I feel this will make him acknowledge some fear he's been frantic to avoid finding." She held it up to me, and I folded it up, wrapped it in a piece of deerskin made with straps designed to keep important documents safe from the elements. Father had dozens of these, as often paperwork for prisoners came and was sent in them.

"Has the professor mentioned anything about Arterous yet? What should be done?" I asked over dinner.

"He said we should keep him in a suspended state until we speak with Klement. He is currently in his room, and I have him in a state where he is floating above his bed. I went ahead and packed all of his things neatly and collected personal things from his horse rigging as well." She didn't eat much and was already drinking her evening tea.

"I found his wand, which we can pack in his things also. It lay broken just outside their basement refuge. It explains why he was unable to survive, heal himself, or last very long. Barthow thinks, and I agree, that he was apparently hit by an arrow right outside the door to the basement and dropped it. He had no choice but to retreat down to the basement, barricading the door with his wand outside. The attackers presumably broke it, since they were blaming the tornado on Father Callious' imagined alliance with magic against them." I explained.

"He was very strong and brave. He stood to protect the helpless priest and did so, giving his life. Protecting those who cannot defend themselves is the instinct of every natural-born soldier." She tried to reassure me.

The problem is, I know that the attackers were unwaveringly brave as well. They were taking the remnant of their tribe to attack what they felt were unimaginable odds that had brought evil amongst them. It is always the failure to try and talk and find common ground that leads to bloodshed. But that is where all humans find themselves, between those filled with rage and vengeance and those defending against the rage. It's in the bloodshed that we struggle between the two. Most folks think it is unimaginable to kill someone else. They do, until someone else is going to kill them. So ignorance of real human nature is just as much to blame.

We waited maybe two hours after dinner, and I had dozed off in a high-backed armchair, when mother shook me awake. "He's here. The professor, bring the letter, please."

I had tucked that inside my vest, or she might have retrieved it herself, but I wanted to try and listen to at least one side of this conversation now. At least eight people had died for this. So I got it out, opened the leather, and handed it to her. She had already shown him the hex jar, which was in the corner behind the chair I was in. I took both and handed them to my mother, and sat on the corner of the table nearest to their discussion. She held the jar up first, I guess to let him know it was still safe. Then she held the letter right on the canvas for him to read. A few minutes passed, then mother gasped.

"Professor! Behind you! It's an... is that an..." She could barely breathe enough to say more, covering her mouth with her free hand.

"What is it, Mother?" I tried, but only got a hand indicating for me to stop. So I waited.

"Professor, he's gone!" Momma said. She looked panicked, trying to peer into the professor's room. Then, she turned to me, went pale, and a paralyzed expression flooded over her. I realized she was looking behind me.

I slapped my hand on the pistol grip, stood, and spun around in a single motion, only to be levitated, and every limb and digit extended as far apart as possible without pain, before I even got turned around.

"Please, Mary and Raileanu, I mean you no harm, be calm," the voice said, and I finally got around where I could see what was happening. Mother then turned towards the portrait, as the professor must have been speaking.

"It's alright, son. This is a friend of the professor. Please, let him speak with us," Momma said.

"I will. I'm okay. You can release me." I said calmly. Maybe someone finally has some darn answers about the things that are killing everyone I know, I thought. I was lowered gently down, all my limbs returning to my own control.

"I am the one who can stop this. I am Kleet. I am a High Elf. If you will allow me to explain, and confirm what you may know, or have seen. Stopping this is why I am here, if you

252

will let me help," the High Elf said. Made sense, so I sat down for what had better be answers. I was ready for someone to make some sense. All I have done is find vague clues, clean up death, and lose those closest to me.

"This man, um, High Elf, was in the painting with the Professor. When he read the letter with the professor, he came here instantly," Momma said. "I apologize, I never, well, didn't even think the High Elves were real. I'm sorry, sir."

This was clearly no man. He was close to seven feet tall, shoulders at least thirty-six inches across, very long, straight, pure white hair, pointed ears, and clothing that, while intended to appear normal, was, well, vague at best. It was hard to focus on, as the light grey was uneven, and even the length of the overcoat varied and changed while standing still. He had very sharp features, and the eyes, from deep within, pulsed to emit their own blue light. His shirt, vest, pants, and boots appeared to be a much older style, and were also varying shades of grey. His boots resembled suede but had no buckles or laces. Another thing, he was controlling my body with no wand, heck, he wasn't even looking at me when he did it.

I sat down on the couch, ready to try and solve, end, whatever all of this mystery. I gave the elf a blank stare. Rare, mythical, unconcerned with the troubles of us or not for thousands of years, it was concerned now, about what was happening with our circumstances.

"I have worked with the professor since the beginning of your father's trouble here. We keep the master copy of the 'book'. We monitor it for traces of ancient, what you call magic. Some of it, after more than thirteen thousand years we have existed, has remained from that time. Some are not designed for good uses, but for harm. We collect and store knowledge. When we find traces of this ancient 'magic' or relics of that time, we retrieve or eliminate them so they can never be used again. What happened to your father, the 'root wand', the human lady and her husband, and even Father Callious being convinced to do it, they were all part of it, part of this system we are bound to destroy." The lack of emotion displayed must be part of their charm, but it was grating on me.

"I am sorry, uh, Kleet, why the hell have you merely lingered around the edges of this while my FATHER, my friend, hell, even Monika are being killed and tormented?!" My unbridled anger animated my hands and movements while seated. It would unnerve anyone, and I struggled to restrain it. "Forgive my tone, but I am sick of digging graves! Please, I want to end all this. I'm upset." I spoke in an unfriendly manner, but not for a lack of trying to be polite; it just came out that way.

"We could not. You must understand. Unfortunately, with dangerous knowledge, there are always those, both magical and ordinary, who will seek to find and use it. Several thousand years ago, one of the 'books' we designed to help us find these things was stolen. It cannot be read as ours, but when it is being used, the writing appears briefly, and can be copied from it, the same as Professor Templeton's copy. Those who seek these forbidden powers have used the book before to try to trap us and collect these things for themselves. We refuse to engage directly or leave our sanctuary until we are certain of events and locations. For us, it is genuinely a risk to all life on earth if we are captured or discovered, but these scattered remnants and the pain they cause are worth the risk. We must be certain before we can try and help. That is all I can say." The High Elf never changed tone, stance, or cadence.

As he spoke, I began to understand. From the beginning, the professor and Klement tried to tell me, this was very important. All of this had happened in a short amount of time, and the professor's increasingly urgent tone was more obvious as I looked back now. I reluctantly shook my head in agreement.

"So this artifact, or whatever it may be, that you think is behind this, where do you think it is? I asked.

"From what that letter indicates, it may be in the room of the basement Father Callious mentioned. I think I know what it is. It will be too difficult to explain, nor should I explain, but if you can take me there, I can retrieve it and remove it to safety."

"I cannot dislocate, sir. I have not been able to, I lost my..." Kleet cut me off with a raised hand and a slow blink as he turned his head towards me.

"Raileanu, I know. I am a High Elf, not a wizard. It's sufficient to say that if you can take me by the arm, imagine the location we must go; I can take myself there. Just as I came here. It is too dangerous now for you to go with me, regardless. You must stay and protect your mother. As I said, the harassment of Monika is proof enough that nefarious magical forces are lurking around this incident. The protection of this place will work for ordinary people, but determined magical persons will not be dismayed by any of it. Please, if you would allow me." he reached for my arm.

I closed my eyes and imagined the mission, the chapel, the back exterior door that led to the basement, and that large wardrobe, the extent of my knowledge of the place he sought, which was described in Father Callious' letter. Then he was gone. No poof, no whoosh, silent, and as though a door - stepped through him.

Mother went straight to the portrait of the professor. She was asking if there was anything else she could know about this Elf, and what else may be known about the killing of my father, how his illness was connected. It seemed he had no more information than we did. Not even the professor had any idea if Kleet was even coming back, here, or to London at all.

****

Barthow had stayed at the mission and was helping the few men from the other mission get settled, knowing that the questions they may have surrounding the death of Father Callious may present themselves later in the evening, and he wanted to ease their concerns before he left. He also had some explaining to do about his duties in the area. These were not magical people, nor cleared to work with them, so he had to be on his best behavior. They were, in fact, brothers from the Carlos family: Juan, Jamie Jr., and the youngest, Javier. They would be responsible for preparing the mission for use when a new Padre would be assigned. Even with the work Barthow had done to clean up, the state of the place had been in decline for some time. The brothers would begin rebuilding tomorrow and making the whole place ready to receive new congregants. Tonight, they shared a hearty beef stew that Barthow had prepared before their arrival, along with two large pots of saltwater cornbread. None of them had any idea of the discoveries of the last few hours.

Kleet arrived in the basement, where I had shown him. He surveyed the room, and with a flick of his eyes, the huge, heavy wardrobe slid across the floor. He was not concerned about the others who were outside. I wasn't sure if they had arrived or if I should mention that Barthow would be there. He pushed it with whatever power he wielded against the far wall. Behind it was a very old door, perhaps even original to the mission, a couple of hundred years, perhaps, in the dry, dark basement. It had a large, heavy iron lock on the bolt latch. Kleet broke that and it clanked onto the floor, again, with no more than a thought. Barthow heard both, but decided to investigate only after the metallic clunk.

He had eaten before they arrived, so he was happily engaging in friendly, comforting talk with the new stewards of the mission. He excused himself, as they were still eating after he heard the sound, and said he would check on it. It could have been a raccoon, possum, skunk, snake, fox, wildcat, or anything snooping around downstairs, so he wasn't concerned about actual trouble. In fact, he had begun packing some of his own shells, a small paper pouch of number four shot held in the bore of the cylinder with wax. He had a mold for that size in his pack, and would always dig out lead from stumps he practiced on, and figured it'd be a better use of resources to make shot shells for his pistol and rifle when it was only small varmints, and this would be a good time to try it out. It also didn't blast big holes in things, as long as he had a bit of distance. So he pulled the lead slug cylinder out and put in his six-shot shell cylinder as he walked to the door.

Kleet went into the hidden room, which was small and quite dirty. After walking into the center, he turned to his left and saw a tarp over something, maybe four feet high and three feet wide. He heard the footsteps coming through the door upstairs, paused, and waited until they were halfway down the stairs. Then, with a thought, he froze Barthow, who could no longer think or move. He had no idea it had happened, nor would he when released from it. Kleet then had the tarp whipped off, making the dust and dirt of decades built up on it freeze in the air until the tarp was on the floor, then it all fell straight down. Underneath was a stone frame over a small copper spout that emerged from the wall, trickling water. At its base was a wide granite basin, filled with water that overflowed and ran into a crack in the floor. In the basin was the source of the High Elf's interest. He recognized it right away. It was a primitive, yet obviously powerful, granite crystal-silicone orb that emitted an uneven, twinkling light from within, visible to magical individuals and Kleet.

****

I had gone to get some coffee from the kitchen stove, while mother was talking to the painting some more. I glanced up as I poured the coffee; they were still talking, so I thought I'd pour Momma one as well.

Suddenly, mid-sentence, she was thrown, or jerked to the left, into the corner of the room away from the painting, and where I couldn't really see, but it looked violent, with a scream indicative of bone-breaking pain. I dropped the pot and cup, drew my pistol, and dashed to the right for a better look at what happened. She was held from behind by a man I'd never seen, with a long, slender-bladed knife to her neck. Who the hell was this, THREATENING MY MOTHER!

I pointed my pistol at his face, confident I could end his depraved mind in an instant. Whoever this was, a line was crossed, and now my mother was my only concern. The long, unkempt, thick black and white hair, scraggly, patchy beard growth, and dark discoloration around the mouth and eyes told me this person had been taking various potions I had seen used before to increase speed, strength, and focus. They're commonly used by assassins, mercenary groups, and thieves, but also showed that he was not ordinary. Then his other hand slowly raised a wand and pointed it at me.

Bandos emerged from the back of the house, through the kitchen, and glanced at me quickly before his yellow eyes darted to the corner he was approaching. He silently moved his legs, his body fixed. I saw all this out of the corner of my eye. His snout was already curled, nose pointing straight ahead, huge wolf teeth jittering with fury, legs only moving from his knees down. Maybe he could give Momma a second to get away, and I could stop this monster, maybe.

The next series of events was no more than three seconds, but moved so, so slowly for me. And it stays that way in my mind, always. I can't seem to remember it any other way.

As soon as Bandos got to the corner, I accidentally looked at him, the bastard wizard saw it, moved the wand to that corner, Bandos jumped at him, a flash erupted, obscured by Bandos' body, exploded no doubt from the wand, Bandos' front right paw tried to go for the knife to knock it away from momma. Momma tried to push the man's arm away from her throat. Her back to him, she couldn't see the marks of added strength and speed. Her effort didn't work. Bandos bit furiously at his neck, for just a moment, until he stopped. He looked as though he was suspended in the air, or on him. The man swung his left arm - the one around Momma holding the knife - and effortlessly flung her to the side, while cutting her throat more deeply than anything I'd ever seen in the same motion. I saw her terror as it happened, as her life ran out so fast. So fast. She lay there face down, slightly on her side with bent legs, for only three or four seconds before she collapsed completely. By the time I had looked back to try and sight down the barrel, my pistol was gone from my hand, floating a foot in front of the still hanging Bandos. That is when I saw the tip of this bastard's wand protruding through Bandos' fur, barely an inch or two. He was killed with a curse and then impaled on the wand. He lowered his arm, dropping a lifeless Bandos and my pistol to the ground. He was wearing a very lightweight but coarse long shirt that was filthy, stained with black fibers. He had a wide belt with large and small pouches on it, and a black leather satchel. His boots were a dark, almost knee-high brown, with buckles. All of this pointed to the common attire of European criminal wizards. He whipped his wand with a flick towards me, and my own pistol cracked me in the forehead, and my head lunged back, I grabbed my head, and knelt in pain. Then he was there, his wand, still dripping with blood from Bandos, onto my cheek, pointed at my left eyeball, the knife at my throat.

"Tell me, boy." Heavy, central eastern European accent, "Where is the Elf. I will not kill you if you tell me now." His breath definitely stunk of vile potions I have no knowledge of. I saw little choice.

"The old Spanish mission. West of here, about five miles." I mumbled with indignant fury. He withdrew the wand and the blade, then thrust it sharply into my right side, and dislocated.

What the hell just happened?? I could feel quite a bit of blood oozing from the narrow slit he left me with. I tried to stand, but rapidly fell from blinding lightheadedness. I needed to get to the kitchen, and there was a jar of dried lion's mane mushroom I knew could stop the bleeding and close the hole. I crawled over to the cabinet, used the counter to pull myself up, reached shakily to the top cupboard, and pulled the jar down with me to the floor. I fought to get my vest and shirt open, and I got a handful of the powder, forcing it into the hole with my thumb until it felt full, then I passed out.

****

Kleet was about to inspect closely the area surrounding the little basin, trying to understand the way this had reached the outside world, when he heard the unmistakable sound of explosive and ripping curses upstairs. He promptly walked into the main room of the basement, just in time to see a massive fireball envelop Barthow, and knock his still paralyzed figure into Kleet, and they both fell on the ground. Kleet saw the figure approaching down the stairs and filled the whole shaft with thunderous streams of lightning. The figure jumped the remainder of the steps to the bottom, still on fire, streams of electricity jumping off him to the nearest chair or wall. Kleet stood, but before he could do anything else, this wizard repaid his pain with a sheet of cleaving electrical fury onto the elf, who caught most of it on his left side. He fell and, with just a glance, eviscerated the man, shearing all his muscles and connective tissues from his skeleton, which fell in a steaming heap on the floor. Kleet stood, snapped his fingers, and a pointed silver canine tooth from this bastard was ripped from his skull, and leapt into his hand. He tried to stand up, but the damage from the strike he took was quite bad, and he stumbled a few times. He wasn't bleeding as much as he was suffering from extreme burns, and parts of his whole left side - leg, arm, and neck were fused and stinking already, crackling the burnt flesh as he tried to move. It was bad, and his concentrating to try and produce some, any, healing wasn't working. Very well, he thought; he would be lucky to get the orb and deliver it to Raileanu and his mother for their protection.

He staggered into the other room, put his hand on the orb, and was back in the Tellafrog's home, lying on the couch, clutching the orb. He looked around in severe pain, only now realizing that his left eye had been wrenched from the socket and burned off, and then winced when he saw what had happened there. He took the tooth he had collected and laid it on the table. He saw me sitting in the kitchen, unconscious. He snapped his fingers and brought me awake.

"Come here, Raileanu. Let me heal that for you," he forced out.

"He had been here, that's how he knew where to find me, I see," Kleet said calmly. "Now you can see how serious this is."

"Where. Is. That. Bastard. WHERE IS HE! He killed my mother! He killed Bandos!" I screamed at him, tears pouring from my eyes as I crawled to him, retrieving my pistol along the way.

"I'm sorry, Raileanu, he also killed everyone at the mission before I knew he was there. He almost killed me. I destroyed him. His body lies ripped apart, flesh from bone on the floor of the basement," he said. When I finally got close to him, he reached over and touched my side, which felt warm and fizzy, and as I watched, closed up with not so much as a scar. Kleet's eyes were closed as he did it, and stayed closed as he put his hand back on the strange orb he had. Half of his body, from head to calf, was completely seared.

"Can you heal yourself the same way?" I asked, as his pain had to be terrible.

"I have tried, but it may not heal. I may die here," he mumbled.

"Elves can die?" I asked.

"Yes, like any other creature God made, yes, we can die. There is, however, no disease or aging we suffer from. Please, I am not able to see very well, and my ears are damaged from the fighting. I will tell you about this orb, and you will need to contact the professor somehow as soon as you can. Please tell him everything as well. I don't have more than an hour, I suspect. The time has come to bring more of you into this endeavor, as we fear the world is proceeding down a dark path that is unavoidable for magic or ordinary people."

Sir, Kleet, my mother is lying there, dead. A medicine man who has become that wolf to try and protect her, lies just there," pointing to them both, still full of fury and eyes dripping with tears. "My father died not a week ago."

"I know Raileanu, we have watched you for essentially your whole life. Let me do what I can. He closed his eyes and was silent for a moment.

"Hey! Wake up!" I yelled at him. Mother lost all her agony in her face, her blood, just a moment ago, splattered all over, was gone. She looked serene and began to straighten her form, settling into what appeared to be a peaceful sleep. Then she began to appear dimmer and dimmer, until she vanished. Then Kleet took a few deep breaths, and Bandos too looked to lose the gore of his demise, and then turned into a white, glowing cocoon that extended to five feet. The light lashed away, and he was his human form again. In full regalia for a ceremonial burial, he, too, vanished.

I looked at Kleet, who had several tears on his cheek running down behind his ear, as he was mostly reclined on the couch. He breathed deeply several more times and opened his eyes. I don't know if he was as emotional at these events, or even his own impending death, or if he was in immense pain.

"What have you done with them!?" I yelled again.

"Your mother lies in repose with your father, the inscriptions on Barthow's tomb updated to show their lives of love and sacrifice. Bandos has returned atop a pyre to his people. They deserve to see his achievements and celebrate his life before he is given back to the universe with fire. I hope this is acceptable, it has taken most of the life I have left in me. They both deserved the best I could do. Now, before I begin, do you wish to write these things down, or would you like me to try for you?"

What follows is taken from my actual scribblings as Kleet spoke, and it may seem disconnected, or confusing, but trust me when I say at the time I was even more confused than you might be. In order to retain the nature of the story and fully explain the nature of the fumblings and errors made henceforth, it is necessary for it to be presented in its original manner as I received it. In further volumes, the gravity and breadth of the High Elf's story will be made plain to grasp.

"Alright, okay, no, no, I can." I wiped my face and tried to compose myself. "Did you see Barthow at the mission?"

"Yes, he, too, I am afraid, was killed. He was there trying to protect them from this vile attack. I am too weak to do anything else with 'magic'. Let me begin." Kleet tried to sit up some, but didn't make it far, and just gave up, resigning to explain from his reclined position.

"Your world is not a straight line from wilderness, or even the Garden of Eden, to where we are now. There were at least three great ages of technological advances of mankind, and we are in the last three hundred years now of this seemingly repeating cycle. With the time I have, I will only discuss the last one, as it is most relevant, given that only two relics from the previous period have been found in the last eleven thousand years. Neither were they functional, nor did they have any use to anyone. Before the last great Calamity, such knowledge and technical ability had been achieved that there were no limits for humans. Almost every living person on earth was able to do what you call 'magic', but to levels even wizards today cannot believe, even if they witnessed it. After the Calamity, the numbers of what you call magical now, were less than a hundred in the whole world, surviving from the time before. The descendants of those hundred are the ones called pure born now. They are a remnant, but no more pure than any other. They were used by the most powerful survivors of ordinary humans, for they far out-numbered those left with magical abilities, as slaves. Around eight thousand years passed, and the world had achieved so much more. We, what you call the High Elves, and oth-er 'magical' races, including shapeshifters, dwarves, goblins, ogres, dragons, all were created in that last hundred years of great advancement before the Calamity. Created by design, by desire, anyone could be anything they dreamed. Some even created machines in human form to serve or fight on their behalf. All of this was made possible by things like this orb. The creators thought it was life, of a sort. They were created intelligences. Many groups of humans made them. Some benign, some diabolical. This one is directly related to you, Raileanu. To your loss of magic. The dragon you saw that day was a copper dragon, yes? It is one of the survivors that was created during that time. They draw power from storms and the heat of volcanoes. He is over fourteen thousand years old. He was created for one purpose: to capture any form of this 'ceegee" that they detected in the heavens, falling to earth. He was trying to catch it when the lightning ripped between you both. The magic being destroyed by the power of the lightning in you disrupted his ability to find this orb. It fell here, in this region, and lay dormant for all these years, until someone brought it to the mission, and unaware of what it was, they stored it in the basin under the chapel." he paused to catch his breath.

"Ceegee?" I asked.

"An abbreviation for Crystalline Integrated General Intelligence. This one is simply CIGI, and it was not the worst of them. There were ones far more powerful, and some of those also are not accounted for. It must have been above the clouds, and for whatever reason, it fell from the sky. More things are circling above the Earth than you know. There are dozens of them still circling the Earth, unable to communicate with or work together, as differing, sometimes warring factions of humans created them. This one seems to be able to communicate only with what you call magical people, and my theory is that after enough time, a single thread of roots, spreading throughout the water table, found its way into the prison, where a person with magical abilities was 'talking' to it. I suspect that both Father Callious and the prisoner were asking and receiving information without knowledge of the other. This orb was just facilitating the connection. Father Callious wanted to help his people. The orb knew the plant life in the water table, and the prisoner, along with records of knowledge in the orb itself, gave an answer that would help him. But these are also dangerous. This one wreaked havoc in this remote area, just doing what it was designed to. Imagine if that monster of a person who just killed your mother had access to one. There are arts and abilities these CIGI know of that you can't possibly imagine."

"Really? Today I can imagine some terrible things, sir!" I pointed out. "What kind of things, like what led to their demise, that long ago?"

267

"Oh, so much worse. How they ended all those years ago is similar to what has happened here. It is that path the world is on now, to the same place. At that time, when we chose to be created in our current form, we do not age or suffer illness." Kleet paused, breathing raspily and deeply for a moment. "Our bodies repair themselves, unless damaged as I am. The sources of this are too complicated for you to grasp now, but they are the same things that are passed along through generations in magical people. It is also how you and Klement have lost your power. It lets us see and control all forces in our world, a feat once thought impossible by science without CIGI. Once the leaders of the world had access to the power of these tools, many of them became concerned with their newfound power and began to delegate important tasks to the CIGIs. Not all were as well-made or reliable; most have stopped working, either due to their own faults, design, or material issues. There are meteors, yes, ones you can or have observed falling in the night sky. Twelve thousand, eight hundred years ago, a city-sized object was coming directly toward the Earth. The leaders had given power to their CIGI to destroy it, years before its suspected arrival. Many of us, dedicated to amassing knowledge and nothing more, had warned of the risks of the proliferation of these tools and the power given over to them, but to no avail. After none of them wanted to stop their pursuits or admit that a seemingly flawless system may have faults. We, along with many others, sought refuge deep within the earth, calculating that the risk was too high to avoid protection from this impending disaster. We were right, but not for the reason we thought." he stopped, wincing with pain, and asked for some water, so I took out my flask and gave it to him.

After a few sips, he rested again for a moment, his breathing worsening. At first, his left hand was the only one showing signs of damage, shaking. Now both were, and his fingers and hands also seemed to be held in unnatural ways. Like a person might if they had frostbite or they had been crushed. After another couple of attempts to drink, but mostly pouring out of the corners of his mouth, he handed the flask back to me. "The separation and incompatibility of the CIGI systems were for everyone's protection, but were also the reason for the disaster. Then the group that had spotted and announced it would deal with the asteroid simply went back to whatever it was they were doing. The CIGI shot huge rockets at the asteroid on time, as planned. I think there were three. One failed halfway up in the sky, but as soon as the three launched, all the other CIGIs who were put in control of defenses in other nations detected the launches, assumed they were being attacked, and launched similar weapons to defend themselves. The power of those missiles is more than any human alive today can imagine. I cannot describe it in a way you can comprehend, I'm sorry. Once every place on earth tracked one launch, they too launched their attacks. It was all automatic. All the CIGIs were doing exactly what they thought they should be doing. Even before the first two missiles that had made it near the asteroid had detonated, most of the Earth's surface was destroyed, or soon would be by fire. Only one made it to the target, and that broke it into a thousand pieces, which fell to the earth, causing even more destruction. Only those of us underground, or near

269

what used to be the poles, survived. It was not easy, and for nearly a hundred years, many of us died trying to survive. Those who did not die, later went out into the world to find it in practically the lowest form of human existence. Very little language had survived; nothing was familiar in the landscape, the people, or anything else. It was during this time that we became known as Fey, or Elves. We were the only fully changed beings that still existed. The other 'magical' races survive, of course, but many of their traits were specific to single purposes, some even created against their will to serve others. Because our power was permanent, and we alone understood the tools and techniques required to allow full mastery of the known universe, we stayed separate. There was no help we could offer to humanity that would genuinely benefit them; it could only accelerate their inevitable path to the same place we are now heading. Our mission, out in the world beyond our enclaves, is to consolidate the old relics, preserve their power from the rest of the world, and store as much knowledge as possible from the beginning of our time as possible. This is why there can be no more elves, why there are so few magical people. We cannot procreate, by design, and along with us, magical people are the only ones with the tools for manipulation of the unseen world built into themselves." Again, he paused, his words becoming softer and further apart.

"The man-made soldiers I spoke of earlier. There are possibly thousands, either buried after the great destruction of the missiles' fire, or the asteroid impact that followed. Some circle the earth, entombed in metal shells above the skies. They are genuinely terrifying, unstoppable, and could be controlled with the matching CIGI that made them. I think the witch, Runetta, and her henchman, who came here tonight, have at least one of those soldiers, and also know that what was going on here is related to what they seek. No wanton bloodshed with such sickening violence has been hoisted on magic or ordinary worlds in centuries as we saw here tonight. They are not to be allowed to get this orb. You must get the Professor here to take it and protect it at all costs. My kind will find him and secure it. You understand now, please say you do..." he trailed off.

"Kleet!, Kleet! I'm here, I understand, and I swear I will, on my whole family, I swear." I said without pause.

"Can we not just destroy it?" I panicked, as if it were a good idea.

"No, none of us can. Take it to the professor, is all I can...." his eyes shut, his hands dropped, and the tension from pain in his body relaxed. This man, this High Elf, was dead.

CHAPTER FOURTEEN

B arthow suddenly realized he was free to move. He could not know this, but the spell that held him expired with Kleet. He writhed around in the dirt, facedown where he fell during the battle, and made sure he had all his appendages, then pushed himself up to his hands and knees, and looked around. He noticed his coat, clothes, and hat were burnt, still smoldering. Leaning back onto his knees and heels, he patted himself all over where he could reach, making sure there wasn't still something truly on fire. Satisfied that the threat had passed, he looked around to see if there was a clue to what had happened. He had been unable to move or hear for what felt like an hour. He couldn't remember anything past coming down the stairs, either. That was clearly a spell of some kind, although he had no idea what kind. He glanced to his right, to find that the large wardrobe had been moved aside, revealing a door. Just to his left was a sickening pile of human bones and flesh. He recoiled up to his feet, grabbed his pistol off the floor, and went straight through that newly revealed door. A quick look showed nothing of note in the dark, and he went up the stairs as quickly as he could, only to find all three brothers had been killed. A black, burnt-looking wound was laid across their eyes, and bloody blistering surrounding that. All three sat in their seats, right where he left them, eating and joking just moments before.

"Well, sheeeit. Oh no. Mother and Raileanu!" is all he said before pinching his eyes shut, and dislocating to their home.

"Mother! Raileanu! Are you here!?" he hollered, having arrived in the front yard, running to the house, stopping in the doorway, to watch me lift my eyes from beside the Elf.

He looked terrible! His hair was burnt, his hat and over-coat looked completely burned from behind, nearly falling off in pieces; his hands were blackened by soot. "Are YOU alright? What happened?" I asked him, looking upset at his condition.

"Yeah, boy," he finally noticed how badly his clothes had suffered, shaking them off, "I'm fine, someone stunned me or froze me or somethin'. I was at the mission, headin' downstairs to check on a racket. I woke up just a minute ago, to find myself almost burnt, a pile of mush that used to be a fellar missing a tooth, and all three brothers who'd arrived were kilt deader than a doornail. What the hell son, where's your momma, where's Bandos, who the hell is tha, whats that big purple split mouse on yer head? Who is that?" pointing to the Elf on the couch, pistol still in hand, whom I was beside. "Is that, is it a uh, is that a dang ELF?"

"Yeah. It is. I can explain, I guess, well, what I just learned was the cause of all this, why it was so important to figure out what happened to Daddy. Wait, are you sure you're okay? You looked like you got chucked in a fire?"

"Yeah, yeah. Ain't no accident my great-grandparents moved to these parts at the end of the 1600s. Ever since they burnt a mess of my kinfolk at the stake back then, most of us have been born fireproof. Must be those strong survival traits we Cordens got. What the hell is that shiny ball thing the elf got?" he pointed at it.

"Honestly, it's the cause of all this. The Elf had been working with the Professor to determine if something similar was present, which might be causing some of this. It's some kinda old relic from prehistory. When the High Elves were pretty sure one was here, he came and met with me and momma, and I told him where it might be, and he went straight there, into that basement at the mission." I turned back to look at the Elf.

"That makes some sense, I reckon. I mean, he coulda froze me. Then that other feller musta kilt them boys and fried me." Barthow took off his hat, surveying the damage it had sustained. "Dangit. My hat."

"Right after he left, that man came, killed Momma and Bandos, and had me dead to rights. He offered to spare me if I told him where the Elf had gone. Heck, froze me, then he pistol-whipped me with my own pistol using magic. Stabbed me. With everyone dead, I hoped the Elf could handle himself, and that with you maybe still there, he would get nowhere." I looked back at Barthow, who was just shaking his head. "I'm not sure what happened, but the Elf came back here, all burned up, barely alive. He buried Momma with Daddy, he sent Bandos back to his people, healed me, and told me about this orb thing. Said I had to get it to the Professor, that he would know what to do. He passed on not five minutes ago."

"That musta been him that froze me then, I was released about that same time, came to, and saw all that happened. That there Elf tore that fool to pieces, left him in a pile of guts and bones." Barthow looked around the area where Kleet was lying. He saw the silver pointed tooth. "That thar tooth musta come out that dirty bandit. Can I see it?"

"Yeah, of course." I waved at it. I turned and sat with a thump on the floor, facing Barthow now.

He picked it up and went over it, looking sternly. "There's a rune or somethin' here, on the front of it. I'm sorry, son, I don't know my runes at all. But there's only one. And this looks like a canine tooth, but longer. This here ain't somethin' you just get out of a tray at some dentist. Some feller made this particular for 'em."

"Lotta good that does me. I can't dislocate, I can't talk to the professor in the portrait, heck, I can't even tell if he's there or not. Literally, my whole family has died in a week, along with virtually every single person I know 'round here, all because of a stupid ball." I held my head in my hands, feeling so much anger and loss at once that I thought my head would split. My fingers dug into my scalp so hard the knuckles all went white.

"Well, look, son, I know this is bad all 'round. I gotta git back to the mission, and clean that up, 'fore someun' comes round and finds signs of magic inside the mission killin' folks! Now you're gonna have to hold on a while, I'll be back and talk to that professor fer ya. Take yer time with yer grief and whatnot. Don't do nuthin' drastic, son, you ain't alone in this, don't talk like that. Here," He reached into his pocket and pulled a small round jar with green paste in it, chucking it underhanded to me. "This is rosemary and western sage oil with crushed leaves. Put this on that lump ye got on yer head thar. That mouse'll be gone in an hour." Barthow, still working like a hero, half burnt up, feeding folks, fighting evil wizards, just patted me on the shoulder a couple of times, and took off. From what I knew, his early years were as bad as mine were now. He knows the world goes on beating away on us whether we like it or not. It's much harder to grind someone down if they're constantly running and working on the tasks God gives us each day. The grinder gets you when you slow down trying to carry the weight of yesterday and tomorrow, and finally give way to the weight of more tomorrows and more yesterdays, and lie down under the burden. So I will try to take the burden of today, of tonight, lay down the burden of the last couple weeks at the feet of God to handle, and be ready for tomorrow, because that's when the task begins of finding these monsters who would employ this kind of trash, and kill them. I took all the hastily transcribed pages of what Kleet had said and put them into my inside vest pocket. If this information was real, which it seemed to be, this isn't the kind of thing to leave lying around. In fact, I considered burning it, as I could remember most of it, having heard it in such a dramatic episode, and I had written it all by hand myself. I decided to keep it safe for now.

****

Klement had several pressing meetings even at the late hour of arrival in Vienna. The troupe caravanned into the city at dusk, with the streetlights already being lit along the avenues. The cargo and workers' carriages and wagons split off in front of the St. Charles Church, proceeding around the back of the block of buildings to the right of the church's front. Their quarters and stables for the animals lay down a narrow alley that split the different important buildings in that area of Vienna, and had sufficient distance from the church and the houses and offices of important government officials, so the aroma of livestock and their care didn't filter out. Vienna was a beautiful city, and crews of workers spent lifetimes cleaning the roads and avenues from debris and horse droppings. Rarely did any remain on the roads more than a few minutes. Horse-drawn carts criss-crossed the streets during all daylight hours, dutifully removing any and all unsightliness. The stables that were allowed in important areas were cleaned daily, and many of the loads were taken to composting pits outside town. Many of those were saved and used when the emperor had his personal garden built almost twenty years earlier.

Moving down the main street past the church, they stopped in front of a building that was part of the block running half a mile, the only one with a permanent cov-ered entrance on the street. Large stone four and five-story flat-faced buildings made up this side of the street. Some were white, some were tan, and some were grey. Some of the stones were large on the ground floors, perhaps two feet high by four feet long. Some had been cut as prisms, some roughed out. Many had scrollwork features under small stone balconies. The one they were parked in front of had sandstone pillar-type blocks around windows, which were all framed with master carpentry of dark brown beeswax-coated artwork. Antiqued copper adorned the exterior hardware of the windows and the flashing hoods above them. A wide, wrought-iron balcony in the center of the third floor had a rounded, standing-seam copper roof. The main door was double, with beveled glass and bright brass hardware, with ornate, large wall lamps flickering on each side.

The doorman, dressed sharply and in military uniform, stepped promptly to the curb and opened the door for Klement's carriage, helping Mrs. Metternich step out. Once the kids jumped out and quickly settled into a proper public state of mind by their mother, they walked up the four steps to the half-round stoop, and were greeted by the head of the house, who promptly led them in.

Their carriage pulled away, and the second one approached and stopped in front of the home. Monika exited, then Wenzel stepped out, and he grabbed the several personal bags Monika had kept with her, joining her as they went into the residence. The entry space was wide, with a statue in the center of the back of the room, made of marble, on a round platform covered in intricate carvings of leaves surrounding a map of the Austro-Hungarian Empire at its center. The statue was of Ferdinand the First, astride a horse arrayed for battle, with a saber high above his head. The statue was a new addition; it was not there the last time Monika had visited. Ferdinand the First ascended to the throne on March 2nd of last year. It was exquisite. The surrounding architecture of the statue was half-round, with ornate staircases circling either side, going to the second-floor landing. The carpentry of the railings and staves was incredible, they were each one a fluted pillar wrapped in climbing vines, the end of the bannisters each a wide, downturned five-pointed leaf bound continuously and flawlessly to the carvings on each vertical stave. From what she had been told, the staircase and its components were original to the house, dating back over a hundred and fifty years, and had taken three years for the carpentry alone. Gold filigree was laced into the designs, looping in and out of the carvings, and along the center of the leaves at the ends, and the center of the handrails for the whole length of the bannister. The walls of the room alternated between mahogany panels and light pine sections, framed specifically to encase important paintings, far too many to name. On each side was a wide solid oak framed entrance to other rooms, parlor on the left, and on the right a room that served for public functions, forty feet across and a hundred feet long, the length of most of the structure. Only the kitchen and preparatory rooms lay behind it.

"Monika, please excuse us, there are two people waiting for Klement, and I must retire and put the children to bed. The same room you had last time you visited has been prepared for you. Will you be alright if we speak again in the morning?" She was clearly tired from the trip, and so Monika agreed.

"Of course, Mrs. Metternich. Thank you for all of your help, and the hospitality of your home." Monika waved as they proceeded up the stairs, the little ones waving goodbye with sleepy smiles.

She, also, was quite exhausted and looked forward to lying down. She proceeded up the stairway to the right, Wenzel five steps behind, carrying her bags.

"Ma'am, are the things you require for tonight in these bags, or shall I have the remainder of your things brought up tonight as well?" he spoke softly from behind, not wanting to have voices carry if Klement was already busy downstairs.

"Yes, thank you. Everything I require is in these bags," she said, surely to his relief. The thick carpeting on the stairs keeps the footsteps quiet. Upon reaching the second floor, she proceeded to the back of the house, down the hallway of about four more rooms, each rather small and intended for short visits from local officials. At the end of the hall, a smaller, less grand staircase led up and to the left to the third floor, where her room was. It was first on the left, and the imperial-quality door, carved with the relief of an eagle, was painted white with enamel and stood open, so she went straight into the sitting room and sat down.

"Where will you be staying, Wenzel? I am sure the conditions of your oath to my protection do not require your quarters in my immediate vicinity, here in this home. I can feel all around me the protections, and they are surely adequate." Monika was trying to let him retire to wherever he felt most comfortable and not encourage undue closeness.

"Yes, ma'am, you couldn't be safer here. I will be in the next house, the quarters for personal security. If you do need anything, the entrance to our quarters is at the back of the kitchen and goes to the back half of the house on the right of this residence, as seen from the street. There is no connection between the rooms of that structure and the front of that house; the kitchen on the ground floor is the only connecting passage. I will stay there until I receive word

280

from you or Mr. Metternich. Have a good evening, ma'am." He set the bags down, turned, and shut the door behind him.

After a nice, relaxing bath, she came out to the sitting room, having smelled food, and found a delightfully cooked hen with carrots and peas left on the table in the center of the sitting room. She wasn't hungry really until she smelled it. So she ate, lay on the bed, and fell asleep right away.

The next morning, she woke up to the morning light filling the room. She hadn't even moved since the night before, and woke well rested. The sound of the maid bringing breakfast had roused her, and from the bedchamber, she could smell it and was instantly hungry again. She dressed and went in while it was being set on the small round table next to the window that looked down on the small central courtyard.

"Sophie, so nice to see you again!" They had known each other for years now. "Thank you so much, I'm starving!" Monika approached the maid, smiling. She tied her robe and pulled out the chair to sit down.

"Ma'am, we are lucky this time of year, we have ample squeezed oranges for juice at breakfast meals. It's divine. I brought you a green pepper and shredded roast omelet, toast, and coffee. Your customary sugar and cream are here also, along with honey. I always like having you here, ma'am." She smiled, curtsied, and left the room.

She enjoyed the breakfast, savoring it while trying to finish before it went cold. She surveyed the room to see if it had stayed the same. The bedchamber was the same: a very large bed platform, perhaps three feet high, made of ornate oak, well-oiled underneath. Square posts at each corner, with sheer cloth draped around them, with brass ring holders hung from the planked top. Some of the furnishings, from desks to the water table, were of different styles, most of which were gifts to the royal family from renowned craftsmen around the world. Each is unique and incredible, though few matching sets. The sitting room featured couches and lounges arranged around the perimeter, most of which were from Italy and France, with several large tables situated in the center. The nook where she was taking breakfast was a cupola, rounded, fully glazed, and such a nice place to enjoy a fine meal. The floors were polished marble, with several oriental rugs covering most of the open areas, pinned to the floor between the tiles so they don't move under duress.

Today, she was hoping to speak with the Professor to find out what else had happened during their trip to Vienna. The room where the Metternichs kept their magical portraits was a rather small, dark, locked room with no windows, converted from an old store room on the fourth floor. She would have to get the key from him to enter. Additionally, there was a merchant in town she needed to visit, who worked with crystal. For that, she would need Wenzel to accompany her.

After choosing to dress appropriately for a guest of the Metternichs, in a city as stupendous as Vienna, she went downstairs and found Klement reading files in his study. Waiting on the edge of the room, he looked up and noticed her and waved his hand to bring her in.

"Sir, have you any word from the Tellafrogs, or from the professor?" she asked politely, not wanting to disrupt any important work he might be doing.

"No, I have not tried yet, and no news has arrived by post either." He finally looked up and over his glasses at her. "Please, come and have a seat. These are files that the security services have compiled on your friend Runetta. I was going over them to see if I could find any compelling reason she might be involved in all of this. Please, take a look for yourself." He handed her a bound set of documents. Monika sat, took the file, and began looking through it. In a few minutes, she had a question.

"Why do they seem to have loose connections, even employment of these types of wizards, who all end up dead or in prisons? Could that have been the connection to John? Perhaps one of his prisoners is related somehow to this?" She asked, still reading through the file.

"I suspected that, as security measures, we keep lists that all bureaus do on magical criminality. I can find no connection to any of the prisoners that have ever been held at Wormwell and this lady. That said, there is no way of knowing every illicit activity of every person, especially those who are well-monied and secretive. Her family is both," he said, still flipping through the pages. "There is a connection, what it is, I cannot seem to nail down, though."

"If she, or they, are so interested in the events around Raileanu's family, why hasn't she just gone there, why linger here, irritating me?"

"I honestly cannot say." he shut the file he had, and stood. "Here, take the key to the portrait room, and see if anyone is available to speak with from over there. I apologize, but for space's sake, I do not have a portrait of John or Mary Tellafrog here. Only the professor, and with the hours he has put in trying to communicate with both sides of the world and scour records of illness, he may not be available yet." He reached into his vest pocket and pulled out a large key on a silver chain, unhooked its keeper through the buttonhole, and handed it to Monika. "You remember where it is, yes?"

"Yes, sir, I do. I will locate you if I find anything out," she said.

"Here," he stacked up the five or six file binders and handed them to her, "leave these in the room as well. They will be safe enough to be locked in there. Thank you, Monika. Hopefully, we will solve this. I have several appointments in town today and will not return until this evening. Have a good day, but make sure and take Wenzel with you anywhere you go outside this house. Oh, and the porter said your crates and trunks are in a small room off the central courtyard. That way, you can work outdoors in the good light, undisturbed by the operations of the house and away from prying eyes. Publishing magical works is big business these days, and I'd hate your and Raileanu's hard work to slip out before you're ready." He left with a smile, out to the foyer.

Monika went straight up the staircases to the room, un-locked the door, and tucked the key under the waist ribbon of her dress so it wouldn't slip out. Inside, she lit the two lamps that were on either side of the room and looked for the professor's portrait. Unfortunately, he was not in it. Just his empty chair. She set the files down on the desk and went out into the hallway, locking the door behind her. When she went back downstairs, Klement was already gone for the day. She looped the chain of the key around the ribbon once more and tucked the key itself behind the bow on her back. She went to the housekeeper, Sophie, and asked her to see if Wenzel was available to go into the town to the shop she needed to visit. After a few minutes, she returned with Wenzel and then resumed her duties.

"Ma'am, while you are stunning and quite metropolitan in that dress, causing a stir with your beauty is perhaps less advisable than a more subdued and useful attire ensemble. Forgive me, but your security is my responsibility, and I think it would be wise," he said as meekly as he could, his head slightly bowed down, his eyes barely glancing at her.

"I spoke for some time with Klement, and he didn't mention anything was wrong with what I am wearing." Monika lifted the edges of her skirt out with her hands, looking over the dress, trying to find a fault. "It is rare anymore I can dress as a lady should, and enjoy the gracious nature of a beautiful city, sir. I don't think I will change," she said sternly and definitively, dropping the edges of the skirt and crossing her arms.

"Ma'am, if you would allow me to explain. Mr. Metternich is still wildly in love with his wife, consistently proclaiming her to all as the greatest lady of Europe ever known. I doubt he is as taken with your beauty as the rest of us are, and my first impression upon seeing you this morning is that you will cause much more of a commotion than we should invite. Please, if I may, I just received word a moment ago in our quarters that the whole entourage of the Metternichs is invited tonight to a symphony at Wienna Musikvoroian by its director Ferdinand Graf Palffy von Erdad himself. For this, you will be required to dress even more grandly than you are now. Mrs. Metternich has already sent word to the city's pre-eminent dressmaker to meet you here at three o'clock this afternoon to prepare one just for you. The symphony is at eight o'clock. Is that alright?"

Both excited and aghast, Monika decided the totality of the circumstances was decidedly in her favor. Compliments intentionally taken as insults are the tools of maniacs, and she would clearly enjoy the day. Besides, these dresses were diabolical to live with in the heat of August, especially if required to do much walking in them. He was right; if trouble did present itself, it would be best not to be bound tightly, restricting movement and activity.

"Of course, you're right. I will change, I need to go to Swarovski Kristallwelten, and I need to be back before that appointment. Should we take a carriage, or are they otherwise occupied today?"

"They are spoken for, my lady. That shop is only four blocks from here, and with appropriate footwear, is not a chore to reach." he gave her a little bow. "I will wait in the foyer for you. Thank you for understanding what I was trying to convey."

"Well, then, to the wardrobe." She gave him a nod, spun around with renewed purpose, and went back upstairs to change. She chose a tight-waisted, dark blue, floral-patterned dress, with a plain black collar and cuffs. The ankle-length dress would hide her wearing her cork and suede-soled riding boots, which had a built-in sleeve for her wand. She wore a wide black belt with a plain steel buckle and a slide purse attached. Her hair was put in a bun on the nape of her neck. Now she looked more like a governess than any person of notable means. Once back downstairs, Wenzel gave her a smile and bow, and they proceeded out the front doors, held open by the military doorman.

Making a right turn at the sidewalk, they proceeded to the end of the block and went right again. Two blocks further, and the pair crossed a street and walked along the side of the Imperial Gardens.

"Ma'am, have you ever been in the gardens?" Wenzel asked.

"No, I have not," she replied.

"Perhaps Klement, or the Professor, might arrange for you to go one day. I recall being a young boy watching their construction. It was really interesting watching the meticulous planning and construction. When we could, my friends and I would often sneak in and play in the great mounds of earth. I suspect some still sneak in, but once construction was complete and the iron fencing was installed, it became considerably more difficult. They say there are flowering plants in there from around the world."

"I shall ask if it is possible later, I would enjoy that," Monika said, peering through the fencing and shrubbery that encircled the whole ten-acre complex.

"It's just up ahead, ma'am, on the right. I will wait outside." Wenzel pointed to the shop, its sign now clearly visible.

"Thank you, I will not be very long." She said, waiting for him to open the door for her, and she proceeded inside. She had been here twice before, both times commissioning lead crystal cases for rare books she had been responsible for during conservation or restoration. She was delighted to see her acquaintance, Maria Staufer, on the floor of the store. She had devised a technique to house the book, incorporating

287

Monika's own design, which utilized small, specially craft-ed stones in a perforated vial to eliminate all moisture from the enclosure. It wasn't magic, but it was tricky potion making.

"My friend, Monika!" Maria smiled broadly and greeted Monika in the appropriate manner. "What are you wear-ing?" she asked with surprise.

"I am trying to appear quite ordinary, if you don't mind," she quipped back, both still smiling. "Is it working?"

"My dear, you could wear a flour sack and still cause irreparable harm to men! Have you any news about Raileanu's father?"

Monika didn't know how to answer. How could she know about that? Did everyone know? Should she know? This was very off-putting, but she recovered and figured the truth would do; it's always how much truth you provide that can cause harm to people who might just be fishing.

"Raileanu is home with them, we're hoping he gets better soon. I wanted to ask you about the possibility of making a crystal horn frog." Monika tried to quell concern and get her friend thinking about something else.

"Horn frog? What is that? I don't believe I have seen one." Maria stated, with a bemused look on her face, as if Monika was making it up.

"Is anyone else here right now?" Monika asked and looked around.

"No, I am the only one working today."

"Alright, I'll show you." Monika reached for her wand, placed her back to the windowed front of the store, and pro-tected the area in front of her on the counter so no one else could see. She tapped the glass countertop, and an image of the Texas horny toad appeared.

"Oh, my, is that a reptile they have in Texas? It's an incredible little thing, how big are they?" Maria grabbed a piece of paper and a charcoal shard, quickly sketching it. "They look like little dragons, don't they?"

"They're only this size, this is an accurate image, and to scale. Do you think you can make one that I can give to Raileanu's mother as a gift?" Monika smiled as she finished her impressive artwork, making notes about scale and details.

"Yes, I can have this for you ready by the end of the week. Will you be able to pick it up, or shall I send it somewhere?" Maria asked innocently.

Monika didn't want to say where she was staying for obvious reasons, so she decided she, or likely a courier, would pick it up.

"I will be back, thank you so much." Monika pulled twenty Guldens from her waist pouch and gave them to her. "Is that enough?"

"It is, thank you so much for trusting me with this thoughtful gift." Maria smiled, slid the coins from the counter, and went straight to work in the back.

Monika went back out front, found Wenzel standing alert in the entrance inset, and they proceeded back to the house. In less than twenty minutes, she was back and safe. She checked the portraits again, still no luck. Shortly after lunch was set on, and since none of the Metternich family were home, she took lunch with the house staff. She refused to have an entire dining room set up for her alone, with priceless dishes and silverware being used and needing cleaning, just so she could eat lunch.

Less than an hour later, the dress designer, seamstress, and ten apprentices and helpers arrived, with five dresses for her to choose from, all the accoutrements to fit and finish them for a formal concert. Monika hadn't seen this many people attending to her attire since her wedding, and really, really enjoyed the attention, advice, and modern designs and materials. Choosing a cream, richly bronze-colored silk embroidered floral pattern, firm to the waist, with a small bustle, square, low neck. The shoulders were slightly oversized for movement and pleated. The heavy white silk embroidery on the sleeves featured ivy, extending down to the wrist cuffs, where they ended in looping fleur-de-lis patterns. A wide silver ribbon went to a reasonable bow left-of-center, with long streamers dangling down the side of the skirt. Because the concert will require stairs to a box seat and hours of sitting, a wireframe was not considered for the skirt. One of the workers had over a dozen shoes for her to choose from, and Monika chose gloss white open top patent leather pointed toe, with a single gold strap and buckle, and a low heel. She was hoping to be able to walk through the Imperial Gardens after the concert. There would be a full moon tonight, and they were also well lit. Not as impressive or moving in moonlight, but it may be her only opportunity. After three hours of deliberation and work, Monika decided the dress was so nice she wanted to pay for it herself, and they came to an arrangement. After packing up and Monika seeing them to the door, the designer said that the payment was so generous that she would send her personal hairdresser over to help her prepare for the evening.

Monika could not have known this yet, but this was the evening when all the horrible events were going to unfold in Texas, beginning with the tornado. She would know something of the events, however, before she even returned to the Metternich's house that night.

Klement and his entire family returned less than an hour before the concert was due to begin. He had arranged three carriages to take all of them the few blocks to the concert hall. Stepping out of the front doors, three low, open-top white carriages were waiting, the imperial crest posted prominently on the sides. Lanterns hung on the front corners. The horses were dressed in full ceremonial regalia, and the driver wore a tuxedo and top hat. Monika and Wenzel rode in one vehicle with the two eldest children, Klement and his wife, and their youngest child in another, and his security in a third. The moon was huge and orange as it peeked over the horizon when they left, and the air was filled with the scent of honeysuckle, wisteria, and warmth, with not a chill to be found.

It was only about a ten-minute ride to the concert hall, and there was a line of carriages waiting to offload their important passengers. Within another fifteen minutes, the group was entering what many consider to be the most acoustically perfect concert hall in all of Europe. Its fixtures and furnishings were exquisite. Everything gleamed and spoke of opulence, and as they made their way to the box seating in the center, left of the stage, they took their seats while the orchestra warmed up. It was undoubtedly one of the most emotionally moving structures; every fiber of one's being could feel the power of the sound in this place. Monika truly wished only one other thing - that Raileanu could be here with her.

The concert lasted just over two hours, and after conversing with Klement at intermission, he agreed to pen her a letter giving her permission to walk the gardens before returning home. The garden was protected from the use of magic of any kind, as it was technically for the imperial family and their guests' use only, so he instructed the carriage driver and Wenzel to wait outside. The entrance was strictly controlled, so there was no need to worry about anything menacing occurring inside.

Directly after the concert, the two went straight to the main gate of the garden. Wenzel got down and handed the letter to the guards, whom he knew personally. After a brief discussion, they invited her in. They unlocked the large iron gate and explained the pathways and which areas were best lit. Monika thanked them and went in alone.

The pathways were wide, meticulously maintained of raked gravel and mortared stone depending on the feature and its propensity to retain water, she supposed. The arbored tree varieties, groupings of striking colors of flowers standing tall on mounds, and flowing down slopes were incredible. When Raileanu comes back, she would have him bring her in daylight, definitely, and educate her on the proper names of every variety of tree and flower. She strolled around, smelling flowers she didn't recognize, and realizing how few of these curated species she had ever seen in moonlight. Near the center of the park was a large stand of knurled, twisted oaks surrounding an ornate bench, so she sat to let her feet relax for a few moments. Monika rubbed her calves, which were not accustomed to these shoes, hoping she didn't already have blisters.

"Well, well. If it isn't my best friend, Monika," a familiar voice said from somewhere under the dark stand of trees.

Monika, still with her right hand by her leg, reached up to her thigh, where her wand was held in place by a garter, and pulled it out sharply. She knew it was Runetta.

"Darling, that won't do either of us any good here, surely you know that." She slid from around the wide trunk of one of the trees, not twenty feet away. "Do you know what this is?" Runetta said, holding a large, clear glass jar with something in it.

Monika was furious that this woman was here; her wand hand shook with fear and anger. She refused to lower her wand, pointing it right at Runetta. Monika stood up, turned right towards her, and approached a few steps.

"What are you doing here? One call and the bodyguard will be here to seize you, which he has the authority to do!" Monika said, glaring at her.

"Oh, dear, I am only here to show you this. Do you know what it is?" Runetta slinked closer, jar in left hand, her wand in right, letting it bounce off her right shoulder. "Here, let me show you." She tapped the jar with her wand, and it filled with white light.

"How did you, what is that in the jar?" Monika kept drawn on her, now with both hands, not knowing if her own magic would work at all, and how Runetta's was working.

"Deary, my family did the enchantments on this garden. I can do what I want here; you, I am afraid, cannot." Runetta made it to the bench, and when Monika backed up a few steps, she sat gently down, letting her right arm drape in a flamboyant, exaggerated way on the top of the bench. She extended her left leg across most of the bench, her right on the ground. Then she looked at the jar with her face turning slowly toward it. "It is a heart jar. I have one for every man in my service. I have a whole room of them, it's how I keep track of who is still doing their jobs."She held it up even closer to her face, illuminating her green eyes as she gazed in. "You see, as long as this copy of their heart keeps beating, I know they're still doing my bidding. This one," she spun it around in her hand, enticing Monika to look at it, "has stopped working." Runetta made a ridiculous, dramatic frown.

"What does that mean, what are you saying??" Monika threw her wand hand down by her side.

"Well, this jar and the heart inside belonged to one of my most productive employees. And it isn't beating anymore. I love to enter that little room I have." She set the jar down on the bench. "The beats can tell me whether they are sleeping, loving, killing, I have learned to know all of their beatings. When I walk into that room and close my eyes, I am filled with the power of life in my service. When one of these stops beating, well, it upsets my happy rhythm."

"That's a human heart!? You're showing me this is now a threat." Monika shouted. "WENZEL!"

"This jar is only the proof I needed to tell you that man of yours is really something. I simply *must* meet him now."

Runetta raised her eyebrow, pursed her lips into a twisted smile, raised her hand with a wand in it, gave it a little swirl, and was gone.

Wenzel and two guards reached her, but a moment later, while Monika was still staring at the jar on the bench, her uncontrollable anger still caused her to shake. She barely remembered to tuck her wand away on the far side of their approach.

"What is THAT?" Wenzel asked, pointing at it, a look of disgust on his face. The jar was still lit for a moment, then it faded. They all saw what was in it. "Was that... her?"

"Yes. I must get to the Metternich's right away!" Monika picked up her skirt and began to run to the carriage. Wenzel grabbed the jar and told the guards to patrol the garden looking for a lady wearing black with dark hair. He said he would take his charge to safety. He chased after her, catching up and taking hold of her upper arm to help her be steadier at speed. The guards had left one person at the gate, but the gate itself was open. He stood at his post, holding a lantern, and asked what had happened.

"A tall woman in dark clothing with dark hair is in the garden, and has threatened my charge! Secure the gate, and let no one in or out until you see your sergeant!" Wenzel told him as they loaded into the carriage.

"Driver, to the Metternich house right away!" Wenzel shouted, and the leads popped the back of the horses, who jerked off the line, jolting the passengers, who couldn't care less. In just two full strides, the horses' shod hooves were rapidly echoing on all the stone buildings.

"Tell me what happened!" Wenzel demanded. "Are you alright?"

"Just get me to Klement. Thank you for being there so quickly." A little out of breath, she managed to get out. "She said that jar was some copy of the heart of one of her servants, who is dead. Then she said she had to meet Raileanu. Something terrible has happened. I know it."

Monika unbuckled her shoes en route and handed them to Wenzel, who was looking very confused. She wasn't taking any additional time to get inside, regardless of social appearances. When they pulled to a stop, she leaped out and ran barefoot to the door, opened it before the doorman could get out of his chair, and ran inside. She considered yelling, but didn't want to alarm the children if possible. Wenzel came in right behind her, jar and shoes in hand.

"Where is Mr. Metternich? I must speak with him right now!" Monika said loudly to the doorman.

"I believe he is in the study," pointing upstairs. She ran straight to it, holding her dress higher to run up the stairs, Wenzel close behind. She burst through the door, and he was indeed, with his head in his hands, and snapped it up when she came to the desk.

"Runetta was in the Imperial Garden. She was able to use magic there," she spoke as she huffed. Wenzel set the jar on the desk.

"Do you know what this is, sir?" Wenzel pointed disgustedly at it.

"I'm afraid I do," Klement was unsurprised.

"What, what is it, Klement, what do you know? What has happened? She, Runetta, said she had to meet Raileanu," Monika demanded.

"Wenzel, would you please excuse us? Perhaps it is prudent to ensure the grounds are secure. Thank you," Klement said calmly. Wenzel bowed and left the room.

"Please, Monika, sit down. I have spoken with the professor. Much has happened just this evening. First, Raileanu is fine, safe, and unharmed. I promise. Something has happened, however, at their home, that is connected to Runetta, his father's illness, all of it."

Monika collapsed onto a couch, exhausted from running, fear, adrenaline, and now this. It is so much that she can barely believe it herself. What Klement went on to lay out for her, however, made her head throb, and then she was acutely hurt. The professor had seen almost everything through his portrait that had transpired at the Tellafrogs. He had known somewhat of the dangers the high elf was trying to identify and contain, but not the extent of the history involved for all of us. Until the end, with the elf's telling of the past, its dangers imposing on our whole world now, honestly, none of us could have known. Runetta and whoever she was working with felt it was just a dark tool of magical power they desired. It is so much more than that. It unfolded to both of them, that willing or unwilling, they were all part of something none could escape.

CHAPTER FIFTEEN

S itting there, bloody from my head wound, with the imagery and smells of death still lingering in my family home, with a seven foot tall High Elf sprawled on my couch, expired from battle with an assassin who killed almost six people in mere minutes, I really wished I didn't know of any of this. My concerns of a week ago were on such unimportant things, plants, genus, seed packets being properly stored, soil samples, ugh, so utterly meaningless. I had no way to contact anyone; my friends in London and Vienna could be at risk. Tears of helpless rage began hitting the floor as I leaned forward onto my knees, and I let out a horrible, primal scream for as long as I could, clawing the floorboards with my fingers. I had to do something, anything. Grabbing the letter from Father Callious, I scrawled on the bottom:

The elf is dead. Mother is dead. Bandos is dead. The three brothers at the mission are dead. Barthow almost died. I almost died! I am all alone here with the dead elf. I have recorded his last words here; they are quite important, and I have no idea what to do now. Protect Monika.

That's all I could think of now. So many times, I should have ignored damned tradition and social rules, and told Monika how I felt. Too many times. Now I am truly alone, and I wasn't going to wait another minute. If I could ever get back to her.

I took a carving knife from the kitchen, and pinned the letter from Father Callious with my note, writing facing the portrait. I didn't even know if it would work. I didn't want to stay inside the house anymore. I needed to calm down and think. Was there anything I could do? I rummaged through the box of my father's things, which my mother had collected from around the house and intended to store later. I found Father's pipe and tobacco pouch. He hadn't used it in years, even though it sat prominently in the room next to his chair, and what was in the pouch was still good. Surely it was a charmed pouch. Papa had grown his own tobacco variety for several years, and since their flowers bloomed year-round and their fragrant aroma was pleasing, Momma allowed him to continue growing it. The bees especially liked it. I took both and went out in the front yard, to the bench table, and sat facing away from the table with my elbows on it, leaning back against the table's edge. I thought about burning the whole house down to try and erase from my mind what had happened, but after some deliberation, I decided that wouldn't help.

I reached into the pouch and found his nail, then cleaned the bowl, scraping the carbon residue from the last time my father had used it. He found it helpful when working on a complex problem. It may have been the only time he did use it, come to think of it. I packed it and lit it with a match, and it did calm me a bit. So I sat trying not to think about anything for a while.

When I had finished enjoying the pipe, I had resolved not to burn down my childhood home. I even struggled with a bout as I had as a young man, with wanting to run off into the wilderness, this time never to return. That would not honor father, mother, Arterous, Monika, or me, and this one was easier to shake off than they had been in my youth. I refused to blame the Elf for doing so little, and, suspecting the dangers, I came to understand his concerns about acting too soon. However, I had also decided to load up every tool of retribution I could find, be ready to travel, and wait on Barthow. I took Momma's pistol, a gift from the rangers, and found my father's old holster belt rig. I hung my saddle holster on it, giving me two. I packed every ball and ounce of powder in the house into my shoulder satchel. I also took my father's magical copy of Bowie's famous knife and his horizontal sheath and hung them on the back of the pistol belt, handle to the right. I packed up some salted pork and sourdough rounds from the house in the satchel as well. I filled a feed bag with oats and alfalfa and tied it to the saddle. I went inside my bedroom and was gathering up my bedroll and coat when I caught a glimpse of myself in the bathroom mirror. I had blood from my hairline running down my face, and over the course of the last two hours, I had managed to smear it pretty much everywhere. I set everything down on my bed and went to clean it up. I consciously tried not to look myself in the eye, because I wanted to see what that vengeance looked like in the reflected form of my enemy's eye when I got my gnarled hands on whoever these people are. But I couldn't help it, and what I saw satisfied me that I was going to be fearfully ready for the next chapter of my life. They would not be.

"Raileanu! You around, boy?" Barthow hollered inside the house.

"Be right down." I dried my face, grabbed my gear, and went downstairs. "What did you find? Is there anything left that we need to clean up?"

"Naw, I was lucky and weren't nobody around thar. I got them boys buried right, and sealed up that secret room good, all rocked up, sealed tight." Barthow whipped around, drawing his pistol in the same motion, pointing it at a spot in the corner of the room, and right there, the professor appeared, holding his hands up high.

"Hold it, Barthow, it is the professor!" I yelled.

"Yes, good ranger, I'm a friend, I've been watching from my portrait. I wanted to wait until you returned before I came. I have someone here who can help us understand what has happened. Please, may he come now?" the professor asked nervously.

Barthow holstered his pistol and said, "Someone better start tellin' us what the hades is a'goin on around here! I had half my hide damn near burnt off, buddy! This boy's whole family's been killed here and has been all clobbered up; he's got a dead High Elf on his darn couch. Hell, this whole place has to be run with magic, and ain't nobody left here with it! I got Camanches, Apaches, settlers, Messican' bandits, cattle rustlers, magical card swindlers, I ain't got time for any more 'round here!"

"Please, sir. May I invite my friend to help explain? It will help all of us I feel." the professor sat gingerly down in a chair and lowered his hands to his knees.

"Do it, git him here then." Barthow sat down, pulled his flask, which wasn't Swiss snow melt, and took a few good tugs.

"Go ahead, Professor," I said.

A thin line from the ceiling to the floor lit up for a second, and another High Elf appeared as the line moved from left to right. This one wore clothing that was sheer white, form-fitting, with a long silvery-grey cloak. His hair was also long, straight, and white. He had the same sharp, long features, lit blue eyes, and pointed ears as Kleet had. He glanced slowly around, and at Kleet. The line of light then flipped horizontally, and went over Kleet from top to bottom, him slipping somewhere else behind the line, and was gone. He turned his attention to the orb next, the line fell on it, and it, too, was gone. This Elf then turned back to us.

"My name is Corfus. First, give me the pages you wrote of what Kleet told you. They are not safe outside our protection. I have watched Kleet trying to help solve this, and I agree with his decisions. Had either of us known sooner, we would have been able to prevent this from happening. We are sorry. You should be aware that this is no small matter. Kleet was over fourteen thousand years old. There can be no more elves. There are a little more than a hundred of us now." Corfus held out his hand, gesturing for me to give him the notes I had scribbled as Kleet lay dying. I pulled them from my vest and gave them to him. He nodded slowly, then continued. "Trying to protect the world God made from the evils the hand of man has wrought is the mission we have assumed all these thousands of years. The time has come for us to involve more of you to help. Changes are already happening across the world that will begin to accelerate towards the singularity that caused the catastrophes of the past. The one that led to the end of the last two ages, for example. We are products of that event. As are all the creatures you call magical. As are all of you who wield what you call magic. Relics of that time are incredibly dangerous, as you have discovered, so we must find them faster than we can alone. While not intended to perform diabolical atrocities, the knowledge they possess and can gift to anyone, able to communicate with them, control of energies and forces that surround all of us, that none of you can imagine."

Barthow took another long nip, closed the lid, and let his hand fall in disgust into his lap. "You must know I didn't understand nuthin' you just said. So you fellers watched all this, and did nothin'?"

"Barthow, to capture one of us would mean the end of all things. That is paramount. It cannot happen." Corfus said with a calm cadence. "May I continue?"

Barthow waved his hand with indignation in the air and looked away. "Even if ordinary people were to find these artifacts, they would be able to learn their secrets in time, and destroy everything through hubris and good intentions. I am asking if all three of you can be trusted to help us in this endeavor. If you are employed by us, you will report unnatural events, strange rumors, and sightings of unusual phenomena observed on the earth or in the sky. If you prefer, we can employ you directly to hunt for these items and those who seek them. The events surrounding Monika in Austria are directly linked. The woman, Runetta, who has shadowed her over the last few days, is linked to a group that possesses some of what we seek. They required that Orb use some of it. What they have, they cannot use as of yet, but this is a primitive version of the CIGI orb technology." I looked at Barthow, who was rolling his eyes and playfully mocking the Elf as he spoke. The Elf couldn't see him, but I could. The Professor waved a stern hand at him to stop, so he took another tug, but he did stop. "We believe there are over a dozen still scattered around the world, inactive, dormant if you will, like this one was until the right circumstances arose. It took requests from the priest, reached out to that prisoner, and, being magical, was able to communicate with him to gain information on the creation of a Root Wand. The particles that travelled through the root system between the two ended up on your father. Those same particles assembled the Root Wand, harnessing the unseen powers of the earth. It was an old magic, where wands made of tree branches could focus and direct these energies. In contrast, Root Wands could discharge dangerous energies, but only by drawing the life from the user until they died. The particles then move onto the person using it, and eat away life until there is no more."

"Is that what happened at the Digger's place? It's what killed them?" I asked, starting to comprehend how it was all linked now.

"There is a truth to your Bible, in that faith must not be put in sorcerers or witches, but only God. In the events described in ancient writings from around the world, although the exact time frames mentioned there may omit the severe expanse of time. This ancient technology led to a level of civilization you cannot imagine. All turned inwards, to themselves, and fell into increasingly animalistic, selfish behaviors, coupled with immense power. The truths, reasons, and my own personal experiences over fourteen thousand years prove that placing power and hope in the creations of man, or in 'magic' at all, leads to destruction. It is simply the focused energies of the world that God made, in ways I cannot explain, yet in a way you can understand. They are not divine, nor are the users of it. They, like we once were, are just people. Only the spirit that we are all given is divine, from God, and to understand the world and our place in it, you must keep faith in Him. Perhaps later, as you travel the world in these duties, you can understand more." Corfus spoke the same way throughout all this, rotating his gaze to each of us equally. It was odd behavior, but their lack of connection with humankind might explain it.

"We High Elves care only about one thing, amassing knowledge, and now securing the relics and artifacts from the previous worlds of men that these tools destroyed. We chose this in the previous time of advanced men, to amass all knowledge, to remain unchanged by time or disease, but in doing so, we cannot comprehend emotion, nor love, nor reproduce. We do, however, hope to stop this procession down the same road as before, without losing all of us before we can. Raileanu, Professor Templeton, will you help us? Barthow?" Again, turning to each of us as he asked.

"Help? Hell, boy, I didn't understand half them words you used, I don't know how much help I could be to a, a, HIGH ELF! Y'all can just wander around doin yer own magic, no wand, what do you want me to do again?" he snorted at Corfus. "I can tell ya when I see stuff, I reckon. Whatever that's worth."

I just sat still, thinking. How much help can I be with problems so significant and worldwide that the magical world doesn't even know about them or what's going on? This is crazy. I had no magic, and the events of this night showed how unfit I was for this. What about Monika? How could I get to her now? That is all I really could think of anymore.

"Barthow, I have not seen a more adept man at tending to the needs of people and important matters over such a vast area in several thousand years. You understand the land here, the people, keeping the peace; you are a great benefit to the Republic of Texas, beyond measure. I would ask no more than you have already done. Here." Corfus handed Barthow a silver medallion, hung from a silver necklace. "All you need to do, if you need me, is to hold this in your hand. The mere heat of your hand gives it power, and when you speak, I will hear it. Nothing more."

"Well, fella, I am susceptible to flattery now, if'n givin' you a holler when somethin's afoot is all I gotta do, well, shoot. I'm in," he took it with a smile, trying to be funny, I suppose.

"How can I get to Monika? Right now, she is all I am concerned about. My whole family is dead, an entire old

Spanish mission's company is killed, you got your Orb thing, can I just get to her first?" I asked.

The professor stood up and said, "Monika, Klement, they're all fine. In fact, I have spoken with Corfus, and you will be able to have a map showing all the runewheels in the world. They are already ensuring that they work for you with no additional preparation. You can go straight to Vienna tonight if you wish." That did calm my thoughts, which were becoming frantic now, swirling around Monika and landing on her, maybe the only person I care for left alive. I felt the panic of her slipping away ease as I heard a path laid out for me.

"I need a way my home here can be sealed off from the rest of the world, that bastard came straight in, dislocating with no trouble. I want to keep my home as it is, but I also want to make it impossible for anyone else to enter without one of us letting them in. If I decide to help in this, finding these things, these CIGI or whatever, I will want a place to rest, to safely call home." I said, surely that wouldn't be asking too much in return.

Corfus tilted his head a little, closed his eyes for a moment, and then looked at us again. "Done. No force known on this world can see, smell, hear, or otherwise detect that this place exists, and the only way in is you, or you in physical contact with another person without duress, through the same entrance you had before. This stands regardless of your decision to help us."

"Please, allow Barthow as well to enter. Corfus, I MUST get to Vienna and my fiancé. Barthow must be allowed to enter and care for my place until I return." I asked with as much humility as I could gather after this day. Corfus nodded, shut his eyes for a moment after giving Barthow a good look, and opened his eyes and nodded again.

"I don't mean to cut this short, but I kinda have to git back to the troubles I had a couple hours ago before all this started. If none of y'all mind," he held up his hand, palm up, checking the room before leaving.

"Barthow. Please, collect and send information. You cannot speak of this to anyone; it would only harm what we are all trying to achieve. Men cannot hear of a power of any kind without seeking it for themselves. Intentions will not save them regarding these tools." Corfus explained.

"Gotcha. Don't go worryin' over me. Most o' the folks I deal with every day wouldn't believe most of what I see and do. I got it." He set his hat tight on his head, winked, and with that, he was gone.

"Would you like to go tonight, to Vienna, or will you need to stay a while here?" The Professor asked. I sat still, looking at the floor where Momma had died, now torn between fleeing this place for Monika or staying only long enough to come to grips with the last few hours. I didn't answer.

"I will be going straight to Vienna with Corfus from here, explaining everything to Klement and Monika as well, they are part of this now as well. What part of it will be up to them, but it is terribly important I relay your hardships and current safety as soon as possible." The professor did want me to go tonight, I could tell. Honestly, I wanted to stay overnight, perhaps in my own bed, in the company of my parents, for a while.

"I'm staying tonight with my parents, sir. I will write a note for you to deliver to Monika for me, if you will please." I said.

"Of course, please, do write it, they are waiting to hear from us now," he said. He had obviously relayed some of the events to them.

I knew what I needed to say. I didn't want to delay them any longer and didn't want to delay what had to be said to her another minute. Here is what I wrote as quickly as I could.

My Dearest Monika,

Please listen carefully to what the professor and Corfus have to explain to you. I am alright, barely. Only through the sacrifice of others, Kleet included, did I survive. They are asking us to undertake a dangerous and imperative path. I have lost everyone, my whole family. I do not want to lose you. I do not want to lose another minute of my life without you. I love you completely, wholly, and will for all of my days. I intend to propose to you immediately upon my arrival. I must mourn here for the night, and say prayers over my parents before leaving and perhaps not returning for some time. I will avenge their deaths by accepting this assignment, but I will not choose this path without you at my side. I will not. Please consider your options carefully, both for my arrival and for the course we take on these other matters as well. Please be safe. I will come tomorrow as soon as I finish saying goodbye here.

All My Love,

Raileanu

I sealed it with wax at Father's desk, where he did all his work for the prison, and took it to the professor. "Tell her, as soon as I can in the morning," he nodded and tucked it into his coat pocket. Corfus reached over and handed me a silver medallion, like the one he gave Barthow, and nodded.

"Raileanu. You are right to tend to your parents' souls, to ensure you are right with them. None of the High Elves ever knew their parents; all of them died thousands of years ago, and we have never known children. Each of us feels the dim shadow of a soul and knows that our very creation was wrong. It is why we endeavor to right the wrongs of the past worlds. The eternal nature of the soul God created is one of the immeasurable truths of all existence. Thank you for honoring it."

"You will take Arterous with you to Klement? Beg him for my forgiveness, I could not have helped, nor saved him in the brave final acts of his life." I choked up halfway through and had to pause. Once I cleared my throat a few times, I decided I had said enough and just nodded. Tears fell from my eyes as I nodded, despite my attempt to hold them in.

"Of course, I heard your mother say he was upstairs. I will indeed take him. Be safe, my friend. I will see you shortly," the Professor said.

With that, both Corfus and the professor left the same way they came. Their arrival in Vienna, I'm sure, will be quite a surprise. I decided to drag a chair and a pot of coffee out to the tomb at the end of the back yard, and stay awake as long as I could with my parents. Their love and wisdom will be the gift I will miss the most in this horrible episode. When the pot was ready, I took an old enameled steel cup and the pot in one hand, the chair back in the other, and made my way past Momma's little gardens to the obsidian monolith. At this hour, it was realistically only a few hours to dawn.

I sat there, swinging between trying to say the Lord's Prayer, tears, thanking them for all they did in bringing me up, and apologizing for losing my magic. Each time, I could feel them comforting me, reassuring me that I hadn't ever failed them. I didn't finish a single cup of coffee. Each time I tried to drink, oh, the mess I made, it just reminded me of how good Momma's coffee was. I gave up trying to have any coffee, even before the pot went cold. I told them what Kleet said regarding the dragon, and I imagined them responding that they knew. Of course they did, now. The last thing I remember was trying to collate and grasp every memory, lesson, and anything else they had ever done for me, taught me, or hoped for me in my whole life, as far back as I could remember, and packing it all into the front of my mind and heart. I would need it for support, defense, cause, and purpose in the new and dangerous life laid out before me.

A rascally woodpecker woke me, hammering away at a long-branched post oak beside the tomb. When McCort saw I was awake, he gave me a good morning screech as well. I was really sore now, cramped from falling asleep in a table chair. The sun had begun crossing the top edge of our dell, and the brilliant colors of it passing along the obsidian also showed the changes Kleet had made. Mom and Dad's names were now interwoven in the center, with their respective dates included. Their likenesses were also made to lie next to each other atop the lid, holding hands. It was more fitting than anything I could have given them, or even imagined, for that matter. I wiped my face with my sleeve; the runoff from my nose and tears had mixed with blown dust, caking my face like a dirty toddler.

"Mom and Dad, I guess I have to be going, those murderous bastards have earned a visit from me and the rest. What they have done cannot be allowed to stand, nor can it be allowed to happen to anyone else. The place is safe, and it's going to be my home now. Thank you, both, I love you, and miss you terribly already." I told them. I slapped my pants with my hat, frowned, and turned around. I gathered up the equipment for the horse and went to saddle up my ride. I took my rope and made a halter for Arterous's horse. I was going to lead her out and let them both loose when I got to the Runewheel. I would switch back and forth between them and get there before sunset today, arriving in Vienna before dark. Hopefully, with the orb thing gone, its tendrils stripped of their power, and heck, half the people in this area killed by that henchman, it should be uneventful.

I felt several times on the trip that I should be more affected by the recent events. Each time I considered this, I realized my brain was reorganizing itself, in such a frantic way that it was almost like watching a shell game involving a thousand cups and a hundred walnuts. All I could do was sit back and wait. I couldn't concentrate on my father for more than a minute without seeing what I now know was ancient, uncaring technology of some kind consuming him. What did any of that even mean? My mother, taken by brute force by people I didn't even know existed, searching for something no one knew of. So many circles and loops being remade in my head, I quit trying. I knew who they were, how they lived, how they raised me, and that they were gone now. The rest simmered at a temperature in my head I couldn't touch yet. I couldn't ever show up as a surprise for them unannounced and see their happiness. I couldn't ever hug them again. Or send letters and posts about the amazing plant life I had found. I wouldn't be able to shop year-round in all the interesting lands I would visit for handcrafted Christmas gifts. They would never see me married or hold their grandchildren. The only semblance of a family I might ever have is on the other side of the world, if she would have me. All I knew for certain now was that I had to get to Monika.

By five o'clock in the afternoon, I had passed the three-quarter mark of the trip. Checking the compass every half-hour after the stop to switch horses kept me heading in the correct direction. I ran across little more than some wild pigs under a clump of low mesquites the whole time. Switching the horses and letting them drink their fill each time from the cornbread pan in my pack, filled from my bottomless flask, the plan was going well. I should be at the Runewheel just after dark, about nine o'clock. I figured that the arrival in London would be unmet by anyone, and God willing, I would have the strength left after that shift to try and go straight to Vienna. The last leg of the trip, I swapped horses with about an hour to go. I passed a creek that had good water in it, not stagnant or full of skeeter larvae, so I let my horse go and went straight on at a good trot to the spot the compass pointed to.

When I arrived, the moon was about halfway to its zenith, and the whole prairie and rock outcropping were lit up like a cloudy day. I took all the tack and saddle off him, gave him another good drink, and thanked him for all his work in our short time together. McCort was back with me now, as it was dark, and nobody would see us together in this place. I told

Arterous' horse to try and find some good folks to throw in with, and to stay away from bandits, as they lean towards mistreating animals now and again. He gave me a snort 'yes' and I rubbed his nose, then turned him away with his mane, and gave him a little slap on the rear so he knew he could go. I packed up the pan and tack, tying them to the saddle, threw the saddlebags and bedroll over my shoulder, picked up the saddle, and rested it on the Runewheel. I checked the compass, found the mark I needed, and held the horn of the saddle with my left hand and traced the rune with my right.

This time, it went smoother, quicker. Maybe like having your whole body sucked through a straw and let loose on the other end, without it hurting. My head really did hurt after, but I may have held my neck tight as I did it, trying to hold onto the saddle and reach too far to the rune. Well, it was alright until I landed and fell on my backside, and the saddle fell on top of me! Quite uncomfortable, I pushed it off and sat up in the dark room.

I was glad the Runewheels were working without all that blood hooey, but I don't care much for fumbling around in the dark. I stood up and let the saddlebags fall off my shoulder to the ground. My right hand fell naturally onto the grip of my pistol.

"Well, hello there, handsome," an unfamiliar woman's voice said. It was unsettling, but not threatening. Then I was frozen in place. Damnit. This had to be the woman tracking Monika, and I can't even pull the pistol that would stop her. She lit up the room with the tip of her wand, filling it with golden light. She was tall, slender, dressed in black, with a devious eye. Yep, that's her alright. I have never wanted to hurt a woman for anything, but I was already considering on the ride to the runewheel what I'd do if I came across her. She was right to freeze me, I would kill this woman.

"Is that little mark on your head my fault? I'm sorry about that." Her bottom lip pooched out like a pouty child. "He was one of my best servants. I'm amazed an ordinary man could have even scratched him. Or was it the Elf? Presumably the Elf. They are so tedious in their unbelief and interference. Shame," she mused out loud to herself.

"Oh, that bastard killed plenty, lady. The Elf killed him, sure enough, but he died from his wounds as well. Had that bastard not been dead already, I would've gotten him myself. I was about ready to rip his throat out with my teeth. But the Elf ripped his meat from his bones first. I'll settle for his saucy puppet master, though. Pray I never meet you again, lady." I seethed.

"No worries about that, dear, you won't ever encounter me again. Your importance has evaporated as far as I am concerned. Just stay away from those relics, if you know what I mean, you handsome devil. I brought you here so we might have a moment to ourselves, so you know to stay out of my way in the future, and as a reminder, as all good lessons have, something to think about..." she drug the bright tip of her wand across my chin, then tapped my nose. Instantly, every single bone in my body began to ache, my joints felt like they were boiling in a pot, pain like I had only experienced with malaria, but this was like two weeks of malarial pain in an instant, then she and the light walked around behind me, and was gone.

I was released after she was gone, and collapsed to the floor in agony, my face distorted and stretching the edges of my eyes and mouth, wincing uncontrollably. I now understood all too well the heebeegeebees Monika had from just seeing her the first time. Gross. She oozed diabolical filth and darkness. Damnit, I was sore, and trying to fight the saddle and runeshift, then fight being frozen and boiled by the witch, I don't know if I have another shift in me right away, from wherever this is. I fumbled around, joints not moving naturally, and although the incitement of pain was gone, the lingering effect was much like a rope burn, but on my whole body. What did she mean by she brought me here? Where is here? I finally found a crack of light under a door and crawled to open it. It was the same basement where I stayed in London with the Professor before. I decided to go find some of the potion the professor gave me before my trip last time. It helped. Fumbling around the room from memory, I found the door to the room I slept in, and there was, in fact, a candle lit on the table for me. It would be very early in the morning here; maybe the housekeeper is awake, waiting for me, so I should go upstairs and announce my arrival.

She was up, reading a book on the magical history of England from the eleventh century, and stood smiling as I came up the stairs.

"Glad to see you made it alright, son. Please, I have a meal ready, it will take just a moment to warm for you, here, sit down." She pulled out a chair. When she warmed the chicken pot pie, I realized I was starving. I hadn't even thought about eating the whole day. I could have had some of what I'd packed, but I was preoccupied.

"Here, I also mixed you an iced tea with that mushroom medicine you had last time. Drink that first while I get your pie and rolls ready with butter." She handed it to me, and I drank the whole thing at once without stopping. By the time the plate hit the table, my head and neck muscles were already relieved. I thought about telling her about that woman in the basement, but didn't want to worry her. She was clearly here to intimidate me, and the professor would be better suited to decide what to tell her or when, so I refrained.

By the end of the badly needed meal, I didn't realize how much I had neglected my nourishment, I felt much, much better, and was fit to shift again. Dawn was breaking here in London, with steaming rain beating the walls, and I didn't want to keep her any longer worried with me than needed.

"Raileanu, the professor said you would need to go to Vienna, and this is the symbol you need on the wheel downstairs for that. It will take you to a building in town, owned by Haizek Moon, a gifted teacher of magical music. The professor said she would be expecting you, and they would come to you as soon as she told them you had arrived." She handed me a scrap of paper with the symbol on it. "He also said you'd lost your mother and father all in about a week. I'm praying for you, and have been ever since you left. I'm sorry for your loss. My mum went on to heaven some five years ago now. It will get easier." She touched me on the shoulder and went to clear the table.

"Thank you. I spent my last night at home praying and saying goodbye to them. It helps a lot to let out what you need to say to that person. I must now address the issues that led to this situation. I feel good enough to head out

317

now. Thank you for the meal. I didn't know how hungry I was until I smelled your cooking. Hope to see you again, stay well." I stood up and went back downstairs, found the symbol, tucked the scrap of paper into my pocket, and picked everything back up, jostling it to adjust the weight better this time. Then I touched the rune, and was gone.

The stone this time was part of the floor of a basement room, and I arrived out onto the dial's face, my saddlebags and belongings scattered across the floor, making quite a ruckus and looking rather undignified.

"Here, let me help you up." A lady standing in the corner of the room said. She was dressed in a black, full-length teaching robe, paired with a blue silk ruffled neck blouse that featured ruffles on the sleeves as well. The striping and crest on the robe indicated that she attended the same school I had, and was a professor as well, although she was at least ten years my junior. Her symbols, embossed onto the sleeve of the robe, indicated a magical music teacher, as the housekeeper had suggested. She had lovely soft features and adorable brown eyes, and was proper enough that no sooner had I stood than I noticed the amount of dirt and filth I had delivered into her basement.

"My name is Haizek Moon. The professor said you should be arriving any time," she said, looking at the dirt and debris I had brought into her home. "I have a private tutoring class beginning in fifteen minutes. Would you mind coming upstairs so your expectant friends can see you've arrived?" She was polite, but in a hurry, I could tell. I'm sure she had no knowledge of the events surrounding me the last few days, and for her safety, I decided to say nothing. McCort

318

was flying in circles, griping about the harshness of that landing, and finally settled on the stone, ruffling his feathers in disgust at the raucous arrival.

"I am very sorry, ma'am, about the dirt and mess I caused landing here. I'll be outta your hair as soon as I can. Thanks for letting me drop in." That was an accurate statement, as the Runestone had virtually shot me out of the top, and my falling and dropping everything was a result of being squirted out a whole foot or so above its surface. I picked everything up, reloaded it to carry, and indicated with raised brow I was ready. She smiled plainly, looking around at the mess, and turned slowly to go up. Yeah, she was mad at my mess. Well, you can't hardly ride twelve hours in central Texas, then runeshift twice and not leave a mess.

She was equally unimpressed as my saddle and bags dragged across, catching everything on the way up the narrow stairs and doorways, which were meticulously maintained, well before I arrived anyway. We stopped in the hallway for a moment, looking at the painting of the professor. Less than a minute later, she gave a big smile and continued on. After all this mess and commotion I caused, I think she decided to make me go out back into her tiny courtyard, because she led me through a narrow hallway and out through the small kitchen. Can't blame her.

"They know I'm here?" I asked, squeezing out the garden door frame, scratching it up as well, into a small enclosed garden, McCort now resting on the saddle I was carrying in front of me.

"Yes, they're relieved and will meet you," she said

"Meet me where?"

"I'll show you. Down here." She opened another narrow door to an angled entrance, to another basement, maybe, that rose from the back corner of the open yard. She held it open, still smiling, and as I stepped into the stairwell and began to descend, she looked at me and said, "Watch your step, Raileanu." She shut the door behind me, and the candles with reflectors lit up, mounted on the walls along the sides. Uh, okay, guess I'm going this way...

The stairs went a long way down, thirty or forty feet deep, and the floor and about half the sides of this tunnel looked carved out of solid rock. The remainder of the sides were stacked dry stone, and the roof seemed to be made of large slabs of slate, which were dark stone, best I could make out in the candlelight emanating from little carved nooks on both sides of the passageway. I had walked about a hundred yards, feeling more relaxed with my elbows out, as the tunnel was a good eight feet across and high, with plenty of room, when I heard footsteps rapidly approaching. Several sets of them. I put the saddle and bags down as quietly as I could, and put my hand on the grip of Momma's revolver. I had no idea who it was, but I wasn't risking another ambush from that woman. I stood straight and dead center of the tunnel, resigned to whatever was coming, ready to fall flat behind the saddle if there was more than one target. The footsteps were getting closer, and they were around the bend to the left now.

As soon as the form crested the edge of the wall, twenty yards away, I could tell it was Monika! I holstered the pistol and ran to meet her, and her arms were high in the air, already crying. I grabbed her with every emotion a man can have, realizing how much hope and love and fear and hurt

I had bound up, and let it all go then. She was the only one who had control of letting it out of me now. I held her for all I wanted to share with her, the hug blending into the hugs I had wanted to give my father, and my mother, and anguish over failing Arterous. I was so happy, so hurt, so sad. Both our hearts pounded, and the crying and shallow breaths were in perfect reciprocation. I stood there squeezing her, holding her feet six inches off the ground for a long, indeterminate amount of time before I set her down. She grabbed my face, and cheeks wet with tears, smiling from ear to ear, just let "YES" pour out. "Yes, yes, yes, I will marry you!" I buried my face in her neck and hair. I quit caring about anything else then. "I am so sorry about everything, about your parents, Raileanu. I never got to meet them. I even had something made for your mother. It hurts to even think of it now."

The professor and Klement, who had stopped short of us, each went to retrieve some of my gear that had been dropped behind me to carry it back. We just stood in their way, oblivious to the whole rest of the world. I did hear the professor say the saddlebags were too heavy for him, and Wenzel picked those up, and my hat, which Monika knocked off when she jumped into my arms. Good thing too, that's a good hat.

"Go on, boys. I'll be a minute. Thanks for everything." I said. They continued to be jovial and silly, happy for us, and tried not to broach the serious subjects or mention the grief at the moment. We stayed there for at least fifteen minutes, alone, staring into each other's eyes in ways we dared not before, for a while, then collapsing back into hugs. I gave her the first kiss of our lives in that dank tunnel, cradling her perfect cheeks in my scratchy, dirty hands. Then, I must have kissed her fifty times standing there. I wasn't nearly as beat and worn out as I thought I'd be; I'm sure Monika had something to do with it. Most of all, the pent-up fear that I might be alone now in the world was gone. When we decided to rejoin the others, I picked her up, cradled in my arms, and carried her the whole way back to Klement's house, forty stairs and all. Emerging in the root cellar under the kitchen, I set her down, but wouldn't let go of her hand just yet.

They set my belongings down at the back stoop for the kitchen, not wanting all that dirt in their house, and we went into the back hallway of the Metternichs. Dusting himself off, Klement said, "Why don't you go up to the room? Monika can show you the way and get cleaned up. Then we can talk. Laughing at himself, he said, "I think you brought half of Texas back with you, Raileanu!" He met his wife Laverne coming around the corner, and she smiled and waved at Monika and I.

"Come on, dear, I'll show you to the room," Monika said and began to lead me to the rear stairs of the ground floor of the house. We went up two flights, and she led me into the same room I had stayed in once before. She let go of my hand to reach for some clothes on the bed.

"I had these brought up from storage. Klement said you'd worn these the last time you visited, and he kept them for you. Said you have the proclivity to wear unbecoming attire sometimes."

"Darn skippy, woman. I only wear that to avoid embarrassing him, but I spend the whole time feeling embarrassed in those clothes.

"Well, I will get your dirty clothes clean while you bathe. Fair enough?" she smiled and leaned on the bed in an unfamiliar manner.

"Now look here, I ain't even proposed properly to you, lady, you'll have to stop all that naughtiness until we are properly married. Don't go stirring up trouble just yet." I tried to appear stern, but she was right not to buy it. So she smiled even bigger, and walked out, pulling the door slowly to watch me, until it closed.

"Jeez. I don't think I'll have any unused emotions by the end of this day. Yes, Lord Jesus, help me. You have Momma and Daddy in your hands, brave Arterous, and all those other folks this week, too. Just keep an eye on me in the days to come." I peeled the days of sorrow and trail filth, my blood, even stains on my pants from Arterous and Father Callious. I threw them off into a pile on the tile floor, where at least someone could sweep them, and I didn't get any blood or dirt on the carpets or rugs. I hung the pistol belt on a hook in the bathroom and ensured the water was hot before taking off my long johns and socks. Even with all those layers, that powder-fine dust in places around my homestead still gets everywhere. I stepped into the tub, and the dirt peeled off into an expanding dirt island as I went in. Great, now I'm bathing in muddy water. Oh well, I'll still be cleaner than when I started. Just as I started to relax a bit, I had a flash of my momma's face when that bastard killed her. I shook it off. I refused to look too closely at the memory because I knew, in that last second, her entire life, every lesson she had taught or wanted to teach me, every hardship and victory, were piled up in her eyes, trying to give them to me. I wouldn't look at that until the right time.

I got out, shaved, and put on the clothes Klement had kept for me: just a shirt, no vest or jacket, though, and certainly not that belly band thing or tie. I went out, knowing where his study was and that he would likely be there, so I headed over. It was locked, so I knocked, and someone came and unlocked it and opened the door. I went in, past Wenzel at the door, and everyone was seated in front of Klement's desk. Monika was on a small sofa, with a seat saved for me, indicated by her pats on the cushion. Joining her, she collected up my hand with both hers and held it tight.

"Klement, I want to say, I'm so sorry about Arterous. I know you sent him to protect me, and in the end, I couldn't help him at all. I know he was so proud to be in your service, and no braver man have I ever met. He went to the mission, knowing the dangers, just to try and help Father Callious after a tornado passed through. The Comanches got him there, and he could have left, but he never gave up, despite being stuck with two arrows and nearly dead when he set up his last defense and fought to the end. It's his bravery in those last minutes that gave Father Callious time to lay it all out. That gave us the final clues to this mystery that killed my father, and to find that orb. Can I speak to his parents before his funeral?" I wanted to make it clear that his heroism and sacrifice were no small matter to any of us.

"I have spoken to them. They have requested to learn about his last moments from you. We will have his funeral in a few days' time. I will have my personal assistant present, as they don't speak English very well, and the confluence of events between the magical and ordinary worlds that lead to his death are nuanced and should be done with precision for them to fully understand. Thank you." Klement said.

As Klement was looking up, I saw him glance to one side, and felt someone appear behind us. Barthow came walking around beside the desk, facing us. Corfus from the other side.

"I have explained, with the professor, all that has transpired to everyone in this room, and answered their questions to the best of their ability to understand. Many things you may encounter, you will not understand, but we will. All have been given similar tokens that can be used to contact me directly. Do you all agree to be sentries on the watchtower of the world?" Corfus asked us all.

Each said yes without consulting each other; Monika even before I did. "Sentries are all I can ask of you." Corfus began, " We will only contact you if we need assistance, but will not allow you to be harmed by more than your share again, this we, the High Elves, pledge to you. By the end of this year, we hope to have established worthy allies on every continent to guard against the rise of the relics and their threat to humanity. You are the first. We advise you to go about your lives as normally as possible to avoid drawing attention from those who seek these powerful artifacts. You, Raileanu, and Monika especially. If they observe any unusual behavior in you, they may return and be less merciful in their pursuit of you. Do not forget, they are not all orbs, nor all intelligences; some of the most dangerous are the tools the orbs controlled eons ago. Trying to explain more will only serve to confuse you further and put you all in danger with knowledge you do not need. I sincerely thank everyone for your help and your pledges."

Barthow came over to us and handed Monika and me a large, circular, silver badge —a ring with a beveled five-pointed star in the center. Around the ring, it said "Texas Ranger" with a squiggly wand symbol in between the words at the bottom. "These will git you clearance fer look'n into anything fishy in the Texas territory. That ain't no small thing. There ain't a dozen of us, not countin' y'all. The Republic of Texas is a bit bigger than most'a these here European countries. I'll be workin' on gettin' y'all US Territorial badges as well, that'll take a bit longer, I'm afraid. Best I can do. Raileanu," Barthow pointed at me, "I'll be a'checkin on yer place as often as I can. I already set up some magic water troughs and feeders for those chickens and goats yer momma had. Also, your ma and pa's owls, along with Arterous' owl, were there when I left. I let them loose, but they chose to stay around a while, so don't be surprised if they're at your place when you git home. Don't you worry, none."

"Thank you. For everything Barthow." I said, looking at the badge.

"Yes, thank you, Barthow, for saving my fiancé's life," Monika said, rightly.

"Now hold on, bubba. You tellin' me there's a wedding coming? I love weddings! Can I bring the missus?" he asked.

"Now you ALL hold on!" I may have overreacted with the veracity of that statement, but I was glad to be here, and Monika was safe. However, I hadn't even spent much time absorbing everything that had happened in the last 72 hours, and really wasn't ready to plan anything as grand as a wedding. I just didn't want to lose her or be alone. "I ain't even asked her properly yet, we don't know when something like that would be happening," I said, trying to calm Barthow down a bit.

"Raileanu, I think we are all tired of waiting, and no one wants either of you to wait any longer, especially after the week you have had." Klement just said what everyone was thinking, myself included, after it came out of my mouth.

"Klement, did you ever check that little pouch you got, like the one I have?" He nodded, yes. "Well, call everyone in here then if it's alright." Wenzel left the room, and Klement came over beside me and put the little coin purse by my shoulder, and I took it. I stood and went over by the desk with Klement to converse privately for a moment, and look in the coin purse. Once the staff of cooks, housekeepers, security, and even two carriage drivers and a carpenter, working late, were assembled, both confused and bemused by this strange happening in the master's study—a room only a few had ever seen, it was time.

I walked to Monika, knelt, and she started to shiver and cry as I took her hand. "Monika Binder, love of my life for as long as I have known you, will you be my partner in life, my wife, for as long as I have it to share with you?"

"Of course I will! Yes! YES!" she cried out, applause from the assembled people excited to witness such a happy moment. I opened the coin purse and removed a glowing copper band with silver braiding throughout it, joining at the setting to grasp a Louisiana Fire Opal. I slid it on her finger and stood to kiss her and hold her for all to witness. I knew Momma and Daddy were happy as well, and at peace now.

The tiny pieces of crusty, green copper I had been finding, which I had sent back at the beginning of this ordeal, were being made into an engagement ring by Klement before any of the terrible events. It included the handful that Daddy had collected, and Momma gave me just a few days earlier. I knew the time had come before I left, and I wanted to make sure she was mine without further delay. Even more so after her resilience through the hardships we endured. We would proceed together into a new life, alert and ready for what lay ahead, with our hands held firmly and horizons that were much broader than they had been even a few weeks earlier.

Congratulations and sincere happiness spread through the room, as hands were shaken and smiles were shared in celebration of this huge milestone of joy in our lives. Barthow took the occasion to give Monika a great bear hug and kiss on her cheek, laughing at his own awkwardness. Laverne, Klement's wife, a vision of control and decorum, was streaming tears of happiness and hugged Monika and me at least three separate times. Their children began running around and jumping on the furniture, excited by the jovial attitude they sensed in the whole room of usually stuffy adults. Corfus stood still and silent, hands behind his back, barely turning his head to watch the proceedings. Then the feeling that creatures of myth -even to those of us in magical worlds, like Corfus, and ancient evils that hitherto were unknown to us that spread so fast and caused so much suffering and evil at the hands of shadowy forces we still didn't understand fully...those thoughts kept crawling around the base of my brain like a tick, and I couldn't shake it. I knew it was only the beginning.

The End of Part One

ABOUT THE AUTHOR

A fourth-generation Texan and U.S. Army veteran, Torin lives with his wife on a small hobby farm in East Texas. A devoted Christian, he is the proud father of four and grandfather of two. His historical fantasy fiction series blends rich historical settings with imaginative storytelling, using science-based explanations to ground fantastical elements in realism. Drawing on his faith, heritage, and life experiences, he writes with a passion for exploring the intersection of science, history, and the unseen.

The Tellafrog Series

Tellafrog: Part One (Released July 2025)
Tellafrog: Part Two (Coming Fall 2025)
Tellafrog: Stringfellow-Moon (Coming Summer 2026)
Tellafrog: The Last Elf (Coming Winter 2026)

www.ingramcontent.com/pod-product-compliance
Lightning Source LLC
Chambersburg PA
CBHW070735180626
46818CB00007B/2853